The Heart Remembers

June Masters Bacher

HARVEST HOUSE PUBLISHERS
Eugene, Oregon 97402

Scripture quotations are taken from the King James Version of the Bible.

THE HEART REMEMBERS

Copyright © 1990 by Harvest House Publishers
Eugene, Oregon 97402

Bacher, June Masters.
    The heart remembers / by June Masters Bacher.
    ISBN 0-89081-846-0
    1. Christian fiction, American.   I. Title.
    PS3552.A257H44   1991   90-20605
    813′.54—dc20   CIP

Printed in the United States of America.

Contents

In appreciation to those essential persons who have reviewed and appreciated my work as recommended reading! God bless you.

A joyous land
Joining the town and just at hand,
Where waters gushed and fruit trees grew,
And flowers put forth a fairer hue,
And everything was strange and new;
The sparrows were brighter than peacocks
*   here,*
And their dogs outran our fallow deer,
And honeybees had lost their stings,
And horses were born with eagles' wings.

> — From "The Pied Piper,"
> Retold from
> Robert Browning

We will run after thee...we will be glad and
rejoice in thee, we will remember thy love more
than wine....

> — Song of Solomon 1:4

1

Destroying Life's
First Chapters

From a distance the two figures perched on the riverbank looked like those of very young girls. One of them clasped her knees in her arms and, folding the long skirt beneath her feet, gazed idly at the tranquil lace-edged swirl below. *Rivers had a personality all their own*, she thought. *Who could guess what lay below the emerald surface?* Today it was all sparkling charm, giving no hint of slumbering passions or lurking treachery with Mother Nature's nod. Rivers could be gentle and benevolent or swollen with rage.

"Rivers are somewhat like people, aren't they?" she mused.

The other girl rose to her feet. "I hadn't thought about it," she said distractedly. In a nervous gesture, she pushed at a strand of dark hair which had managed to escape the polished pompadour.

"Just what *have* you thought about, Yolanda?" her companion laughed. "I've waited an hour to hear what was so urgent. Another cry of 'wolf'?"

"*Wolf* may be the right word," Yolanda began, only to become evasive. "Know what I wish? That life were a book—and one could just rip out the beginning and plunge into the climax—the here and now of where life has brought me. I'm scared—just plain scared—"

"Of what? Or whom? Come to the point."

"He's back."

The way Yolanda said he identified the man of her fear. She had every right to be frightened. Rachel felt her own scalp prickle. Some men are born devils, Aunt Em claimed. Maybe she was right. Otherwise, how had this one escaped prison? And what on earth brought him *here*? *Tell me, Yolanda*, her heart willed. But the lifelong friendship which had woven a bond of understanding between them, made her know that Yolanda would not be rushed.

"Jules—" Yolanda said suddenly, "that's the name he goes by. It sounds more dignified, more respectable maybe. But inside the man hasn't changed—never will—" Yolanda's voice rose like mercury in a thermometer. "Julius Doogan's here to ruin my life—ruin my marriage—"

"There's nothing he can do to alter your relationship with Maynard and you know it," Rachael soothed. "It's as sound as my marriage to Buckley—or Aunt Em's to Brother Davey, providing—Yolanda, forgive me, I have to ask you this—providing you told Maynard about—you did, didn't you?" *Oh, please, Lord, let me sound calm!*

"I did, oh, I did—that is, all that mattered—"

Yolanda was holding something back. But this was not the time to press her, not when she was near hysteria. Rachel looked up at the June-bright sky where a single sun-split cloud wandered across the blue. "Remember how we used to watch cloud animals, Yo, pretending they were cavorting in a circus parade? Now, you really wouldn't want to rip out beginning chapters, would you?"

Rachel's voice was lighter than her heart. Was she trying to allay Yolanda's fears? Or was it her own? If Julius Doogan, by whatever name, was in Lordsburg, he was on thin ice. What could be important enough to make him take such risk? Thank goodness, she herself had nothing to hide from her husband. Buck had been wagon master when the troublemaker split up the wagon train on its journey from East to West. Cole's train . . .

Cole. Memory of her first husband still hurt. Many nights she had awakened trembling from dreams in which he had walked, along with young Doctor Tim, Yolanda's intended husband, straight up Superstition Mountain and into the fiery inferno that once was its peak. Buck, Cole's best friend, always understood about those dreams. Taking Rachel's sweat-soaked body into his arms tenderly, he would whisper, "I know, I know, Darling—I loved him, too. But he died heroically. 'Greater love hath no man than this, that a man lay down his life for his friends.'" Dear, dear Buck. Only he could restore her sanity. . . .

Wouldn't that be the section she would remove if life were a book as Yolanda suggested? Or would it be the memory of her drunken father's attempts to marry her to any man who could support his appetite for rum?

Rachel forced herself back to the present and its blessings. Now, she must comfort Yolanda in spite of her own apprehension at the return of Julius Doogan, the traitor. "Remember, Yo?" she said of their childhood cloud games. "Surely you wouldn't want to remove that chapter—or the ones in which we shared our dreams of white knights?"

"I remember—but the animals changed shapes right before our eyes when the wind clawed at them, just as our dreams have faded. Oh, Rachel, Rachel, what am I going to do? You're so smart, so wise—"

Rachel rose to stand beside her beloved friend. Being casual wouldn't work she realized. Yolanda needed a loving arm just as she herself needed to be held closely and reassuringly when the bad nights came.

She laid a gentle arm around Yolanda, feeling her body relax a bit. "I'm not smart, Darling—and only God is wise. Let's pray."

2

"Yes, It Is True"

Lordsburg's usually busy streets seemed uncannily still in the amethyst twilight. Almost as though it were holding its breath—waiting. Waiting for what? Her return? Rachel shuddered, her steps lagging. The copper sun, from behind the mountain to the west, was preparing to punch the day's time clock, its work finished. Her work had only begun. How was she going to break the hateful news of this dangerous man's return? Julius Doogan's presence here was too long ago for Mary Cole to remember. The twin boys, born after Doogan had forged papers, sworn falsely, and resorted to murder to lay claim to Blue Bucket mine, had never heard the name to her knowledge. Star was the one who concerned her deeply. She remembered.

"Yoo-hoo! Dearie!" Emmaline Galloway's familiar voice interrupted Rachel's thoughts. "You girls were so late, I was gittin' worried-like. Come on in."

"I should be getting home. As you say, I'm late," Rachel began, only to have her protest interrupted by the older woman.

"You wasn't makin' much progress. Now, do like a tell yuh—I got hot apple pie with th' name 'Jones' stamped on it plain as the nose on yore pretty face. First green apples uv th' season 'n me'n Davey-Love both be rememberin' how yore Buckley takes uh shine t'green-apple pie."

She was right of course, this dear thoughtful soul who had taught her so much about life when, as a frightened child-bride, she had left the New England fishing village to make the long journey to the Oregon Territory. What would she have done without her? Even now ...

"You bless my life, Aunt Em," Rachel said with a catch in her voice. "The pie will be wonderful."

"No problem a'tall—watch yore step, Dearie. I been tryin' t'git that man uv mine t'trim them purple iris so folks kin find their way to th' cafe—ruin our bizness, otherwise. 'Course, he's been busy with th' sign."

There was obvious pride in Aunt Em's face as, wiping her hands on the Mother Hubbard apron, she scratched her nose with the back of her hand and pointed to the enormous sign. Still wet with black paint, it was surprisingly well-lettered: AUNT EM'S EATERY.

Rachel gave her beloved friend a warm hug, accepted the still-steaming pie, and turned to pick her way through the riot of flowers bordering the bare-ground walk. Unconsciously, she was hurrying. To get to her family, yes, but to avoid questions as well.

She was about halfway down the walk when Aunt Em called, "Be careful—will yuh now? I mean, I worry 'bout them dark woods—"

Her voice trailed off significantly. There could be no mistaking a new note of concern in her voice. It had been years since Aunt Em had used words of caution, worried about her safety. "Mothering" to the middle-aged woman spelled anxiety. He *was* here. Had she ever doubted it?

The deep green pines, firs, and cedars were filled with imagined demons—claws outstretched to steal her attempted calm. She found herself increasing her stride and then breaking into an unwarranted (she was sure) run. Panting, she jerked open the screen of the cozy cottage and stopped short to gain control. Her pounding heart continued to outrun the swinging pendulum of the great Swiss clock which dominated the entrance hall.

"I'm home!" she announced in an unnecessarily loud voice.

"I know," Buckley's dear voice came from the shadows, "and welcome, My Darling." He laughed. "Come closer so I can see you—you sound excited to be coming home to me."

Wonderful, faithful, patient Buck. Never questioning. Never recriminating. Just accepting her as she was, trusting her. She need not look up to see the adoration in his eyes. She *felt* it, and it always brought peace to her heart.

Rachel took a few steps toward his bent-over body, a shadowy silhouette about to light a fire against the slight chill that clung even though the season said summer. He struck a match to the fir boughs serving as kindling to send a rosy glow against the book-lined walls of their inviting living room, then straightened to hold out his arms.

Was it the reflection of the chuckling fire in the great fireplace or didn't his smile fade and his eyes glow fiercely? It was a foreign expression—a little frightening, even exciting.

Rachel took a few steps forward, haltingly, as if her husband of 10 years were a stranger.

"Well?" There was a command in his voice—no, a demand as if he needed reassurance, too.

Rachel hurried forward, drawn by an internal magnet, pressing her head against his shoulder as he caught her in his arms. "I love you, Mr. City Manager," she whispered, realizing suddenly how very, very much he had come to mean to her.

"I needed to hear that, My Darling," Buck whispered huskily. "There is something I need to talk with you about—something which I had hoped would never resurface. But it has—and there must be no secrets—"

"Yes," Rachel said against the warmth of his chest. "I considered keeping still until I—we—were sure Yolanda was right—that he—"

Try as she would, Rachel was unable to say his name.

"Julius," Buck supplied. "Is it still hard for you to talk about Doogan? The man is unspeakable. But you *were* going to tell me?"

She nodded. Being Mrs. Buckley Jones had taught her the invaluable lesson that withholding feelings was often not a virtue. "It's true then? Julius Doogan is back?" Rachel queried.

"Yes, it is true." Calmly. Quietly. Just a statement of fact.

Incredulously, her panic vanished. She recognized the look he had given her now. It had said what this wonderful man, not given to eloquent speech, was unable to put into words—that he loved her with a love that comes once in a lifetime; that he would be lost without her; and that, with God's help, he would protect her against all evil.

Strengthened, Rachel drew back and looked deep into his eyes, seeing an entirely new depth to their love. What a strange time to realize that it was all right to love again, to give herself wholly to the man who adored her, who held marriage to be the sacred thing God intended, who (tears welled up in her eyes) built his entire life around her and the children—something an empire-builder like Cole could never do. Her heart would remember forever her all-consuming love for her first husband, but she could put it in proper perspective now, folding it away gently, so that she could give herself unreservedly to Buck.

Without words between them, Buck understood. His face alive with pleasure, Buck laced unsteady fingers at the back of her neck. There was a touching huskiness in his voice. "I brought you something," he said with boyish shyness.

"Oh, Darling, you know I love surprises. Tell me—I can't wait!"

She didn't have to. From behind the bucket of pine cones on the hearth he pulled an unsealed cardboard box. "It's already wound."

Wound? What on earth?

One! Two! Three! Four! Five! Six!

The big Swiss clock intoned the time. And, even before Buck could lift his "surprise" from the box, the doors of a miniature chalet-style clock swung open to allow a wee bird to hop out as if embarrassed at being some two seconds late.

"Oh, I love him!" Rachel squealed excitedly (unaware that this was the first time she had let herself go so completely since she had lost her first husband). "He understands me—I'm late, too!" she finished above his six triumphant cuckoos.

"You have made me very happy, Rachel," Buck said simply.

"*Happy*? You? Oh, Buck, try to realize how happy you have made *me*. How could you have known what this would mean— especially now, when I felt that everything was falling apart?"

The little bird, having proclaimed that dinner was late, hopped back into obscurity, closing the door behind him with a clatter. Human beings were a strange lot, he seemed to say, so completely absorbed in each other instead of themselves. Rachel and Buck laughed together. There were some things they could tell him, too!

"We'll let the children help decide where to put the clock," Buck said, pulling it from the box and letting the chains serpentine to the hooked rug, untangling themselves before resting in a shining heap.

Rachel stood watching spellbound, hesitating to end the moment which outshone the chains. *The children.* Where were they? How could she be sure they were safe? Even before she could finish her thinking, there was a sound just outside the living room window.

"Buck," she whispered through dry lips, "that sound—and *he's* back—"

3

The Wisdom
of a Child

Rachel would hold memories of that evening forever in her heart. It ran the gamut of emotions, changing showers to sunshine so rapidly that she could only recall the beauty of the rainbows in between in retrospect. How quickly Buck had turned the fears shared with Yolanda to peace, which turned to unexpected excitement. Next, just as fear surfaced, how quickly their children painted the world with laughter! Then, as added bonus, came the element of surprise. That tender moment when, in each other's arms, Rachel and Buck marveled at the wisdom God had given their child.

Estrellita! Their miracle. Their Star.

It was Star who led the other three, whooping with glee over their conspiracy, tumbling over one another and in to join their parents. All talked at once.

"Did we surprise you, Mother?...Did Daddy keep the secret like he was supposed to?...Did Mother know that they had helped pay for the cuckoo clock?...Me and David had Mr. Mead keep back a little bit every time we delivered telegrams (Saul)... I helped Star dis–dis—what's the word, Star? But let me tell it (*Mary Cole*)...*distribute*, go ahead, Mary Cole, tell our father and Mother Mine...distribute newspapers...Daddy said we had to be quiet as mice at the window, till he gave us the 'come in' sign and we never made a sound till it was over, then we just about fell through the window watchin' for Daddy to motion us in." Chatter, chatter, laughter making the rafters ring with its silvery tinkle.

Rachel hugged each of them with misty eyes. How silly she had been to allow fear to reach out and clutch the peace Buck had restored.

Supper was festive. Allowing Star to wrap a pink frilly apron around his still-lithe middle, Buck sang lusty songs picked up along the Oregon Trail when he was Cole's trusted wagon master. Having appointed himself cook for the evening, he scrambled eggs and clumsily set sourdough biscuits to rise. All the children helped, but Star was the focus of Rachel's attention as she made a centerpiece of wood hyacinths and maidenhair ferns she had gathered from the stretch of woods separating their large, but cozy haven (one of the few remaining log structures in the area) from the growing city.

Star was a child of nature. One of several matters which concerned Rachel. The question of how to caution the children—particularly this one—to be on guard—was a delicate matter—a matter of protecting them from whatever trap Julius Doogan was here to set, without alarming them unnecessarily. Star had been his pawn in schemes to get even with Cole, who had fired him along the trail West; to gain control of the lost mine; and to climb to power.

Star, the child of mystery, the lone survivor of an Indian raid, was lovely as a five-year-old orphan; and now at the tender age of 16, she was beautiful in the way a delicate blossom on a slender stem outshines even the most flamboyant surrounding flowers. Her dark Spanish eyes always seemed to see something beyond other mortals' cone of vision. Those great hauntingly-beautiful eyes set in the oval of her face, crowned by raven hair, gave the illusion of smoke. And, Rachel thought for the millionth time, she was as difficult to hold on to. Her brilliant mind was forever drifting into the stratosphere, seemingly to gather wisdom for the other children, who were earth-things to a flaw—always tormenting one another, teasing, experimenting, while whooping in their rough-and-tumble play. Each one so dear, so special, so unique. And each loved equally by adoring parents. How could God be so wise, placing exactly the right child in the exact order to meet needs beyond what mothers and fathers could have asked?

Her mind had wandered so far that Star had to take her hand when she failed to hear their "Soup's on!" announcement. "Come, Mother Mine, it is you who must cut the pie, por favor."

"Oh—oh, yes, of course," Rachel murmured in a voice too low to be heard above the laughter of the children. *The language,*

Rachel's mind persisted, *adds to the mysterious charm of this miracle child.* How glad she was that nobody had tried to rob Star of the music of her native tongue. She meant the world to Rachel...and now her safety might very well be threatened again...perhaps her very life. The thought was unbearable.

When the last crumb of the pie was finished, Buck sent the children scampering to bed. He and their mother would do dishes he said, overriding their weak objections. Even Star made no protest. With that faraway look in her olive eyes, she kissed first Rachel's cheek and then Buck's.

"I will listen to their prayers," she said, "so the two of you may have time to talk." *How could she know? How much had she overheard while hiding at the window?*

Everything apparently. And it was enough. It was she who would resolve the problem burdening her parents' hearts.

"Story—can't we have a story?" That would be Saul, eyes so like his father's, whatever they lacked by way of color compensated for by irresistible gentleness—now rounded in appeal. "Yes, *please*—pretty please—*por favor*," chimed the mischievous Mary Cole and David. Those two would do anything to delay bedtime.

Star was accustomed to their wiles. But tonight was different. "Yes," she said quietly, "there is a story you need to hear."

4

Star's Story

"Once upon a time," Star began, her voice, though low-pitched, drifted clearly into the kitchen's open door where, this time, it was her parents who eavesdropped, "there was a very wicked man..."

"Is this a Bible story?"

"No David, and neither is it a make-believe one. It is real, very real."

"I won't like it." There was the hint of a pout in Mary Cole's voice, her way of wheedling—a ploy which Star ignored.

"Yes," she said solemnly. "You will like it. It is about *us*."

"Us?" Rachel could almost feel their huddling closer to hear.

"Yes, about you, although it begins before you were born—back on the Oregon Trail when I was very small and very lost with only the stars and God's hand to guide me. God is good and has much wisdom. Without Him, I would have been left wandering in the vast wastelands without food or drink, eventually to perish like a flower in the desert—"

A pause.

"Isn't that the way it is with us all?" Mary Cole had grown very serious.

"*Verdad*, the thought is somewhat the same—"

"But we would never have had you—and how could we do without an older sister to teach us things teachers don't know!"

David, dear nine-year-old David. The thinker, who was trying to imagine a world without his idol. Rachel shared the child's question in her mind. She listened now as Star, in simple language, candid, open, taking the compliment graciously and without denial, explained that God would never have permitted that to happen.

"He had a plan for me so He spread His wings which cover the world with caring. He shielded me from harm and He will shield us all from this wicked man—"

"He's still *alive*? He's *here*?" Saul, always the doubter, was all ears now.

"Don't interrupt," Mary Cole's excited voice commanded. "Let Star tell her story—and *then* we will ask questions."

As ugly as the truth was, Star told it eloquently, painting the world in a God's-eye view. She could change the face of the world, Rachel recalled Cole's saying as he looked with fatherly pride at her endless stacks of colored drawings—each bearing a title as touching as the work of art itself. "Baby's First Smile." "Fingers of Silver Frost." "Fragrance of Gingerbread." "Peal of Church Bells on Christmas Morn." "Color at a Quilting Bee." "Eyes of the Lost Puppy Found." "Heaven's Harp." "Farewell of the Rose."

The drawings (paintings as Star grew older) were so beautiful they made Rachel's heart ache. Cole was right. Their love-child would be a great artist one day. She painted from the soul. Listening now, Rachel saw the picture of their past unfold—the polished stones of memories, the cornerstone of a more nearly perfect today.

Poignantly, Star told her sad-sweet story admitting that there was, as "our Grandma Emmaline so dear would say, 'trouble a-plenty in the big world outside our world woven of love.'" But, in language the other children could understand, she explained that the Creator-of-all-good-things provided the human heart with the inner resources to find happiness, made up, like beads on a string, of little things. And they must remember that good-will always triumphs over evil. "*Comprende ustedes*?" And there was a touching chorus of "*Si, si*— now tell us more."

The wagon train was getting ready to descend the steep canyon wall in preparation for crossing a tributary to the Kansas River when Rachel had felt the tug of Star's wee hand. A pair of dark eyes, great burning lamps, betrayed no emotion when she inquired softly, "Will the men drown, *Señora*?" It was only a simple question the frail brown waif asked, but in it was a restraint far beyond her years—and an unspoken need. Feeling that the child would vanish at the slightest puff of wind, Rachel knelt beside her, brushing the curtain of blue-black hair from her pixie face . . . soothing . . . probing gently in an effort to establish the identity of the child whose eyes begged for love. "Mi madre—" the tiny figure now crouching like a frightened animal began, then, changing to well-practiced English said simply, "My mommy was killed. My father runned. *Estrallita*, me—I hid and asked God for you." *A survivor of an Indian raid!* Rachel's arms, like her heart, reached out....

Star's story made no mention of the cloud that hung over the immigrants' wagon train, formed by the heavy-lidded wagon master. She was too young and too fascinated by the journey with her new parents (God's answer, she said) to take note of Julius Doogan's insults, his jeers, and his improper advances toward Rachel behind Cole's back. Rachel recalled it all with a shudder. Buck (who had been "Buckeye" on the trail) noticed and put a comforting arm about her shoulders. Dear, wonderful Buck who, taking Doogan's place when the conniving man—upon being fired—took half the confused travelers with him, stood by and watched with pride as Rachel and Colby Lord took the orphan child into the circle of their love. Now he shared with her precious memories of seeing the child, who appeared out of God's mysterious nowhere, become a flesh-and-blood daughter. No longer a child of vapor, Little Star became a part of them all. To have, to hold, to cherish, to love. And he still did. How precious to share memories of the heart....

Rachel lifted her head from the comfort of his chest. Star had resumed her story. It was important to know just how much she revealed. It would help in dealing with the situation at hand for the rest of the story dealt with the terrible disasters resulting from the half-beaten enemy.

From the beginning, trouble had stalked the dissidents who were misguided into following Julius Doogan, Star's "man of evil." Word had it that all had perished either from starvation, illness, or Indian raids. Not so. Doogan had deserted his followers and sought out Cole's train, finding them where Cole had begun his dream, the establishment of a city. But Star remembered only when he came out of nowhere and snatched her away, kidnapped her for ransom, people thought.

"Daddy Cole," the still near-translucent child was saying, still pronouncing his title as *Dad-dee*, "was away on business and Mother Mine was very lonely. Without protection? No, Uncle Buck—now our Daddy Buck—was always there. But as the sun sank low that terrible night, the evil man stole in to take me far, far away, up high on a mountain surrounded by a rim of fire. He hid me beneath brush where I waited and prayed. God had brought help before. He would bring it again.

Mary Cole, Davy, and Saul were excited by the drama, apparently having forgotten their fear.

"Wow! *Kidnapped!* What a story!" Saul punctuated his words with a whistle.

"Were you afraid, Star? Oh, I am glad nothing happened," David said thoughtfully.

"She prayed for help, silly," Mary Cole said with a touch of scorn. "And it came, Star?"

"Yes—but not before something *did* happen—not to me but to Daddy Cole's town. You see, the evil one hid me away so that almost everyone was searching—but he didn't kidnap me for ransom. Worse! The man broke dear Daddy Cole's heart by burning the town."

"Burned *Lordsburg*...the evil one did that?...Then how could it be here?" All were questioning at once.

"Daddy Cole built a new dream."

No mention of the countless other heinous acts of Julius Doogan. Killing. Stealing. Swearing falsely that he alone held claim to Blue Bucket Mine and stopping at nothing to steal it from the shareholders. Nothing about Yolanda's shame—a young, inexperienced girl in love with love and victim to Julius Doogan's uncanny way of leading the innocent astray. Her "elopement" which proved to be no elopement at all, simply another way to gain access to ownership of Superstition Mountain. There had been no marriage and, thankfully, no relationship of any kind. Yolanda, discovering that Julius Doogan's intentions were less than honorable, fled. Rachel, remembering, doubted if Star knew. In fact, so few did. Perhaps only the Lees, Yolanda's parents, and Rachel herself. Judson Lee gave every appearance of being the hardheaded father whose vocabulary did not include the word forgiveness. But he met his prodigal daughter with outstretched arms. And the matter was closed. The problem was that Yolanda Lee could never forgive herself.

No mention, either, from Star about the fatal explosion which changed the course of Rachel's and Yolanda's lives forever. All of which was well and good. The children had heard quite enough for now. There was nothing left to do except gently remind them to be cautious. *Julius Doogan could be here for no good.*

The story hung unfinished. The conversation had gone other-directional by a question posed concerning how they could all bear the name of Jones. And that was Star's favorite story, so proud was she of her beloved family.

"God gave me to my new parents—"

"Please, Star, you never told us if you remembered your other parents."

Star thought for a moment before answering Mary Cole. "I *think* I do sometimes. They are only shadows that come and go. Oh, I will share the pictures I sketched when the shadows took on substance—"

"Yes, show us!" the listeners pleaded. It was Saul who introduced a new idea. "Do you have a picture of the evil one—so we will know him and can outrun him?" His voice said this was a game.

Star's answer indicated otherwise. "Yes, Saul, I do. But he will be changed in 10 years. Just trust me to know him—"

"He sounds like Satan—slinking around, never revealing his-self—*him*self. Grandma Emmaline says we don't all see him and that's why we let him lead us into trouble. *Is* he like Satan, Star?"

"*Si*, like Satan or his helpers, Saul. Shall I continue *por favor*?"

Yes, and then the pictures.

"Well, Mary Cole was next, the only child Daddy Cole and Mother Mine had. The twins came in answer to prayer after Mother Mine married Uncle Buck. That was after Daddy Cole had gone to be with God. And so we are all Joneses—all coming in different ways. We do not have to be 'birthed' to be loved."

"But I wish God sent *me*." Mary Cole's voice hinted at a pout. Her pouts were hard to resist, lips pursed as appealingly as a lilac bud. And so Star's answer held a smile. "You were, Darling, we all were."

5

Confrontation

It was ironic that five days later Rachel was compelled to put into practice the advice she gave Yolanda only half an hour before....

Eager as she was to share Star's story with her friend and ask questions herself, there had been demands she must meet beforehand. The matter of enrolling the children in summer Bible class took more time that it should have. Couldn't Mrs. Jones teach? Not this year, Rachel declined. She would be a behind-the-scenes helper, which was the exact truth. She would be watching and listening for the intruder who might be a threat to the children—only this she would be unable to share. Rumors were as dangerous as facts. Either one could incite panic, the very thing they needed to avoid. Buck would work toward the same end, keeping his eyes and ears open to any small incident mentioned at the City Council meetings. With Cole's death, Rachel had backed away from the business of organizing city government; but now she was involved of necessity. Then, there were the grapes which burst with summer goodness earlier than usual and must be jelled.

This day she felt an urgency to take the woodsy path to the imposing (somewhat boastful in Rachel's mind) house built and occupied by Dr. and Mrs. Maynard Killjoy. Fleetingly, Rachel wished that she liked the doctor better, then loyally put the thought aside. He was Yo's husband.

She looked over her shoulder at the garden she and Buck had worked together to perfect. The sights, scents, and sounds of it always put her thoughts in proper perspective. This morning the air was particularly fragrant with blossoms and drowsy and with the busy hum of bees from Buck's hives. It was good that the unpretentious log house, with its weather-worn shingled roof, was blest with more than its share of many-paned windows. All of the windows looked out on the flower-filled garden, often pitted with shadows and patched by sunlight. Columns of wild larkspur, ranging in every conceivable color from deepest purple through shades of blue to pink, bleaching to pure white. Yellow field lilies, which neither Rachel nor Buck had the courage to separate, clumped together triumphantly like stars in the Milky Way of white wood-violets. How fortunate to have a natural stream, spanned by a mossy bridge, laugh its way to the larger stream below, where it laughed even louder as if reunited with a parent. A quaint arbor, sweetbrier-rosed, arched in welcome to the garden path leading to the vegetable garden in back. Such a contrast to the Killjoys' formal grounds where exotic flowers were screened from view by carefully-pruned shrubs. Nothing was visible except for the very top of the goddess, Venus, which held forth a pitcher from which a tiny flow of water dripped uninvitingly. Rachel often wondered if Yolanda truly enjoyed the pomp of it all after her rough-and-tumble upbringing in a homesteader's cabin too small for the 13 children, but filled with love.

Yolanda met her with a little cry of joy. "Oh, Rachel, you're *here*—and we're alone to talk. Let me get the coffee going!"

They were stirring their beverages and making small talk when Yolanda stopped in mid-sentence, her spoon allowing the amber contents of the priceless china cup to drip unnoticed onto the white linen tablecloth. "I saw him," she said as if her sighting spelled the end of the world. "Up to then it had been rumor—I mean, most of it—but now I know."

"Julius?" Rachel forced her voice to sound light. "Jules—or has he decided to change it again? He's an old hand at that, you know. Remember his half-dozen or so aliases?"

"He just added another one, changing his surname from Doogan to Dunigan. He didn't see me," Yolanda said disjointedly, wiping absently at the enlarging puddles of coffee.

Rachel, in deliberate slow motion, took a swallow of coffee. "So Julius Doogan becomes Jules Dunigan. Does that change *him*, make him more respectable? And," she tried for an offhand manner, "anyway, what's it to us, Yo?"

Yolanda's spoon fell to the floor with a clatter. "It's everything!" she cried out as if in physical pain. "Don't you understand?"

"No," Rachel said flatly, picking up the spoon. "No, I don't."

She had dealt with Yolanda's hysteria before. But the other occasions had been different. There had been real crises.

"He's here to ruin my life—to—to destroy it, get even. He holds me responsible for foiling his scheme to take the mine—thinks I influenced Pa. And he'll never forgive my rejecting him. He'll destroy my marriage," her voice rose still higher, "do harm to Roland—"

"Aren't you being somewhat paranoid, Yo? You have no proof."

"How can you defend him—after all he's done to you? You know the man is capable of anything—*anything*!"

"Be reasonable, Darling. I would be the last one in the world to defend such a cad. And don't you think I remember all I suffered at his hand—even before you met and became infatuated with him?"

"Don't you *dare* refer to that!" Yolanda hissed between clenched teeth. "Oh, forgive me, Rachel—you are my dearest friend, the one who has stood by me through thick and thin, all my life. *Forgive* me?"

At the sight of her tears, Rachel rose and, covering the short distance between them, knelt beside Yolanda. "There is nothing to forgive," she soothed, putting comforting arms around the thin shoulders and rocking her back and forth as she would rock a child. "But, Yolanda, we do not have the facts yet. Julius Doogan has no claim on earth to manhood—but, whether we like it or not, he has paid his duty to society and managed to be released before completing his sentence. As to why he's here—well, time will tell. By the way, have you told Maynard the entire story? Be honest with me—so we can deal with it."

Yolanda's head dropped in shame. "No, not everything. I—I—was too afraid of losing him. He and Roland are all I have—*Roland!*"

Yolanda pulled away and stood up, wild-eyed with desperation.

"Sit back down, Yo, and stop getting yourself worked up! You'll be ill. That's it, sit until we've finished this conversation."

"But—but," Yolanda complied with Rachel's near-order but stopped her sentence in confusion, only to burst out, "How can I deal with it?"

"Openly—or else you have no marriage at all. You must tell Maynard."

"And Roland—how can I protect him?" she whispered.

"You won't have to protect him. Roland knows, unless I miss my guess. Star told the story to Mary Cole and the boys. Don't you know they would break their necks in a wild rush to tell their best friend?"

It had been a joke, Rachel remembered, everybody trying to see which of them, herself or Yolanda, the stork would visit first. The legendary wide-winged creature must have delivered them all in one load! They were born just hours apart.

"Did she—Star—tell about *me*? Oh, Rachel—"

"Of course not. Even if our Star knew, do you think she would say anything to upset the other children or hurt *you*? She omitted the dingy part. But Yolanda, aren't you holding something back?"

Her silence was an answer. *How white her face is*, Rachel thought, *and hasn't she lost weight?* Concern for Yolanda caused Rachel to question no further. Had her agitation brought this on?

"You know you can confide in me and I will understand—anytime. But for now let's put our minds to rest. Only promise me one thing, Yo. You *will* tell your husband?"

Yolanda's hands twisted in her lap. "If only I knew how . . ."

"By looking the matter straight in the eye. Direct confrontation is best." She wanted to add that any loving husband would understand, but secretly Rachel doubted that Yolanda's marriage was as secure as her own. And then she remembered something important.

Rising to take her leave, she said casually, "Do you remember our list of qualifications for a husband?"

Yolanda stood, too. "That was a long time ago."

"Yes, another time, another place—way back in our romantic dreamtime when we were girls in the proper East. But the listing made sense and is as true today as then. What headed the list?"

"I—I have forgotten whether it was trust or respect—after love and shared faith. Does it matter?"

"Not the exact order, but the qualities, yes. I know you respect the man you married, so trust him to understand. Confront him, Yo!"

Leaving the main part of town took Rachel by the telegraph office. The telegrapher, William Mead, his weathered face obscured by the usual sunshade that revealed only his tight lips, which, usually still, were busy now, deep in conversation with—yes, it was. It *had* to be Julius Doogan. Garbed in fine clothes, his back to her yet somehow she knew.

If only she could hurry away. But it was too late. Mr. Mead, spotting her, stopped his conversation (what could they be discussing?) and waved. The other man turned on his heel. "Why, good morning, Mrs. Jones!" he greeted her brazenly.

Confrontation, she had said.

"Good morning," she said coldly, aware that his eyes followed her.

6

A Decade of Change

"I am concerned about Yolanda," Rachel said as soon as she was able to talk to Buck privately, following her upsetting talk with her friend.

"Do you realize that you make the best sourdough flapjacks this side of the Mississippi, Mrs. Jones?" Buck's bronzed hand reached the honey jar, gold-glinted by the early-morning sunbeams dancing in their small breakfast nook.

"Some compliment. Sourdough is unheard of on the other side. *And* these are *pancakes*, not flapjacks—buttermilk, too, instead of sourdough. But the recipe is an immigrant. Make you feel better, Mr. Jones?" She pushed the jar conveniently out of reach. "Enough—and I've found that my husband cannot listen and chew at the same time."

"I can so!" Buck's teasing voice sounded like the children's. "Quote: 'I am concerned about Yolanda.'" He laid a triumphant hand gently over hers. "And *I* have found that my wife cannot worry when I hold her hand."

It was true. Buck was stalling purposely, a ploy which set her thoughts other-directional. How good, satisfying, *wonderful*— how much richer marriage was when it began with friendship and respect and flowered into romance where others began, then faded with age. *Like Yolanda's!*

"Want to tell my why?" Buck's manner was no longer playful.

Rachel related details of her conversations with Yolanda. He registered no surprise. "I think she has every right to be frightened, Rachel. Cautious, anyway—we all have."

Rachel's back stiffened. Then the stiffening departed, leaving a trembling void—if a void could tremble. She was hearing what she did not want to hear, news that could destroy 10 years of hard-won peace. Beneath the sweep of the tablecloth, her hands knotted into fists. Hoping that Buck had failed to see, she thrust them into the patch-pockets of her white morning-frock. She had forgotten how hard her heart could pound.

"I was hoping..." she began hollowly, then could go no further.

"That I would say everything is all right? I wish I could. We who remember Julius Doogan were foolishly in hopes he would drift out as he drifted in, given time to strut around a little. But deep in my heart I guessed there was a deeper motive—not an honorable one, naturally. Suspecting he might have escaped, I had William Mead wire both Salem and Washington, D.C.—"

"Are you sure he can be trusted, Buck—Mead, I mean?"

Buck looked at her in surprise. "Have you reason to think otherwise?"

"No," Rachel admitted slowly, "just a feeling—forgive the interruption. How *did* Doogan complete his life sentence—or," she felt her face pale, "—er, escape?"

Buck spread his hands in despair. "His record's clean on paper. Got an early pardon, according to the new law, on good behavior."

Rachel groaned. "But why here—here of all places?" Buck scratched his head. "I have searched my soul for an answer. By the way, Mead's report verified that the name *is* Jules—Jules Dunigan, granted by the courts. I do know that the man is dodging me. And we both know that he is capable of anything, even taking over a town!"

Yes, she knew. How well she knew! Dear, wonderful Buck had believed her story so long ago. A story so incredible that even she wondered if it was a dream....

Where did one draw the line between a dream and reality? Rachel had wondered then. She wondered now. Brother Davey, against all advice, had gone to Portland and failed to return. Used to his antics, nobody had worried except Aunt Em and Cole. Cole always cared. But this was one of his rare times at home with Rachel and Star; and surely a man like the spunky little preacher could take care of himself. Only he couldn't.

Would she ever forget? No. Memory of the urgent telegram Willie Mead delivered which had summoned her husband had lodged in her heart. No explanation. Just that he must come if he hoped to see his lifelong friend alive. Cole went. Other brave men joined the search when there was no further word from Cole. They returned bringing a near-senseless, rambling-of-speech Brother Davey. But not Cole!

Surely *somebody* knew *something*. If she could get Brother Davey alone, try and coax *something, anything* from the disoriented man....

Marshal Hunt, then as close to being a symbol of law as Cole's city could come, had brought his wife to the pioneer beginnings of civilization, only to have her, too, become confused and frightened. Her claims of having been taken prisoner and seeing the men there lacked credibility. It was then that the dreams commenced. Or were they really dreams?

Lucretia Hunt sedated by some doctor who had tried to extract information as to the true owner of Superstition Mountain.... Brother Davey—chained, beaten—threatened with death by starvation. And Cole—oh, how her heart chafed with the memories! Cole strung up, beaten, *killed* (according to Lucretia). By a *judge!*

Yes, it could happen. A man *could* take over a town. The man who took over as judge, jury, and executioner was—*oh, dear God, do I dare remember?* her heart cried out in silence—none other than Julius Doogan. And he was back in Lordsburg now!

Believe, darling, believe, believe! Buck, wonderful Buck, who always stood by for her. Believe? Yes, she would believe—even when other people's faith wore thin at the elbows, she would believe.

And God had brought her husband home. Home to his loving wife, his daughter who hurled herself at dad-*dee* to announce, "Mother Mine is going to bring us a *bambino!*" Home to wait for Mary Cole. Home to his friends who prayed without ceasing. *Home*...to be...be...killed in the *horrible explosion* which took his life and that of Yolanda's intended husband. Maybe at the hands of the man who had returned to finish them all. Small wonder Yolanda was terrified....

Buck coughed to regain her attention. How long had she been drifting like the fluffy meringue clouds now visible above the treetops? Not the decade it seemed, for the last of her coffee was still hot in her mouth. At the risk of choking, Rachel swallowed.

"I don't know what to do," she whispered. "I feel as if I'm battering my bare hands against a stone wall of despair, not even knowing what we are fighting."

"Maybe it would be wiser not to pursue the question too far."

Rachel felt a jolt of surprise. "You mean ignore the threat of his emerging from a background of crime?"

Caustic words burned her mouth, begging for release. But Rachel thought better of impetuousness. One look at the indomitable set of Buck's jaw and chin reminded her that moving cautiously meant that, like a bird of prey, he would assess the victim until, sure of itself, it grew confident and bold. Then, armed with truth, Buck would swoop down and the victim's futile clutch at its slippery perch would spell its doom.

"Not ignore, My Darling," he said slowly, "quite the opposite. Observe. Watch and pray, as we are told to do. Meantime, we need support."

"Support? I don't understand. Why, we have the entire city—"

She paused. Even before Buck spoke she realized that she was little more than acquainted with over half the population and (the thought startled her) there were many whom she had not met.

"A lot has happened in the last decade, Rachel. People have come and gone. Old-timers remember, what few remain, but without malice. That is as it should be. We share the same history of the past and the dream of the future. But the newer people know nothing of our past—and they need to know if we expect them to join us in solving problems for this generation and those to come."

"You mean *protect* ourselves, don't you, Buck? Just say it."

"That's part of it, yes. We need their confidence, but we must earn it. We need even more—we need their friendship—something we have paid less attention to than when we needed each other so much. There has to be a common cause, a meeting of the minds— the hand of fellowship."

It was true. It came as a shock to Rachel that she, too, had grown self-satisfied, maybe even somewhat selfish. Church used to bring them all together and hold them together. Now, each of the four churches enjoyed the full fellowship of its members; but something was lost when the community limited its concern rather than enlarging it. That, why *that* could spawn prejudice—widen the gap. "But how—?" she began, then paused.

"How to begin to renew what we have lost?" Buck finished. "We know who the old standbys are—those who traveled with our wagon train so long ago, the established merchants—including," he grinned, "Brother Davey, our bantamweight who claims to be able to lick his weight in wildcats. I wonder if he realizes how few that would be!"

The image restored Rachel's smile. "God bless him and his Emmy Gal," she said with a catch in her throat. "But Buck, what can we do?"

"Ready for this?" At her nod, he continued, "I would like to have you accompany me to the meeting of the City Council next week. What's more, address the group. You're the closest we have to a founder having finished Cole's dream."

"*Me?* The only woman? I—I—yes—yes, I will. History *is* a start."

7

Demonstration
of Courage

The warmest shade of hazel might have been matched to her hazel eyes, warm, friendly, and understated, Rachel thought as she laid out the plaid tunic she planned to wear to the council meeting. The imitation leopard-skin collar and cuffs knew no season and Buck always said they added even more highlights to her already wispy curls which still managed to play hooky like a schoolgirl from the heavy golden braid encircling her head. Looking her best would give her needed courage. It would be no easy matter to give Lordsburg's history without undue emotion—making it interesting enough to hold the attention of the men, while avoiding the dramatic which ultimately would lead to panic, fear, or suspicion. That was exactly what she did *not* want.

Now, to call on Aunt Em. She must tell her about the plans and ask her to keep the children for the evening. They must not be alone, a fact Rachel kept under wraps, along with other signs of caution.

Emmaline Galloway's hair had whitened, but time had been incapable of slowing her pace. The woman who had served as Rachel's beloved surrogate mother on the Oregon Trail was pathetically glad to see her. Gathering Rachel gently to her warm, amply-endowed bosom, her gray eyes grew moist with tears. "Oh, come in—you *are* in!" Aunt Em's voice divided equally between laughter and tears. "It's been too long between visits. Fine kettle uv fish when friends git so tied up in worldly matters they's no time fer one another."

"I know—and that's precisely what I'm here to discuss, get advice on—"

A look of pleasure crossed the other woman's face. She loved giving advice, Rachel remembered affectionately. "Would another time be better?"

"No time like th' present! Now, set yourself down at the cook-table fer coffee—" Aunt Em paused to sniff. "Do you catch uh whiff uv somethin' burnin'—Oh, my prune cakes!" Rachel smiled. Aunt Em didn't burn food.

Pulling the fragrant cakes from the oversize oven and lining them up neatly on the windowsill, she replaced them with more batter-filled pans. "We'll downright be compelled t'sample these. Could be bottoms are burnt and customers wouldn' take uh likin' t'that. Anyways, we got us some competition now—just like th' church. Too bad, us bein' compelled t'compete."

Rachel nodded as Aunt Em poured coffee and tested one cake with a broomstraw, found it done inside but declared it was too hot to slice up nice. Rachel could just be taking one home. 'Twas a favorite of Buck's.

"And now," she picked up the thread of conversation, "what's it you need advice on, Dearie?" she asked, plopping herself into the chair nearest Rachel.

Rachel told her about Buck's invitation but stopped short of referring to the exact purpose. "Do you think it would be proper?"

"Proper and overdue. Why, you run this town after we—uh, lost Cole. My Davey-Love and me, well, we could'n figger why you bein' so dedicated—there I go, meddlin'—"

"Dedicated? I was *obsessed*—and came frighteningly close to letting Cole's dream become an idol," Rachel admitted.

"Drink yore coffee, Dearie. Don'cha know Aunt Em understands her baby? Wore yer frail little old body an' keen mind to uh frazzle, that's what. But, Darlin', we lose somethin' special when you go 'n completely cut ties—"

Ties. That was it, the thinning of friendships which bound them endearingly close. Friendship was like a cable, Rachel thought, like a habit, one wove another thread to it over and over, until it became impossible to break.

"That's what we want to rebuild, Aunt Em—recoup what we have managed to lose. We *must*. If we can recapture it, don't you think we will be pleasing in the eyes of the Lord, to whom we dedicated Lordsburg? And certainly we will seek His protection—"

"It's Doogan, ain't it?"

Rachel jumped, then felt herself unwind. "Am I that transparent?"

"Yer open, that's whatcha are—open and frank—'n borned t'be uh gentle leader. Iffen it took that scoundrel's sneaking back in here t'arouse them God-given gifts, so be it. Word's got 'round amongst us that Doogan's put th' mark uv th' beast on what he's here about."

Aunt Em rescued her second batch of cakes and put sourdough biscuits to rise. "Where's he hiding?" Rachel asked Aunt Em's back.

"Jest about next door—at th' Welcome Stranger Inn, th' one my competitor runs. Oh, there she is—right nice woman or 'pears t'be—'n I'm guessin' she don' know nothing 'bout th' sins uv this viper callin' hisself Jules Dunigan." Aunt Em scratched her nose then pointed a flour-dusted finger.

A silver-haired, rosy-cheeked, fairy-godmother-like woman, whose figure had seen better days, emerged from the open door of the Welcome Stranger Inn. "That's her, Miz Lily, ever'body calls 'er. 'N right busy she is—'specially since that Doogan—Dunigan—whatever 'is filthy name is, come back. Men folks a-comin' 'n a-goin' all hours. Davey-Love speculates most is teamin' up with 'im. Troublin', ain't it now?"

"Of course it could have no meaning," Rachel answered, wondering whether it was Emmaline Galloway or Rachel Lord Jones she was trying to reassure. She succeeded in convincing neither because at that precise moment a bearded, gaunt, middle-aged stranger emerged behind the landlady. It was almost as if, like a penguin, he watched to see if the lady made it before plunging into the water himself. Coatless, hatless, checkerboard vest flapping open, the loose-jointed figure gave every indication of leaving in a hurry. The man's enormous ears and jumping-jack gait appeared designed to be comical. His eyes did not. Bright, snapping, and appearing to take in everything at once, he looked more like a terrier—the breed that snaps at the heels when one is not looking.

There was tense silence in the Galloway kitchen as Miz Lily reached behind her to hurry the stranger along. Panting, she looked somewhat like a plump tugboat dragging a too-heavy load. The woman pointed to a boat anchored behind a screen of weeping willows leaning over the stream.

Rachel was watching the door of the inn, wondering if others would emerge when Aunt Em pointed at the clump of willows. "Look! Men everywhere. *Look quick!*"

But when Rachel spun in her chair, there was no sign of life. The willows went on with their weeping without motion. "Are you sure, Aunt Em? It's hard to see in this bright sunlight. Could it have been—"

"My imagination? Rachel, you disappoint me. My vision's not failin'. I could spot uh needle on that sandy bank 'n you know it!"

"I *do* know, dear Aunt Em—forgive me. It—it's just that I feel like a child waking up from some ugly dream, one that has been going on for years—and—" Rachel felt a sudden chill traverse her spine. What if—oh, how foolish—but what if—? She could go no further.

"What, Darlin', what did you see?" Aunt Em took her hand and held it.

"This Miz Lily—is that her first or last name?"

"First." Aunt Em's nostrils flanged out, her face blanching.

"And—her last?" Rachel's voice was barely audible.

Aunt Em was breathing heavily, and then eventually she said, "Dunigan."

Outside, merchants were locking their doors in preparation for the noon hour. Rachel hurried through an alley, a shortcut to the grove of firs fencing the Joneses property. The children would be home from Bible class and maybe, just maybe, she thought, Buck would be back from Salem where he had been checking on forms of city government. Brother Davey who had tagged along could have been at the livery stable caring for the team. She hummed, near-skipping in her rush.

The sun, as if suddenly aware that it was July, cast a simmering net over the city. But the grove offered cool green silence, broken only by a rhythmic swish-swish lullaby of the stream below as it licked against the ferny banks. How peaceful, inviting—and safe from harm.

Why, then, was there a sudden crackle of dried pine needles disturbingly close by? Rachel paused. The sound paused too—only to resume with her next step. The first time she had been uncertain, but now she was sure of both the sound and its origin. *Footsteps* on some obscure path in the tanglewood between herself and the stream. The very air around her seemed to pulse with warning and a raven swooped down. She was not alone—that she knew. But, refusing to panic, she kept up the same gait. The forest relapsed into a doze while the raven widened its search-of-death circles, gaining altitude above the sun-burnished treetops where a few clouds scribbled in the sky.

Home. She was home! As were her husband and her family—*safe!*

The afternoon went pleasantly and all too quickly. Rachel wanted to share her sightings and suspicions with Buck, but he was more excited than she could recall having seen him. It was as if someone had pushed a button, signaling him to explain every detail of his findings.

"It is good to see you like this, Darling," she said in growing excitement herself. But she doubted if he heard. Anyway, she was calmer now and realized that keeping still would be a greater act of courage than diverting him. The afternoon wore into evening. And then the Jones family walked happily beneath a mother-of-pearl moon toward City Hall.

8

Revival
of the Spirit

Rachel glanced about the council hall with appreciation. It was so dearly familiar that time telescoped, making the then-and-now of her life one. The long table around which all men of the community used to gather now dominated the far end of the room to face guests who would occupy seats set up in neat rows. Council members, papers scattered before them, would claim the seats-of-honor around the time-polished table. The smell was the same—stale smoke and leather.

Coming early tonight provided opportunity for Buck to prepare his opening statement while Rachel, who would sit in the front row (unobserved, she hoped, by the all-male audience), reexperienced the feel of the hall. The only thing new was the fanlight window behind the podium to the right of the front table. The semicircular light, with its clear-paned glass between the rib-like sash bars, reflected silver slashes of moon-glow in spite of the glaring light from the ceiling wheel of gasoline lamps. Shadows danced in the corners. Strange, this feeling she had, a stranger at home.

The room filled suddenly and conversation flowed around her. "Lots to consider." "Yep, incorporation's got its good points—higher taxes but more protection." "Well, men, we'll be more informed afore castin' votes." "Votes? We gonna vote?" "Man's privilege."

And then two disturbing comments and responses.

"*Man's?* Rumor's got it that some of the mouthy women've got the unreasonable idee that they should oughta be listenin' in!"

"Honest Injun? Women?" A chortle, followed by "Woman's place is in th' home 'n that settles that."

"Without uh vote? You a-puttin' women down, man?" Brother Davey!

Rachel had recognized none of the other voices. Neither did she recognize this one: "Mr. Dunigan says it's quite common elsewhere."

"Dunigan!" Brother Davey exploded. "What's that termite got t'do with our bizness?"

"You know him?" Facing straight ahead, Rachel was unable to see the speaker, but she felt a prickle of fear traverse her spine.

"Maybe I do 'n maybe I don't. But we foundin' fathers don' need no stranger buttin' in—jest could be he's uh sheep in wolf's clothes."

Rachel, wiping damp palms, wished Aunt Em, who had given her the French-knot-embroidered handkerchief, were here to say, "'T'other way 'round, Davey-Love." By her own admission, Aunt Em was the only one who could "turn his damper down."

There was more in the verbal exchange, but Rachel missed it because the city manager brought his gavel down. He stood tall and straight, quiet but commanding. She had forgotten how handsome he was in a rugged, outdoor way—forgotten, too, how well he thought on his feet and how convincing he was when he spoke. *Forgotten?* Had she ever known, really? She remembered only his brief instructions on the trail West and, yes, that she had admired his low-key style that garnered attention. Colby Lord had depended on his friend so completely....

"Ladies and gentlemen," Buck began.

The crowd grew quiet. Rachel's heart did not. *Ladies?* There were other women present? She conquered the almost overwhelming desire to look over her shoulder. If she had, she probably would have been unable to deliver her speech. But, yes, there was another woman in their midst—lost in the shadows of the back row....

"As you know, we are gathered here to discuss an important debate—to incorporate our growing city or to postpone incorporation. We had pigeonholed the issue until I could conclude a study."

He paused to take a swallow from his water glass—just long enough for David Saul Galloway to mumble, "Pigeon-*livered's* more like it—stallin'—"

Buck, undisturbed, half-smiled and continued, "My work in Salem is finished, an interesting experience—"

His explanations were concise, clear, and to the point. There must be a vote, followed by filing of a petition, after which they must decide on the form of government. Was it the pleasure of those present to take a straw vote? Or did they wish to gather signatures on a petition?

If the straw vote they decided upon was an indication, there could be no doubt that incorporation was favored. Rachel was pleased. That meant more law and order. It meant—oh, how important!—that some self-appointed leader with what Brother Davey referred to as a motley band of "Robbin' Hoods" would be unable to stampede a peaceful city, unsuspecting and dozing in the sun, and take it over at gunpoint. It means so much more than many in this room had never had to endure—some surviving by submission to wearing "the mark of the beast" (figuratively); others, by drowning in their own blood which "flowed through the streets" to a chariot-wheel depth like the biblical description.

She shuddered, remembering.

"Do we have volunteers to circulate petitions?"

Hands waved like a flag in the wind all over the hall. The meeting was going well. So well that there was a clamor for options regarding city government. Buck, obviously pleased, turned palms up in mock surrender. "Well," he half-teased, "first there must be a governor, then a people willing to be governed. We can turn that around since—"

" 'Barcus is willing!' "

Dr. Killjoy! Yolanda's husband. Rachel wondered why she was surprised at his presence and even more surprised that he would speak up—and with the glib quote from Dickens. If Yolanda had shared her past as Rachel advised, certainly it must have gone well.

She turned her attention back to Buck's explanation of choices which, he emphasized, must wait until after approval of the application. There followed a lively discussion, a few arguments (quickly settled), ending with an agreement that a Mayor-Council arrangement was the choice. Of course, there had to be a City Manager—and his name would be Buckley Jones. Why change horses in the middle of a stream?

"How we gonna go 'bout choosin'?" Mr. O'Grady had ridden all the way from his homestead? Rachel was startled by the realization that somehow she had allowed herself to neglect the fellow-travelers seeking a new start in the Oregon Territory. Why, she had forgotten the man's first name! But she did remember

Elsa, his courageous wife, who had delivered a baby during a flood which held them up for days. She *must* renew friendship with them all—Elsa, Mandy Burnside, Opal Sanders, the Farnals. And how long had it been since she called on Nola, Yolanda's mother who had been such a solace when mother died back East?

With an effort, Rachel's mind came back to the meeting. "Yes, voting would be better," one of the men was agreeing. "You mean voting on councilmen—then again on mayor? How long would each serve?"

"Good question," Buck answered. "Another decision. We could rotate members of the council. And as for the mayor, well, yes, that could be a separate election. Or the person receiving the greatest number of votes on the ballot could automatically become mayor."

There was a chorus of approval. But what to do right now? Couldn't Buck appoint one?

"Gentlemen," Buck reminded them, "we are not a city yet."

"Sounds complicated-like," one of the men mumbled in a head-scratching tone.

"Yes, but that's the way a democracy works. Now, I suggest that we move along with the agenda." The other members of the council nodded.

"There is a guest speaker I wish to introduce. One who can fill you in on an important matter—our shared past. It is important that every resident in our soon-to-be-incorporated city appreciates our history. It is a legacy we will wish to pass down to our children. May I present Rachel Lord Jones? Mrs. Jones?"

"Thank you, *Mr.* Jones."

Rachel was smiling as she turned to face a sea of gasping faces. A woman? A woman *here*? Thank goodness there was no hissing, not so much as a ripple of whispers. On the other hand, the dead silence was not easy to address. A spattering of applause would have helped, but she had not expected that. Again the *déjà vu*. Time's calendar stopped, then began flipping backward. She was speaking to an audience of long ago—one she had faced as the only woman present, saying nothing, simply holding tightly to Cole's hand. And eventually, after his untimely death, taking over completely. Now she must prove herself once more. This time she would never let go again. Women must have some rights— maybe even vote—but first, she must gain favor in the eyes of these men. Feminine, but not kittenish—meeting the criteria of the "weaker sex." Apprehension turned to amusement—not diminishing her sincerity.

"For the benefit of you whom I have not met, once upon a time I was Rachel Buchanan—before my marriage to Colby Lord. It is with pride that I stand before you to claim the full name of Rachel Buchanan Lord Jones," Rachel began softly and sweetly. "The name of Lord stands out as a legend in our city—it was Cole's dream to establish a town free of crime, a city of true brotherly love and concern, dedicated to God. Please understand, then, that the name of Lordsburg is *not* because of *his* name but in honor of the Lord who led us through storms, Indian raids, and near-starvation along the frontier trail to the Oregon Territory."

Pausing a moment to steady her voice, Rachel saw a flicker of interest in the eyes of the strangers who, moments before, had registered shock and something akin to resentment. "Only faith saw us through."

"Amen!" boomed David Saul Galloway.

"Thank you, Brother Davey," Rachel said humbly. And to the audience, she added, "Brother Davey made the perilous journey West with us—drove one of the lead wagons and comforted the bereaved when they laid their loved ones to rest along that lonely trail. It was this dedicated man who performed marriages, blest newborn babies—and prayed fervently. It was he who saw Cole's dream come true."

"*Amen, amen!*" came a surprising chorus. "We wuz thar, too—"

These were her friends—hers, Cole's, and Buck's. Oh, praise the Lord for every single one of them. They gave her the strength to go on—to tell her story objectively, without undue credit to any of the founders, and give insight to the bloodshed and iron tears which went into building the lovely city of today. A story of ultimate triumph....

The faces of her audience faded away. And Rachel Buchanan Lord Jones no longer struggled with the present. Apprehension, amusement, and unworthy thoughts were but withered grass. She spoke as if guided by God's Spirit. Surely it was He who rolled back the scroll of time before her. In a vision, all things past were her present. The words she spoke were prophecy....

She stood once more in a place not of man's creation. Sky-brushing timber untouched by human hands, waiting to be hewn into logs. Logs to be fashioned for constructing cozy cabins, the excess sent down the water ways for other pioneers of the raw, rich land. And the one rounded hill in the midst of oak, hazel, and all kinds of underwood. Could the survivors of the long journey be so heartless as to hack away the haven for deer, bear, wolves, and elk? Heartless they must be, for there was no way of surviving without housing. Anyway, the timber was considered worthless without a way of hauling it away. There would come a day—but for now, there must be houses, churches, schools.

Then what a welcome from those who had come before, including Judson and Nola Lee. And once again came the old sense of adventure which had brought the newer settlers West. Yolanda Lee's letter had not exaggerated. And, oh, the togetherness spirit of it all.

Cole's dream began to materialize. Homesteading, mining, trapping, *and dreams* demanded supplies. And so a first store, a second, all organized around the teaching and preaching of the doctrine of love, which drew hordes to each other's houses.

And then the discovery of Superstition Mountain and its legendary Blue Bucket Mine at the very peak, the cradle of crime—*real* crime. The arrival of the militia . . . kidnappings for ransom—proving once more that "the love of money *is* the root of all evil." The building of this very hall for men to meet in and make decisions such as: What to do about the spread of pestilence and how to handle the undesirables who raided homes and blamed their crimes on the Indians. . . . The fire—the awful fire—which licked hungrily at Lordsburg, leaving the dreams of Colby Lord in ashes. And finally the still-unexplained explosion atop Superstition Mountain . . . burying forever all signs of the lost mine . . . sucking brave men into the roaring inferno in search of others. Among them Colby Lord himself. . . .

A deadly hush covered the earth and the shocked-silent ghosts of mankind moved wordlessly in the eerie twilight of crumbled dreams. . . .

Moaning, then raging, and finally, a turning back to God, gripping His Almighty Hand, asking His guidance in restoring their faith, in their hopes of piecing together a dream which only He could bring back from the dead. . . .

Each rainbow has a reflection. Rachel caught a glimpse of it first, passed it along to others, and love—too long folded away in bitterness—came back. In a delicious afterglow, she took her late husband's place—advising, engineering. Oh, he had trained her well.

"And what you see here," Rachel ended triumphantly, "is the fulfillment of that dream—a dream we must keep alive, guard, and cherish. Sometime I will share more," she promised, "but for now, I beg you to carry on responsibly. Like God and country, our heritage is worth our all. Let us live in peace, with no division over code, creed, color or gender. For those of us who have sacrificed our all, feel—no, we *know* that we are God's chosen ones, not because of our goodness but His!"

She had made a soft landing into the real world of today. Once more she could feel, see, hear, *care*. And care she did when there was applause. Not the spattering she would have laid down her life for preceding her speech! *More*. The men were standing. Standing in ovation while their hands clapped out a glory which made the rafters ring!

What they said Rachel would never know. Blinded by tears of joy, she made her way toward the back of the building where— would miracles never cease?—Emmaline Galloway was entering with an enormous granite pot of steaming coffee in one hand and a tray piled sky-high with tantalizing gingerbread in the other. A spicy aroma filled the hall.

"Oh, Aunt Em—God bless you! It was wonderful, the way they received me—and more wonderful that you emphasized my daring suggestion that we ladies be accepted. To have another woman—"

"Two uv 'em dearie," the older woman, whispered breathing heavily from her burden. "When yuh can, sneak a peek there in th' corner—now, whar in tarnation is my Davey-Love? I'd be dead on my feet iffen I hadn' ordered these Mother Comfort shoes."

"Let me help."

"Come up front and hep me serve—no, not afore lookin'—"

Rachel needlessly smoothed her hair, using her elbow to shield her eyes as they searched the shadows. And there she stood—the woman Aunt Em had pointed out. Who? Oh, Dunigan, Lily Dunigan. But what was she to Julius Doogan alias Jules Dunigan?

The woman, stooped as if to make a quick exit, was making her way through the throng toward the door. And what was this? She was surrounded by men of a different breed—hard, shifty-eyed, so dirty and unkempt that Rachel's nostrils picked up the foul odor. She must escape or she would be sick. In her rush, she bumped into the Dunigan woman, their eyes meeting. In spite of the raw fear Rachel saw there, she saw what surely must be a gentle woman. The type of woman fashioned purposely to care for others . . . tuck in babies after bad dreams . . . fry the holes in doughnuts while young children watched...kiss away bruises, and, above all, be loyal to those she loved, child or adult.

She hurried away before Rachel could greet her. And then a familiar figure sliced between them. "Good evening, Mrs. Lord Jones," he said with an insolent smile, his sharp eyes admiring her insolently. "How wise of you to keep some things to yourself—" Jules Dunigan's sentence remained unfinished. Rachel rushed out before the benediction.

9

Yolanda's Secret

The petitions were finished. Lordsburg citizens were off and running, as if vying for the crown of laurel leaves before the "Go!" shot was fired! And now, this morning before the Joneses' Rhode Island Red rooster announced the approach of dawn, Buck had saddled up and taken the papers to Salem. Rachel was excited along with him as they had a quick breakfast. But there came one bad moment when it was time for goodbyes. Riding away had been Cole's lifestyle, but Buck—Buck had been such a stay-at-home—always at her side—

Again, the feeling of *déjà vu*, which was interrupted by an able-bodied whirlwind as Star, David, and Saul bounded down the stairs with the newest pet yapping at their heels as they flung themselves upon their parents. All were talking at once.

"Mother promised we could—("*might*," Star corrected)—go on the Bible-study picnic. We have to pack a lunch 'cause the Reverend's wagon leaves *re-eeal* early. And we wanted to say goodbye to Daddy Buck—and can—("*may*")—the dog go?"

Mary Cole ran to join the family. She had taken more time with her hair and looked for the world like a "Sleepy Doll" featured in the latest catalogues—all pink and white with an oversized bow holding her dark curls. She darted to Buck and administered a strangle-hold, as the puppy nipped playfully at her heels.

"Hey now, you four! Have mercy—give me air, will you, Duckies? Want me to strangle before hearing what you named that mutt?"

Their young voices grew shrill with laughter. "He's no

45

mutt—he's a fine dog from a good family!" David said solemnly. "And he—"

"—*has* a name!" Saul interrupted. "He's a Scotty and—"

"—so we named him Scot,'" Mary Cole shrieked in Buck's ear as she continued her grip on his neck and, hair ribbon forgotten, pressed even closer while caressing his neck with the top of her head.

"Scot." Buck tested the name as if giving it all his attention. "Now that figures," he grinned then singsonged:

> "Once I had a dog and his name was Scot—Which
> most Scotty dogs are named, I guess, than not!"

"Oh, *Dad-dee*," Star laughed her seldom silver-spoon laugh. Eventually freed, Buck motioned Rachel onto the front porch.

"The children adore you," Rachel said softly. "Oh, Buck—"

"And the adoration is mutual," he said huskily. "Now, take care—"

"I will—oh, I will—for you, for them—" Rachel's voice was muffled against his starched shirt. Then, looking up into his eyes, half expecting to feel herself drowning in the blue depths of Cole's eyes, she saw instead a dipperful of stars reflecting in the kitchen window. It was then that the two men merged into one. Adventure, excitement, and peace overwhelmed her. There would be no more terrifying dreams. Love had washed them away.

There was still time for an early-morning walk after the family left. Buck would see his charges through the woods where the wagon was to meet them, and then ride on. The sound of childish laughter and the rattle of wagon wheels had been reassuring. Oh, how she loved them! And what a glorious morning it was! And how thankful she was that she and Buck had had the long, long talk—telling each other every detail—before he left. Blessed intimacy of marriage—something Yolanda lacked in her life. But why?

It was at that point that Rachel decided she *must* see her friend. She turned toward the still-shadowy path leading toward town, then cautiously turned back. Why not climb the slight incline and enjoy the glorious view? The mountains in the distant east looked like a purple camel kneeling for the rising sun to fling a soft pink saddle over its highest hump. Below, houses, some straining at grandeur, nestled with tall church spires reaching heavenward, their very tops painted crimson by the rising sun.

The writhing loops and bends of the dirt road, like dusty-brown snakes seeking shelter before the sun-warmed surface heated their bellies, looked out of place as it found its way to dark, wooded expanses, patched by emerald fields of wheat. And, feeding it all, the ultramarine stream singing its way to the river. One could learn much more from nature, Rachel reflected. Hurrying as it was, the rippling stream always had time for a greeting, pausing at every root and fern-clump along the mossy banks.

Prosaic windows flashed gold briefly—and then the sunrise.

Reluctantly, then expectantly, Rachel turned back to the trail and hurried toward the formal garden surrounding the home of Dr. and Mrs. Maynard Killjoy. Yolanda ran to greet her before she knocked. A busybody breeze ruffled her dark hair, made her look childish in her long pink nightgown and wrapper. But the strong light of the morning sun revealed the shadows around her dark eyes and accentuated the furrow between her heavy brows. Her face had lost its healthy glow. Something *was* wrong.

"A thousand pardons," Rachel said as lightly as she could force her voice to be. "It is far too early. Were you and your doctor-husband discussing something that upset you?"

"My doctor-husband is not here—seldom is." There was bitterness in Yolanda's voice, but she tried hard to recover. "Coffee—you and I—like old times. Come in, Darling Rachel."

Rachel was buttering her second cinnamon roll when she noticed Yolanda had pushed her own roll aside, untouched. "Should I fear for my life, Yo? I should have brought along our new dog. You know, let him sample, see if he survives—"

Yolanda was not listening.

"Yoo-hoo! Does my friend live here?"

"What? I—er—" Yolanda looked startled. And hadn't there been a momentary flash of fright in her eyes? "I don't feel hungry, a touch of the flu, I guess—"

"Is that why we haven't seen you at church or you haven't dropped over to chat?" Rachel laid down her knife and observed her intently. "What does your doctor call it?"

A tomblike silence prevailed as Yolanda's face looked even more pallid beneath the two bright circles of red that stood out on her cheeks like heavy rouge. When she spoke, there was no mention of Rachel's question—just a quicksilver change of subject.

"The children kept their promise, didn't they? I mean about going to the picnic? I refused to let Roland go—until they promised—"

"You would have denied him *that*? I'm surprised at you! Of course they went. Wild horses couldn't have held them back, but why—" she began, only to have the answer flick into place. "Safety in numbers?"

"Something like that, Rachel," Yolanda burst out with sudden emotion, "somebody—you know who—has been tormenting Roland, insulting him, absolutely dogging his footsteps, poking fun at his glasses—threatening to break them—as well as his *bones*, every time he takes the trail beside the stream. I—I'm terrified—"

"The plot thickens," Rachel murmured theatrically in an effort to coax a smile. She was unsuccessful, a fact which triggered determination to get to the bottom of Jules Dunigan's guarded activities along the stream, even though she might well be leaping headfirst into a maze of brambles. But a maze had to end somewhere....

"What's wrong, Rachel?" Yolanda's anxiety-filled question dragged Rachel's thoughts from her imagined search alongside the stream where, trailing a thread of evidence, she had been stalked.

"Just thinking," she answered truthfully. "Rest assured Rowie will be safe today. The Reverend's strict orders are that the children cling together like vines—no wandering away. *And*," she smiled, "you know how they stick up for that son of yours. Personally, I would rather be tossed into a lion's den like Daniel than be attacked by the four Joneses! Could it be that we're making too much of this?"

"Too much? You don't know him like I do—" Yolanda's voice trailed off as if he were too horrible to talk about.

"That's true." Rachel drained her cup, her mind searching for exactly the right words. "Yolanda, I'm going to ask you a question—and *please*, I want a straight answer. Have you told Maynard?"

Yolanda looked as if she did not recognize the name. "He—I—"

"The truth, Yo!"

The answer was a breathless, "No! It would be like clipping the last thread that holds us—not that we're lovers—"

It was Rachel's turn to be breathless. "Yolanda, what are you *saying*? Forgive me—sometimes even best friends meddle—but if I can help, won't you confide? Sometimes just talking about it—"

"If you want to help—just catch me up on everything about him."

Him had to mean Jules Dunigan. Rachel, knowing it was futile to question further, quickly recapped all that had happened then reassured Yolanda that some, perhaps most, could be only suspicion. "Besides, maybe Dunigan will move on as soon as he finds whatever he's after. Incorporation's sure to take place. Then we can have some restrictions—that is, keep such people from setting up any kind of business."

"It's too late. Jules Dunigan is already in business."

"He what?"

Yolanda's voice could have come from a grave. "He owns the Welcome Stranger Cafe—at least, he lays claim to it—and something's going on there that's dangerous. You *know* that, Rachel."

"I *think* there is, you mean. We'll see. But, even if it's true, what's troubling you so much? The men can handle it—and we'll help just as we always have. Tell you what," she said brightly, "why don't you and Maynard get away for a time? Remember all those plans he had for taking you to Europe—and how excited you were? You," she attempted a giggle, "were going to discover an exotic island—"

"Stop—*please* stop. You're torturing me." Yolanda burst into tears, her frail body shaking unmercifully.

"Oh, Yo!" Rachel was around the table immediately, kneeling at Yolanda's side. Drawing her head to her tenderly, she begged forgiveness then said, "It was cruel of me to pry. Does your mother know how upset you are? Why not spend some time with your parents—get away—"

"No! I—I—c-can't. They'd know—"

"Know *what*, Yo?" Rachel pushed a tear-dampened strand of raven hair from Yolanda's face as she released her. "Nothing could be that awful. Something's wrong—but, believe me, Maynard needs to know. He acted happier than I have ever seen him at the council meeting—as if he had the world in his pocket. Make me understand! I refuse to leave until you do."

"I'm pregnant!"

Rachel rocked on her heels in shock. Pregnant? After ten years? "Did you tell him *that*?"

"He told *me*. He's a doctor, remember? And don't tell me to be happy!" Her voice was filled with loathing.

10

More and More Questions

Buck was delayed—too long it seemed to Rachel. She postponed plans for calling on friends lest she miss a message. But there was no letter. No telegram. Just waiting.

Bible school was still in progress. Rachel accompanied the children to the church, did her shopping—often stopping to chat with Aunt Em and Brother Davey—and then returned with Star, Mary Cole, and the twins. They were chatting, always chatting. But Rachel was ever on guard, the familiar stretch of friendly woods through which they must pass seeming now to change into an impenetrable forest where, soundlessly, a thousand menacing eyes watched and waited. The site had grown even more threatening when Star confided that a group of men on horseback had followed the wagon the day of the picnic. "They thought we did not see—and they were right about most of the niños, so busy were they in their talk. But my eyes saw. And the Reverend saw also. *Padres* know things. . . ."

"Did you talk about it, Darling?" Rachel queried, her heart almost stopping "And the children—did you share your picture of the man?"

"The evil one, *si* but not with the Reverend. You told me to keep quiet—and I shall obey. Mary Cole and Saul paid little attention, perhaps because I was most careful lest they be frightened and have bad dreams, *verdad*?"

"*Verdad*, sweetheart. And David—what about him?"

"David was more solemn. He thinks more—*verdad*?"

"*Verdad*," Rachel repeated. "What you say is true. Maybe I should make the warning a little stronger."

The way Star's dark eyebrows knitted together suggested that the child knew more. Just enough to make Rachel more apprehensive.

It was in the middle of the third week that the telegram came. That particular day she had paused again to look down upon the sprawling city. First to feast her eyes on the unbroken greenness of the fields, then to see the church which glowed like alabaster in the bright sunlight. And then came the unmistakable rustle in the bushes along the banks of the stream. Men, a dozen at least, were pushing a boat into the midst of the bushes. What was the mystery? And what part did she play in it? The only thing she knew for sure was that she *was* a main character. . . .

Today Aunt Em would be baking her special raisin pies. Rachel headed toward town. It was a good day to drop by to sample them and exchange news. Only there was more to be shared—

"Mrs. Jones!"

Rachel jumped at the sound of Willie Mead's voice and whirled quickly. So quickly that she caught sight of Jules Dunigan's back as he all but slunk from the telegraph office. Rachel was sure that, as the telegrapher ran an ink-stained finger along the single strand of hair remaining on his pink skull, he, too, turned eyes toward the retreating figure. Willie had removed his sunshade but his round, blank face revealed nothing. At that moment Rachel was certain of what she had suspected all along—the man, so seemingly unaware of what went on about him, saw and heard it all. Why did that disturb her?

"Telegram from the mister," he said, handing her a yellow envelope and watching her face as she read the contents: COMPLICATIONS STOP BE HOME MONDAY STOP CALL CLOSED-DOOR COUNCIL STOP LOVE YOU STOP BUCK.

The man seemed to wait for her to share what he had already read.

What she said instead caught him off-guard. "What's the man we once knew as Julius doing here?"

Obviously flustered, Willie Mead said, "He—why, I don't know—I mean, he's staying at the Welcome Stranger—"

"Which he owns. Don't look so surprised. You knew, Mr. Mead. I advise caution—you know his history. *And* make sure he knows nothing of this telegram!"

"You can trust me."

Rachel was not sure at all.

Minutes later Rachel was relating the incident to the Galloways. Brother Davey's gray beard actually bristled on the sides before settling down to droop beneath his chin. "Sometimes I git th' feelin' thet feller Mead's th' ravenous bird from th' west Isaiah talked 'bout—"

"From th' east, Davey-Love," Aunt Em dusted flour from her hands, causing a white cloud to float momentarily then settle on the apron encircling her dark sackcloth "uniform." " 'N speakin' uv directions, will'ya be good enough t'hand me th' raisins on th' south cook-table—without nibblin'?"

The grasshopper-like little man moved to obey his beloved Emmy-Gal. "East, right—'n Willie *did* come from th' east, but I'm a'doubtin' iffen he brung along much righteousness. I know he claimed he wuz on th' Lord's side 'way back yonder, but sumpin' allus whispered uh warnin'— like he wus uh follerer 'stead uv uh leader. Not so's it'd show, but stripped down to his nakedness—"

"Now, now, Davey-Love, don' go judgin'," his wife scolded gently. "Hit's this man a-callin' hisself Jules Dunigan that's got me worried."

"Ain't no proof on thet *mushroom* neither."

"Mushroom?" Rachel all but laughed.

"Yeah, uh real toadstool. Th' rest uv us is trees, puttin' down roots solid-like. While he's uh real fungus—springin' here, thar 'n ever'whar, spreadin' pizon then hidin' out lack Adam 'n Eve."

Emmaline Galloway rescued the first batch of pies, bubbling up in miniature russet geysers through slits in the crisp brown pastry. Her husband, on her heels, shoved six more pies into the giant oven. "Trouble is," he mumbled, "he's clean as uh whistle on th' surface. Me—I watch 'im day 'n night—"

Aunt Em plopped into the nearest chair and fanned herself with a courtesy fan from Handy Drugs and Sundries. "Fer as we kin cal'clate, this so-called new-man version uv Julius Doogan ain't connected with the gang uv hoodlums messin' round th' streamside. Se we don' so much as have circumstantial evidence—ain't thet jest what th' big-town lawyer called hit—th' one who read our Cole's will—and then General Wilkes'?"

"I seen 'im yesterday!" Brother Davey announced importantly.

James Haute! Across the screen of her mind, Rachel saw the man who had brought the sad-sweet tidings that both men had left her their love—and their possessions. Short of stature, black hair glistening with oil and carefully plastered to turn upward like question marks, as if to balance the waxed mustache. Thir-tyish then, he would be pushing 50 now. Looks were deceiving, Rachel had learned from Mr. Haute. The man was no longer comical when, intelligently and efficiently, he went into action, reading the papers which left her more than wealthy and appointing "one Mr. Buckley Jones" executor of funds specified for construction of a new church, school, and completion of the city-to-be. Those memories still hurt....

"James Haute," she breathed. "What is he doing here?"

Brother Davey frowned. "Upset me, too, Rachel. I got t'thinkin' 'bout th' party uv th' second part 'n all them fancy words—'n how th' man danced 'round th' candle 'stead uv comin' right out 'n sayin' sumpin' 'bout—whut wuz hit, Emmy-Gal? I d'clare the ole noodle's failin' some."

"'Bout lack it allus wuz, Davey-Love," Aunt Em winked at Rachel, breaking the tension. "Conflict uv int'rest—meanin' thet claim Julius Doogan faked. S'pose he's follerin' Doogan—Dun-igan?"

Aunt Em stopped fanning, contemplating her own question. Brother Davey was quick to answer for her. "Could be, jest could be! Thet blood-suckin' bedbug's like uh shiftless ant packin' 'round a bunch uv aphids t'do 'is work whilst he busies hisself spreadin' disease—"

"The disease of man's inhumanity to man," Rachel finished in a dead voice. *Oh dear Lord, must I go through it all again?*

"Eye fer uh eye—and in this case I'd enjoy hit!"

"Davey-Love!" Aunt Em gasped in shock. "You bein' uh man uv th' Word—"

"'N uh man uv th' law!" David Saul leaped to his feet and, grabbing his back with one hand, hammered the table with the other. "Y'er uh dead man, Jules Dunigan!"

Rachel and Aunt Em stared at him in disbelief. "Jest thinkin' out loud—jest prophesyin'—" Brother Davey said, eyes on the scrubbed floor.

Rachel refused the pie Aunt Em set before her. Murmuring that she wanted to see the Reverend, which was true, she made a quick exit.

Brother Davey was right. She too felt that danger was immi-nent. Loathing the thought, wishing nothing more than to banish it, Rachel could not. In one way or another Jules Dunigan would undo them all—unless—unless—

Oh, no! She must not entertain such thinking. And yet, some-how they must find a way to legally corner this man, the refuse of the world, and turn the tables. Cowardice settled nothing, begged disaster.

But how?

A temporary relief from panic came when Brother Davey called seemingly from another world, "Want I should call th' meetin'?"

Rachel waved affirmatively. Togetherness, that was the key. *Togetherness and renewed faith,* she thought as she hurried to the church. . . .

11

Old Times
—Good and Bad—
Revisited

The Reverend Luke Elmo had changed little. His head, always bare of hair, rose like a full moon above the black robe the one-time circuit rider still clung to. Rachel knew, however, that his strength was failing—as was his close-up vision.

"Rachel?" he queried uncertainly, even though she was within a few feet of him when she called out a greeting. "Welcome, my child."

Rachel brushed an affectionate kiss against his still-unlined face. The elderly minister would ever hold a special place—a hallowed place in her heart—as did this site. It was a mistake, however, to raze the original building—because of the decreasing attendance and, in a more personal sense, the memories the other church held. It was there that she and Cole had privately renewed their vows just before Yolanda and her young minister took their own. There, too, that—after their shared journey through the long, dark tunnel of despair—the two girls had taken their present husbands, to have and to hold, in a double wedding. . . . What would life have been like had the horrible explosion not snuffed out the lives of the men they loved? Rachel, just as she had emerged from the tunnel before her beloved friend, had been able to put her heart back together—let it love—before Yolanda. Now she wondered if Yolanda ever would completely. Flames from the burning mountain still raged within her—the desire to replace the love she had lost and get revenge against the man she held responsible. She was approaching another crossroad. . . .

"I thought perhaps Yolanda would be with you. Somehow the two of you belong together," the Reverend Elmo ventured.

He paused, motioning Rachel into his small study. Her nod indicated that she did not wish to discuss Yolanda. "Call on her sometime," she suggested once they were seated.

This time it was the minister who nodded. Glancing out the window, his gentle eyes panning the area, he explained that the children had stayed overtime while Star completed a picture. Familiar setting, of course, but did Rachel have any idea who dominated the scene? Rachel did, but the name hung between them unmentioned.

Luke Elmo pressed his hands together, tips of the near-transparent fingers barely touching. "And you know who else has returned?"

"Haute—James Haute. I'm wondering how long he plans to remain—and what he is doing here," Rachel said faintly.

"I am unable to answer your question as to his purpose. As to his plans, he wants to stay—has rented the offices adjoining Dr. Killjoy's. It is I who will be moving along—"

Rachel grabbed at the sides of the peacock chair Frank's Fine Furniture had donated for lady guests as an advertising scheme. "You—you're going?"

"Don't look sad, my child. I have seen you sad before—and now rejoice at your happiness. I am weary, Rachel, bone-tired—and have abused your hospitality. I came only to fill in—and have overstayed—not so much as paying my board and keep—"

"You are our guest—not a boarder!" Rachel protested. "You are needed here—more than ever now—with—with the return of these men—"

"May I quote the words of our Lord—say that I will not 'leave you comfortless'? I will announce my plans to enter a retirement home this church has contributed to when the deacons meet and at the same time recommend a new, young minister. Come, come, let us be glad. Now, what brings you here? I feel that you are troubled."

Rachel avoided his eyes and his questioning tone. "I need to visit some of our members whom I've neglected shamefully. Buck will be home—telegraphed me—" her voice took on excitement, "and I—we, his family—will be *so* happy! He wishes to meet with the council, so we—that is, you and I, could go calling—if you will come along?"

"Of course."

"We can alert the men and, Reverend, I so want to see the Lees—that is, for a visit. Yolanda hasn't visited *and* refuses my invitation—there! I've said too much."

"Not at all. As a matter of fact, I do not wish to have you traipsing those lonely stretches alone—not until we, uh, know."

How understanding he was, Rachel thought as she rose to go. Outside, "Miss Callie," Yolanda's "baby sister" could manage the children with the help of Little Star. Rachel knew that Yolanda adored her carbon-copy sister, her identical twin—except for the 20-year difference in their ages. Why had she neglected to contact *her*?

With that question, Rachel's thoughts rolled backward like an enormous rock which, jarred free of a mountainside, plummeted down . . . down . . . to where she had sublimated the memory of Callie's birth. Who was the "medicine man" who appeared to deliver the baby on Christmas Eve while the rest of the family attended the Christmas program? *Who was he*?

On impulse, Rachel stopped by Yolanda's. No, she could not take time to go in—just give Yolanda another opportunity to see her parents.

Rachel's knock went unanswered. But *why*, when she was sure she heard voices when the garden gate clicked behind her? Had the click triggered a warning of danger? The glass curtains between the heavy brown brocade drapes moved ever so slightly as if touched by a small breeze. With a feeling that anxious eyes had peered cautiously from behind the shield of the window dressing, Rachel knocked again.

This time there was instantaneous response. "Auntie Rachel!"

Rachel stooped to put her arms around Roland, noting, as always, the quiet intelligence in the deep-set eyes behind his glasses. "Too big for a hug?"

Roland smiled shyly, "Not from you—I'm hurrying though. I want to see Star's finished picture."

The boy bounded down the path, dodging the fountain, just as Yolanda's pallid face came into focus. "Rachel! My word, you scared me out of my wits. My mouth's so dry I could spit enough cotton to knit a sweater!"

Rachel burst into laughter, born of amusement at the unique language and relief. The old Yolanda was back! Maybe only for a visit, but who knew where it could lead? Yolanda was laughing, too. Laughing until tears rolled down her cheeks, clinging to Rachel, while the two of them rocked back and forth for the first time—how long had it been? Since they were girls?

"Hey, it wasn't *that* funny," Yolanda gasped, wiping her eyes.

And then she was weeping. Rachel reached out and embraced her again. "That's right, Darling—cry it out—just don't shut yourself off from me. Not ever again, do you hear?"

Yolanda nodded, still weeping uncontrollably. "It's a 10-hanky crying jag—I—I—" she hiccuped, "have held it pent up for so long—so, so long—"

At length, Rachel whispered gently, "What is it, Yo? Be specific."

"J–j–just everything. Oh, don't ever stop loving me—no matter what happens—or what I do—" Yolanda's voice traveled to another world.

"Fat chance!" Rachel said hastily. And then the words soaked in. A thousand frightening images flashed before her. *No matter what happens? No matter what I do?*

"What is it you plan, Yo?" she asked in what she hoped was an offhand manner. Then, teasingly, "Maybe we can conspire together."

But the moment had passed. The old Yolanda was gone. The newer version had stolen her away, leaving a frightened woman whose two charcoal eyes were as blank as last night's ashes.

"My husband and I no longer love one another," she said as if some ventriloquist were speaking through her motionless lips. "I guess we never did. He is in love with his work—without loving his patients. They mean no more to him than white rats, held captive in a maze to be used in his experiments. *I* am just another one of them—bearing a child at my age—" Yolanda's voice grew shrill, hysterical.

"Your mother did."

"I am not my mother. She, too, was a victim. But at least she bore the 13 children on a regular basis—my womb is closed by time—and choice. Oh, women are prisoners, Rachel—white rats and mere toys!"

Rachel grabbed the white-knuckled fists that flailed the air. Gently, she uncurled the bloodless fingers. "You don't mean that—just tell me what's wrong. Why were you afraid to open the door?"

Yolanda's eyes rolled back in her head. "I was afraid—afraid of *him*—and afraid of Jules Dunigan. Maybe they're into something together. Both of them are watching my every move—spying—*I saw them!*"

"Yo—Yo, listen to me. You aren't making sense. Listen to me—" Rachel gave the thin shoulders a gentle shake, but deep inside her

her an unknown terror was building. Yolanda was emotional, but she would never fall to pieces like this without cause. "What proof do you have?"

"Come outside—you'll see." At least her eyes were focusing.

Yes, she saw. Outside each window there were tracks. Several sizes. But all were tracks of men's shoes.

"But you, Yolanda, what's happening inside *you*? What do you plan to do?"

"I am not going to give birth to this child!"

12

The Imposters

With a fine sense of the dramatic, the sun rose in all its glory. Like molten gold, it laced the ragged bonnet of snow remaining atop the far-distant peak of Mt. Hood, while to the west, its still-warm fingers picked out blotches of color along the slopes of Superstition Mountain. But even as Rachel and the reverend clipped across the thirsting countryside in Rachel's buggy, a ghost-like fog appeared from nowhere, lending chill to the air. Sure signs of fall, perfectly natural. But Rachel wished the day could have remained bright. Yolanda had darkened it.

Well, at least the dear man beside her lent brightness. He was a good conversationalist and kept up an even flow of talk about the growth so obvious all around them. Cabins dotting the land where once there had been isolation. Fields of grain, still trying to stand at attention while awaiting harvest. As the fertile valley, centered by the rise in terrain which boasted Lordsburg, yielded to rolling hills and timbered uplands, the minister pointed with pride to the new crops only a few years ago unheard of: filberts, hops, berries, vetch (good for hay, grazing, and soil enrichment—a legume which furnished nitrogen). Nitrogen? Rachel's mind drifted elsewhere. Didn't lightning do the same? Almost as if nature considered the thought a summons, there was a distant rumble of thunder. Oh dear, did she recall how to raise the buggy top? She had brought no umbrella and—

"—and wish that Yolanda had accepted your invitation." Rachel had missed the preceding words. And here they were at the Lees' home!

The house was newly-whitewashed, she noted, and there was a whittled-out picket fence surrounding the aging split-log house. The pickets were rough, ranging in size from cordwood then dwindling to little more than toothpicks. The fence, nevertheless, was a dream come true for Nola Lee. And Judson had his coveted roads through the vast fields. They zigzagged drunkenly through cornfields, orchards, and gardens filled with every vegetable Rachel could name—and a few she could not. Reeling its ribald way to the sheep meadows, the road's forks came together at the great once-red barn on which was painted: Dr. Sweet's Chill Tonic—Ask For It By Name!

What on earth?

Luke Elmo answered her unasked question with a hint of laughter. "The makers of that concoction paid Jud to advertise—money he used to fence the place in and do a few things for Nola. They refuse help from the children—too bad about some of them—"

"The boys?" Rachel's voice trailed off. "I'm afraid I've lost track of them. It will be good for me to get back in touch. If I'd kept in closer contact with Yolanda, maybe—"

Rachel could have bitten her tongue off. Nobody else suspected there was a problem. How wrong she was!

"I feel a grave responsibility, too, my dear," Reverend Elmo said, as he alighted and extended a hand to her. "Watch, your skirt's caught on the fender." As she untangled it, he continued talking in a low tone. "A minister does feel closer to couples he marries, witnesses that total joy as they commit their lives to God and one another. Ah, if only young people could remember that the *we* in a wedding comes before the *I*. But," his voice sounded tired, "the union is such a private matter. We servants of the Lord can help, if asked—otherwise, we run the risk of interfering— 'putting asunder'—"

If he said more, the words were lost in another burst of thunder, closer this time, indicating a strike nearby. A speckled cock squawked a warning to the variegated harem. The hens foraging at his spurs took to the air with a chorus of cackles then, reassured by his vainglorious stand, came back to earth apologetically behind him.

The commotion brought Judson and Nola to the door. "Inside— inside!" Mr. Lee was waving his broad red-haired hand in welcome, the very walls appearing to vibrate with his excitement. And yet his eyes scanned the sky and focused on the buggy.

Quickly, but not quickly enough to convince Rachel of his purpose—it was Yolanda, not a storm, the big Irishman checked on.
But pride would not allow him to ask. Fierce pride which he tried
covering with blarney.

A hungry-looking hound rose from his bed in Nola's jungle of
flowers and, scarcely glancing at the guests, raised a speckled
nose to the sky, giving a single, unenthusiastic bark. "Shet up,
Houn' Dog! *Now* ye be barkin'!" then addressing Rachel and the
Reverend, "Good fer nothin' 'ceptin' treein' squirrels—got some
fer dinner, fact is, ain't we, Wife?"

The angular woman's once-dark hair was totally white now.
And time's gravitational force had pulled her body unmercifully
to the right side, shortening one leg. The intelligent face revealed
pain with each step; but it did not slacken her pace as, dark eyes
bright with unshed tears, she hurried forward to embrace
Rachel. Rachel understood the tide of memories which must be
washing back to the past. "What would I have done without you,
dear Mrs. Lee?" Rachel had asked so many times, only to have her
reply, "You mean the company I kept with your dear mother in her
last days? We needed each other—and what would I have done
without *you* to teach our Yolanda so much?"

Rachel took both her misshapen hands and, in an effort to hold
back her own tears, sang out gaily, "Um-mmm, is that rhubarb I
smell?"

Yolanda's mother smiled shyly in appreciation. "The same—
you mean you'll stay for dinner? It gets lonely—" she broke in
mid-sentence when Judson cleared his throat.

"Wife here needs t'git out some—'taint writ-down nowhere
thet wimmen folks keep on a'cookin' 'n cleanin' onct th' brood be
gone, all 'ceptin' Abraham, Father of th' Multitude. He took a
hankerin' t'th' soil—me oldest—son, thet is. Say, would ye be
willin' t'make th' sourdoughs fer us, girlie, like—"

Like Yolanda used to do. Judson Lee was grieving for his
daughter. Undoubtedly thought she had become "uppish,"
ashamed of her own kin. Rachel longed to assure him, to explain.
But she had promised. . . .

"Guess I shouldn' be askin—" Judson's voice underlined his
need of his daughter.

"Of course, I will, Mr. Lee. In fact, surprise! I brought buttermilk—remembering how you enjoy buttermilk-beaten biscuits.
Want to guess what else we have in the buggy?"

"*Pour.* Ye be bringin' me pour, girlie?" His Irish-blue eyes were
dancing. And his legs ready to jig as well.

Luke Elmo had gone for the dairy gifts and Judson Lee was still talking. "Why would folks be ruinin' rich, heavy cream in its natch'ral state? Whip hit, me foot! They be takin' out their spite on what nature's prepared perfect-like. Nothin'," he licked freckled lips, "like rhubarb cobbler with me pour! God be blessin' ye, girlie!"

Being "company," Rachel and the Reverend would sit at the long, homemade table with himself and his brawny, red-haired son. His wife would serve, after roll call and prayer. "Abraham, Father of the Multitude," Abe mumbled, eyes on his brogues. "Rachel, the Ewe," Rachel said, repressing a smile. Reverend Elmo caught the pattern. "Luke, Lukas the Physician." And then he prayed.

"Want'a set uh spell, Wife, after refills on coffee?"

His wife declined with a shake of her head. Years of serving had conditioned her to a "woman's place." It was too late for change.

Judson did not insist, but spoke of the benches he and Abe had handmade, a far departure from the pitch-oozing fir stumps which served as chairs surrounding the table on Rachel's first visit.

"Come uh long ways, we have—me'n the boy here. How's crops on yonder side uv th' homestead, Abraham?"

Abe forgot his shyness as he told of the abundance—more than the whole settlement could use before some went to waste. "Can I be makin' uh suggestion, Paw?" As permission was granted by the ruddy-cheeked giant who was his father, Abe blurted out, "Seems uh bit t'me we oughta have Preservin' Day like onct we done—'member, Miz Rachel, how we used t'can 'n dry—allus savin' enough fer birds t'winter on? Whatcha think, Paw?" The boy's eyes were shining.

"What uh good idee, Boy! See," he said proudly, "how enterprisin' me lad be?" Pride in his son turned to doubt as he scratched his red thatch of hair. "I dunno—maybe them city folks wouldn' be likin' common food now—all them stores offerin' fancy canned goods. But begory! (brightening) oughten we be tryin'?"

"Indeed we should!" Rachel said happily. "In fact, we all need to return to some of the older ways, get to know our neighbors—a part of Buck's plans. Just set a date. Right now, I will help Mrs. Lee with the dishes—and, oh, Reverend Elmo will tell you about the special council meeting—it's urgent." Excusing herself, Rachel rose.

Mrs. Lee sat alone, elbows on the oilcloth-covered cook-table in the kitchen. Her food was probably cold. She refused to allow Rachel to "get those beautiful hands all red." No to Rachel's suggestion that her food be warmed, just a fresh cup of coffee—what she needed was to talk—privately.

Rachel poured coffee for them both. "About Yolanda?" she said as she seated herself. "I see her so little—"

Mrs. Lee cast an anxious glance into the dining room. "Oh, the men are looking at the fields—and we'll talk quickly. I—I just don't want to talk before my husband—it hurts him so—"

"He loves her dearly, Mrs. Lee—and she loves him, loves all of you. In fact, she is longing to see you, but . . ."

God would have to help her find the words to comfort the mother while guarding the daughter's confidence. *Lord, please!*

"There *is* a problem. But why won't she come?" Nola's voice was sad.

Surely the Lord heard her plea. Rachel suddenly found a possible solution. "Why not go see *her*, Mrs. Lee? She needs you."

Color flooded Mrs. Lee's face and her voice was so low Rachel could scarcely hear. "Me? I—I have nothing to wear. Oh, here they are—"

Judson Lee appeared to be in a very jovial mood as he bade them goodbye. "Better be goin' for shure—could rain. You be knowin' Oregon's weather—whole lot like th' squalls over th' moors 'bout th' time hay's mowed. Ah, dear ole homeland, me Emeral' Isle—"

He was still talking as the Reverend helped Rachel into the buggy. Rachel understood when she saw him hand a note to Luke Elmo, his talk obviously an attempt to divert the others' attention.

The minister scanned the ragged piece of lined paper then handed it to Rachel once they rounded the bend of the road leading downward. Disappointment was her first reaction. She had hoped the note was for his daughter. Instead, it was a request for them to choose a dress for his Nola. "Somethin' real nice, so's she be goin' t'church and be th' bes' dressed wife hereabouts on Preservin' Day."

The money wrapped in the scribbled note was pitifully inadequate, but it caused Rachel's mood to soar again. Aunt Em was a talented seamstress and was not a whit opposed to "borrowing" styles of dresses she saw in the ladies' fashion stores. Rachel would buy the material—the fabric, trim, and notions. Judson need never know.

The Reverend broke into her thoughts. "Judson will attend the meeting. What's more, he will notify the Burnsides and Farnals. We will visit another time. Right now—*gitty-up, Nellie*—we'd best try to outrun this storm."

At that very minute, a single drop of rain, fat with warning, plopped on Rachel's face. Had it not been for that small trick of nature would she have realized that something was happening which somehow, she knew, tied in with the other strange happenings in and around Lordsburg? They had stopped at the base of Superstition Mountain.

"You stay put," Reverend Elmo said quickly. "Wrap yourself in the blanket. I will try my luck at getting this pesky top up."

Rachel, eyes drawn involuntarily to the mountain, so long ordered closed to curiosity seekers, for a glimpse of the site of so much tragedy and the final resting place for Cole and Timothy Norval. A *No Trespassing* sign forbade intruders to go beyond the fence which stood as a guard—with one exception, that of a trail on the other side of the mountain, reserved for the Indians' use only. Superstition Mountain was the ancient "Happy Hunting Ground" resting place of their ancestors. Periodically the tribes gathered, each paying homage by means of tribal dances and songs in languages dating back to a time before the appearance of the "Pale Skins."

Some magnet with an irresistible force drew Rachel's eyes to the top—only to have it disappear in a sudden drift of fog. The cloud cover that followed all but obscured the peak. Her heart skipped a beat and then seemed to stop. A light! She had seen a sudden flash that lit the premature darkness. Immediately there was an explosion of thunder. Had there been a preceding flash of lightning? Reason told her that that was the case. Her heart told her otherwise.

With indrawn breath, she waited. The light appeared again. And this time there was no thunder. Her heart resumed beating, now in a tempo which caused her eyes to throb and a dozen blotches of light to bob up and down. Lanterns! It had to be lanterns. Indians did not carry lanterns. Neither did they venture out when it was dark. *Who...why?* Imposters, but what right had they to be on hallowed ground?

No answer had come when suddenly there came the sound of hoof beats—close at hand. And above the rider's head was a lantern. The others had disappeared. And then there came the welcome voice of Judson Lee! He skidded to a stop, his horse's ribs heaving in and out to tattle the speed his owner had demanded.

"Th' weather don' be behavin'. Wife wanted I should be bringin' protection fer ye—so here be uh quilt—lantern—'n th' like. Wanted the two o'ye be havin' this doodad—wimmen's trifles—"

"Th' two o'ye" had to refer to herself and Yolanda, whose name he was unable to mention. Anyway, what Rachel saw as she unwrapped the quickly-wrapped package would hardly be a "doodad" for a minister, she thought with a smile, as she examined the daintily-embroidered bertha-shaped collars. Beneath the lantern light, Rachel could see minute seed pearls scattered at random. Something, she guessed, from a treasured garment of long ago—perhaps her wedding dress. Surely the gift would win Yolanda's heart, its puritan pattern and stark white color making her look like a little girl who wasn't finished growing up. Which, to Rachel, described her friend—

The light again! The men, busy with the buggy top, did not seem to notice. "Did you see it—the light there at the base of the mountain?" she blurted without thinking.

The men, busy with bolting the top, still did not look up. "Happens sometimes—jack-o-lanterns an' this be th' kind o'night. There! Reverend—now git goin' afore th' storm be bustin' loose fer shure. Got t'git meself back—wife's 'fraid uv storms—'specially when them evil fireballs be playin' 'roun' uh cemetery. Portends trouble—"

With that Jud was gone. So were the lights. Reverend Elmo was still fumbling with a contrary bolt and missed the repeated flash when it came again. Rachel, feeling a surge of adrenaline, grabbed the blanket he had brought and pulled it over her head then leaped from the buggy. Squatting near the fence, the blanket making a dark tent around her legs, Rachel knew she was near-invisible as the light came closer—almost close enough for her to unravel the mystery.

"Jack-o-lantern," Mr. Lee had said, the name for swamp gas, common in his homeland and the southern lowlands. Many a legend surrounded its origin among the superstitious Scotch-Irish. And scientists called it "St. Elmo's Fire," having to do with weather combined with electricity. Well, conditions were right—but, her heart gave a painful lurch, its gases, which formed into a luminous ball, made no shadows! And shadows were dancing from the mossy ground to the tops of the treetops, now reeling in the wind whose whine would have drowned voices of those in the buggy. The lantern. She could only hope that the imposters had failed to see its glow—

Without thinking, Rachel scrambled to her feet. Later, she would realize how shocking a black ghost's appearing from nowhere would be, draped as she was from head to toe beneath the dark quilt.

Zing! Something whizzed past her ear—too fast for a bull bat. *A bullet!* And she was the target!

There was no time for fear. Vines, set in motion by the wind, cast sinister shadows over a chalky face, clumsy hands shaking as he tried to hold the lantern in one hand while gripping a gun in the other. A frightened *boy!*

"Bart!" Rachel gasped—Bartholomew, One of the Twelve, Judson Lee's second-born son. "Have you taken leave of your senses? What on earth are you doing here—and why did you shoot at *me?*"

"Miz Rachel—Miz Rachel, ma'am—I—I wouldn' be firin' et you—"

Rachel listened to no more. "Drop that gun!" she said in her best schoolteacher voice. *"This minute!"*

Sheepishly, Bart obeyed. With a fearful attempt of nonchalance, he slid his right hand into his pants pocket and made muddy caves of the ground around him with a clumsy shoe.

The other lanters had disappeared, a gang of cowards, undoubtedly, making a quick getaway to save their skins—abandoning one of their own like rats leaping from a sinking ship. But Bart's head was still held high, his left arm too stiffened by fear to lower it in all likelihood. By the pool of light the lifted lantern made, Rachel could see his young face turning sullen momentarily and then crumpling in shame. If only he would tumble into a bewildered confession—but she must take no chances—

"Kick that gun to me, Bart. Thank you," she said, as she stooped to pick it up. "Now, I think you'd better explain what you are doing here and who your accomplices are. Yes, *accomplices*, for you are here for no good. You can trust me—"

Bart Lee looked as if he would drop dead with fear. "I ain't into nothin'—honest, Miz Rachel. I wouldn' lie t'you—not you. An' I dunno who they are—nobody tells me nothin'—we—we jest do target practice—'n git paid fer hit. I don' even know who—"

"Target practice—at *night?* You know that makes no sense—*and* you know you're trespassing—" the sentence lay unfinished. The wind puffed out his lantern ... and Luke Elmo was calling her name....

13

A Choice
for a Change

Talk had gone far into the night after Buck reached home at lamplighting time with gifts for the family." The children screamed with delight and the dog ran in senseless circles, barking until, finally, he grew hoarse.

"Now—to bed with you—*all* of you!" Rachel said firmly at last. "No whys. Daddy and I have business to discuss in preparation for tomorrow's meeting." The children went. But there was a conspiracy in their eyes. They would talk on and on. Well, so be it.

Alone, Buck drew Rachel to him as a hungry man grabs for food. "I'm just no traveling man. I need you with me every breath I take—"

"Which is perfectly all right with me—" she murmured, knowing that they must get down to business. She needed to be prepared for the council meeting—to know what was so urgent—

With a sigh, Buck released his grip, but his arm remained intimately about her shoulders as they sat down on the nearest sofa.

"Catch me up here first, then my report from Salem."

Rachel did the best she could, sidestepping details as if she were dodging puddles following a storm. More strange sightings along the river front...Yolanda's equally strange behavior... the trip to Yolanda's parents' home...and the discovery of invaders at Superstition Mountain. The hardest part was the shooting incident.

"Rachel! You could have been killed. You are too bold. Who fired the shot?"

"Bart—Bartholomew Lee. But Buck, the boy has fallen into a trap. He has a leader in all this, but doesn't have an inkling who. I am convinced that some cowardly creature one could hardly label a *man*, is training himself a firing squad—paying them—"

Rachel heard his sharp intake of breath but was unable to see his face, head cuddled closely to his heart as it was. "Where was Reverend Elmo? I fail to understand—"

"Putting the top of the buggy up—but, please—let's get on with *your* news. Oh, I must tell you, though, that he's leaving—says he's going to a retirement home around Salem, I think—"

"I found that the retirement home hasn't been completed. Not one board is cut—it's washed up. I have an idea, but it will have to wait. What I have to say now takes priority—"

How right he was! Incorporation? Permission granted. ("Oh, Buck—Buck Darling!") But, pushing her head back against his chest, there was work to be done—decisions to be made. She *had* notified the present council? Good! And yes, of course, the original members, the founders: Brother Davey, Chaplain...O'Grady... Farnal... Burnside—those who had followed Cole's wagon train instead of following the divergent "cowless column" led by Julius Doogan.

It was Rachel's turn to suck in a lungful of air. Thought of the traitor's name—and now his presence and acceptance by the newer residents never failed to cause terror to course through her veins. How many were following him? *And why was he here?*

Why, she was behaving like Yolanda. With an effort, she put away thoughts of the man. "Yes, Buck, Brother Davey and Judson Lee helped me spread the word. Mr. Lee being named Lord Mayor." The self-chosen title brought a shaky smile...his sitting on the pinnacle of pride. "I took the liberty, too, of inviting Reverend Elmo. Maybe he could offer the benediction—and Brother Davey can have the honor of saying the invocation. It would be like stealing candy from a child to deny him that.... Oh, forgive me...that sounds so trivial...."

"Trivial? No prayer's trivial, my darling. And believe me, we'll need all the help we can get. You see, we were right about Doogan—Dunigan. It's a long story, but among the many other troubles that man stirred up was a train robbery—recently—"

Rachel jerked erect. "Robbery?" she whispered, *"recently?"*

"More recently than the other felonies, the ones which he prides himself for having 'paid his debt to society'—pleading 'not guilty' of course. He has no right to be free—but that is history. What we must do now is look out for the present."

"I don't understand."

"Nobody does for sure. In fact, he may not be the man the government's looking for. What I mean is that those of us who know him *are* sure, but there has to be proof—and he's a master at covering his tracks. Like Satan himself, he can lead others into trouble but never leads them out!"

"But—but why is he here?"

"The money, it seems, is buried here. It happened while he was imprisoned, so how can we prove he's involved? The government suspects him of masterminding the whole thing *before* he was apprehended. Could have boomeranged, as those who did the actual train robbery were all shot except one. He had time to stash the money away—possibly here—and then he was—I would rather skip this—"

"No!"

"Hanged when caught."

Rachel was sick. The room whirled and she dropped her head back to the sanctity she felt against the warmth of her husband's chest. Did he say more? Probably, but mercifully, she slept. . . .

• • •

And now the council meeting was about to begin.

Being the only woman present put Rachel's teeth on edge. She was on guard from the moment she seated herself. True, she was treated with respect, held in great esteem in fact, by Lordsburg's "inner circle." An ingrained sense of "right" set her apart from others of her gender. After all, it was *her* husband who founded this flourishing city. And it was she who had the courage to pick up and carry on after his death. That alone decreed suffrage. But, more than that, she was downright likeable, real genuine-like, not a "she-male" the way some women in her position would be. Otherwise, would she have handed the gavel over to her present husband so graciously?

In an effort to regain her poise, Rachel allowed her eyes to circle the table where the men sat waiting for the arrival of the city manager. She wondered what was holding up Buck. What could he and the new lawyer be discussing that they could not discuss here? Members of the council were growing impatient—mumbling and grumbling. Retired Judge J. Quentin Hathaway, in his quiet way, was his own man. Style or no style, he disdained facial hair, his face as smooth and pink as that of a newborn. He viewed the world through bespectacled, pale blue eyes, and when he spoke, he seemed to calculate each word as if preparing to weigh the case at hand. But he was fair and completely objective. Jim Culpepper, who recently opened the hardware store, distinguished himself by sitting on the edge of his chair, like a bird prepared for flight, impatient, always impatient. The man at Culpepper's right was a stranger to Rachel as was the next member of the council. Why was he so tense—looking wound up to run forward or backward, depending on how the majority voted? She had to stretch her neck to see over the enormous brown crock filled with October's harbinger of autumn, vine maple leaves gathered and arranged by Aunt Em's capable hands, she was sure. But her eyes locked with those of the man she had sought, Hezzie Maxton, the innkeeper. Hezzie was out of place in the group. Pugnacious by nature, surly and obnoxious by choice— always waiting just long enough for an opinion to find expression so he could contradict it. In Rachel's mind, his manner was downright rude—that of a man who is unsure of his manhood and his standing, attempting to *appear* secure beyond question. He took great delight in baiting anybody around him in order to take careful aim and fire at a target. And, good gracious, his eyes were focused on Rachel!

Maynard Killjoy rose and, standing tall, stretched his tall physique even taller, his keen eyes searching the room. Was he expressing irritation with Buck's tardiness? Or could he be on the lookout for some unexpected presence? Rachel had never understood the man completely. He could be totally arrogant, sometimes understanding, but always impatient. Her first impression of the doctor had never changed—the time he was treating Yolanda for shock, bordering on insanity, after the explosion. He did, she admitted to herself, have a surprisingly successful talent in that field, in spite of his need to cultivate a more gentle bedside manner. Why, then, as Yolanda's husband, was he so blind to her emotional needs now?

Rachel's thoughts were interrupted by Buck's long-striding entrance. Dr. Killjoy checked his pocket watch as Buck made room for James Haute, the short-of-stature attorney who had handled Cole's business affairs as well as General Wilkes'. But— *oh, dear Lord, don't let me remember*—the capable lawyer had also served Julius Doogan!

Concentrate on other matters . . . think of tonight . . . forget the memories of the past . . . widen the heart because of what it remembers. . . .

She forced herself to look at Mr. Haute. His hair, always thin, had given up, leaving a bare skull and he had shaved off the question-mark mustache she used to find comical. But his intelligent brown eyes still reminded her of a field mouse as they darted every direction, assessing the group. She had learned to respect him—except for his dealings with Julius Doogan.... Quickly, she glanced back to Maynard Killjoy. There seemed to be a need—something that she should remember and couldn't.... It was he who spoke. "Shouldn't we get started?"

"Cool yore taters, doc!" Brother Davey retorted. "We'll be startin' when th' timin's right—no sooner—"

"What makes *you* go defendin' him? Why, you'd vote 'firmative iffen he wuz t'go proposin' uh fornicatin' house on Main Street!" a newcomer exclaimed.

Brother Davey leaped from his chair and sprang at his foe, jerking his shirt sleeves above the garters to show arms about as muscular as jaybirds' legs. "You wuz sayin'?"

"I said it!"

An audible gasp circled the table.

"Gentlemen!" Buck's voice carried a command, "control yourselves. And, as long as you are here, Brother Davey, prepare yourself for the invocation while we call the roll."

Both men glared at one another, each a self-proclaimed winner.

Roll call began. The man to the right of Jim Culpepper was the new barber, Calvin Merriweather, who blanched when his name was called. Dropping his pinch-on nose spectacles, the man reached to retrieve them with a loud scrape of his chair, heavy jowls bagging in the process. "Heah," he said in a syrupy drawl which sounded as if he'd crawled beneath the table. " 'N I wan' y'all to be fixin' your mind that I cut hair 'n throw in uh shave on Wednesdays."

"No advertisin'!" Hezzie shouted.

Buck rapped the table with the gavel. There was silence.

Brother Davey's prayer was brief because, he said, "You know they's big problems waitin' fer solutions."

"Now, please, gentlemen," Buck said without recrimination, "this is a time for unity—so let there be no more bickering. Let's not allow this all-important discussion to degenerate into wrangling. Let me lay the problems before you, one-by-one, *after* I tell you that we have approval to go ahead with incorporation."

Raising a hand to stop the stomping and yelling of approval, he continued. Of course, that creates more problems. They would be on their own—deciding on a tax base, a form of city government, what they wanted by means of law and order . . . how elected. And *very* important, setting up a building code determining desirable places, run by responsible merchants—

Was that essential?

Yes—unless they wished to have the city doomed to failure, have it pushed off the map by hoodlums, become the Sodom of Gomorrah—

"It is my prayer that you take advantage of our choice for change *now*—rule out more growth at present, allowing those who are in business to remain and voting on new applications after careful consideration."

"What's th' all-fired hurry?" Hezzie interrupted.

"Because," Buck said slowly, "of what I am about to reveal— what this emergency meeting is all about."

Quietly, solemnly, and with dignity, Buck explained. "Lordsburg cannot be the city we envisioned for our children, the place where business people, old-timers, and immigrant families can settle and prosper unless—unless it is kept law-abiding and civilized. So it is best that we move swiftly to set down ground rules. You see, there is reason to believe that there *could* be an enemy among us, hiding from a robbery . . ."

There was stunned silence. Brother Davey was first to speak.

"This city's blest by th' Lord Hisself. We lissen fer His voice—'n I'm a-tellin' you, what be Doubtin' Thomases, doubt *me*, well, I'd build uh ark on top uv Mt. Hood iffen I heerd th' Lord say to. So count me 'n my Emmy-Gal in on th' side uv salvation—"

Carried away, the bantam-sized preacher looked ready to crow. To Rachel's relief the group sat quietly. No scowling, no sarcastic rejoinders, and with little interest—if they heard at all.

But it was the quiet before the storm. Without addressing the chair, the men exploded at once. They already knew who the culprits were, the scoundrel who slipped in like a thief in the night and his weak followers . . . spies, they were . . . and they would identify them. One was . . .

Buck's sharp rap of the gavel stopped them. "How *could* any of you know for sure when the government's secret intelligence has run into blind alleys? *Please*—no attempt at identification now— just decide on our procedure *now*, draw closer to our neighbors and with bridles on our tongues, be on guard. Nothing can be accomplished without unity. I—I hesitate to say this—but our very lives and those of our families may be at stake!"

The nervous perspiration beading his square-set jaw convinced them.

Decisions were reached quickly. Good representation—by popular vote, of course—selecting the best leaders from founding fathers and merchants. Yes, a moratorium on new enterprises for now. Better send a telegram explaining intentions including the need for officials of the law as well as a request for state monies—and reasonable taxation. "Les'sen they wanted t'pay out a potful uv cash money." "Top dog" in election ought to be declared mayor—yep, even if 'twas a *woman*, since she couldn't cast a vote anyhow. Clear? Clear as Hobson's bell. There was a titter, eyes flashing back and forth as if attached by a single string...

Stunned, Rachel sat rigid. And then terror struck her heart.

"Dunigan's our man!" someone said.

14

Appealing
to Yolanda

Yolanda was quick to answer the door this time. Obviously she had been watching the window, hoping for a visit from Rachel long before now. Rachel felt a prickle of irritation pass through her. After all, a walk would be good for Yolanda. What was she trying to do? Isolate herself from the whole world? It was impossible, she thought with a flash of insight, to insulate oneself from one person. The attitude was ungodly and spread like the disease it was—destroying the mind, body, and the spirit—rendering *total* insulation—even from God.

"Why haven't you come sooner?" Yolanda demanded.

"*I*," Rachel replied with a hint of irritation, "have been busy! What's *your* excuse?"

"Oh, Rachel, don't be cross with me!"

Rachel sighed. "I'm sorry—it's just that I am disappointed in my best friend's becoming a whiner. May I come in please?"

Yolanda brushed two fat tears from her cheeks with her free hand as she pushed open the door with the other. She murmured an apology while motioning her guest to be seated on the love seat, where fingers of autumn's gold sunshine poked inquiringly as if to find a mirror for reflecting its warmth and brightness. Well, the room had need of both.

"You just don't understand what I'm going through—how awful—"

With the adroitness of a listener who has heard the complaints over and over, Rachel quickly changed the subject. "I came to bring news. May we open the drapes? Unless you choose to prefer darkness to light because your deeds are evil?"

Without waiting for an answer, Rachel struggled with the tasseled cord. Finally, *finally* with a rusty protest, it slid along the rod.

"Yolanda, you're turning into a mole! Come on now—a smile!"

The sound of footsteps in a back room drew more attention from Rachel than Yolanda. "Do you—is there somebody else here—company?"

Yolanda sniffed. "Mrs. Maxton—*company*? That woman's no company. She has about as much imagination as a stump—and wouldn't recognize humor if it chucked her under the chin. Sort of a combination housekeeper and nurse. I'm *delicate*, you know." Sarcasm put the word in italics. "Just somebody my caring husband engaged to spy—only she's too dumb. She's a calamity."

"Yolanda, my patience is thinning. The way you talk is—well, downright sacrilegious. Now do you or do you not want the news?"

Yolanda leaned forward, the old light of interest catching Rachel by surprise. "My parents? Did you go? You—you didn't tell them—about this experiment I'm carrying inside me?"

"I'm finding it hard to be civil with you. Snap out of it, Yo—or no more news and I *do* mean what I say! Experiment indeed! God has blest you richly—" Rachel switched tactics. "Mr. and Mrs. Lee are fine, bless their dear hearts, but puzzled by your behavior. You *must* get in touch. They'd welcome news of the baby—and besides—(*help me say it, Lord!*) you are the one to tell them—you're family—"

"Tell them what—what's wrong?" Fear flared in Yolanda's face.

"About Bart—yes, something is *very* wrong."

Wide-eyed, Yolanda listened as Rachel reported the incident at Superstition Mountain. "I'm—I'm sorry. When was I ever there when they needed me? I'm so ashamed, but—" with a lift of the rounded chin, "I'll go even if everybody else breaks out with spotted fever and the doctors hang a quarantine sign on this house!"

"There's my Yolanda! But, Yo—what do you mean *doctors*?"

"Maynard has another doctor with him," she said absently. "I know nothing about him—not even his name—don't care really."

Rachel let that pass. "Oh, your parents want to renew Preserving Day—Abe's idea really."

"Abe, Father of the Multitude, remember?" Yolanda smiled. Sadly, but a smile all the same. "You know what? That would be a good time for me to go. Actually, I'm afraid to go alone—and this way I could just melt into the crowd—"

"Until there was a chance for privacy. Wonderful! Subject closed. Now for a report on the council meeting."

Quickly, she told of the decisions. Yolanda listened intently and said she would have known nothing about the incorporation otherwise. Rachel bit her lip to keep from reminding Yolanda that Maynard was there. It occurred to her then, that the one man whose name she failed to catch must be Dr. Killjoy's partner. Further mention of Yo's husband was unwise. And yet something niggled at her brain. Important. Demanding. Something from out of the past.

Then, like the fragments of dream, the pieces fell in place... a scene from the past which resolved a question, only to create a much greater one revolving around Julius Doogan. Oh, yes, she remembered—

Maynard Killjoy was leaning over Yolanda, listening for even one promising word of coherence as she drifted in and out of consciousness. Listening, without sleep, as he had since the explosion robbed her of her intended husband and her sanity as well. Yolanda, beautiful vibrant Yolanda, a scarcely-breathing skeleton, silenced due to the shock which was too great to bear. And then the miracle! Yolanda's touchdown into the real world. Or, at least, into the netherworld preceding it. Complete recall demanded that she reach into the far corners of her mind. Her youth with Rachel... the dreams... the corncob dolls. Was she being foolish? Not at all, Maynard assured his patient. In a low compelling voice, he had urged her to talk on—and on... and then... (oh, how had she forgotten?)... mention of Julius!

"I envied Rachel—wanted to be loved." And, still struggling to catch up to the present she must face and conquer, Yolanda told of her shame. "Only—only—nothing happened. I don't want you to think the worst—I remain the foolish virgin."

How tenderly Dr. Killjoy had answered. Rachel, standing outside the bedroom where Yolanda lay, heard his shaken voice murmuring: "That is nothing to be ashamed of—"

Maynard Killjoy *knew*. And he understood...

"Oh, Yolanda, Yolanda, everythings's all right! You *did* tell Maynard. You must have forgotten!" Joy spilled from every word, joy which was short on longevity.

"So?" The terse word cut. "I told you I had."

Rachel shook her head in perplexity. "I—I guess you're right. I *don't* understand."

Yolanda's troubled eyes darted to the window. "Please," she whispered, "close the drapes—and the door to the kitchen—"

Rachel complied quickly, before Yolanda could change her mind. Somehow she knew that Yolanda was ready to talk, just as she had confided in the man who was now her husband.

"I told you," she whispered so low that Rachel had to bend low to hear, "Julius Doogan was here to ruin my life—rob me of what little dignity I have remaining—take away what facade remains of a crumbling marriage. Don't interrupt—I must talk quickly— let you know that I am not hallucinating—"

"I never thought that—"

Yolanda's lifted hand silenced her.

"He's here almost every day—and when he isn't—" Yolanda was breathing in little gasps as if she'd been running, "he's lurking nearby to carry out his threats."

"What threats?" Rachel, too, was breathing heavily.

Yolanda squeezed her eyes shut. The lids quivered. When she opened them slowly, they contracted as if she were in physical pain.

"Threats on Rowie's *life*—says accidents can happen so quickly in a frontier land where there's little law and order." She paused.

Rachel longed to reassure her that the problem was about to be resolved. But she dared not interrupt.

"Threats on *you*—you and your children. And Rachel—oh, dear God, *Rachel,* he—he says he will not hesitate to claim he is the father of this child!" With that, she began to sob.

The last word hung in frozen silence between them. Neither was able to move or speak. Yolanda's hands were clenching and unclenching and all blood had drained from her precious ivory skin. She needed help. And, for the first time in their lives, Rachel was unable to give it. A thousand questions paraded through her mind. And yet, in some far corner of her numbed senses, she understood in part. Julius Doogan was capable of intimidating a woman. How well she knew—

At last she spoke through lips that throbbed with the pain of gradual thaw: "What—what does he want?"

"In exchange for my silence?" Yolanda's tongue was thick. "To be allowed to stay—prove he's a changed man—"

"It's blackmail!" Rachel was recovering. "But he couldn't know about the baby unless—oh, Yo—Yo Darling, he hasn't laid his filthy hands on you?" The possibility set her heart pounding, making speech impossible. Yolanda seemed to have heard only the first question.

"He knows," she said bitterly. "Maybe—at one time—this beast could have been human—even a doctor. Trust me, he knows."

Yes, he knew. The mysterious "medicine man" who had delivered Yolanda's baby sister. The man who, although he had abducted Little Star to retaliate against the "injustices" Cole inflicted on him along the Trail, was gentle to her. Yes, he knew. . . .

"Now do you understand my fears? And why I have tried to lock him out?"

"Yes—and no. How *has* he been gaining entrance?"

"Mrs. Maxton helped maybe—or the new doctor. I trust *nobody*."

"Then he *has* been here? Oh, Darling, don't you know you're contributing to the credibility of his lies? You alone—house all dark—but (brightening) your husband knows better. He will believe you and well, you were very personal with me about Star's father—even about my relationship with Cole before—before we consummated our marriage—so I will be just as open now—"

"And ask about this child's father. It's as if Julius Doogan could see through the blinds—knows Maynard and I do not live together as man and wife—that I have locked him out of our bedroom. Lovemaking is out of the question."

The situation was suddenly funny. "Yolanda, for goodness sake, do you think I haven't discarded belief in the *stork*? My children even know better. Now, what is it you're saying? What are you holding back? It's impossible for me to help unless—"

Rachel expected a tirade of words. Instead, she saw a nostalgic look, a look of longing for something unexpressed, cross Yolanda's face. "There was a rainy night. I was afraid of the lightning—and—but who would believe that one night could—could be enough?"

"*I* would. It happened to Cole and me. But, Yolanda, you *must* make things right with Maynard. I beg you to. No arguments. It takes two to kill a marriage. Go to him. Don't answer—just pray!"

15

New Acquaintances—
and Old Ones

There was a flurry of excitement in Lordsburg. Old-timers looked forward to the renewal of Preserving Day while newer settlers welcomed the opportunity for a glimpse of the city's history-in-the-making. Mrs. Jones' report had sparked their interest. And now with elections and the like just ahead, this would offer a chance to act out their history lesson. Business flourished at the hardware store for jars. Then the General Merchandise ran "plumb out" of sugar. And, admittedly, stores stocking dry goods had never done so well. Neither had the ladies' ready-to-wear. The situation was humorous really. Those who patronized the ready-made shops did an about-face, deciding to act out the early days with proper attire—checked gingham, ground-sweeping dresses with matching bonnets. And, in contrast, those who had helped build the town opted for a "good dress." Yolanda' mother, unaware of what lay in store, was going to have the best of the two worlds. Aunt Em had chosen various shades of blue in a soft percale and would add tucks and laces as featured in the "better stores." But, busy as she was, would Rachel lend a hand with the baking? Of course! Nothing could please her more.

"So tickled t'git th' chance t'show off my wares," Emmaline Galloway confided. "Let's do up all kinds a tarts, cobblers, doughnuts— *everything*, includin' th' seven-layer devil's food," she said above the whir of her sewing machine. "Frankly, Dearie, bizness has slowed some—due (she lowered her voice) I'm a-thinkin' t'that Dunigan place. That lady looks like uh plump dowager angel with that snowy thistledown hair 'n apple cheeks.

Still 'n all, you know a lot's goin' on that should'n. He—you know who—has sneaked in uh rareeee-show—"

"A what?" Rachel stopped swirling frosting on the chocolate cake.

"I keep forgittin' you're uv a new generation. Uh raree-show's uh disgrace—uh, well, kinda *peek* show, usually uh street show uv disgraceful women, jest 'bout stark naked—cheap 'n somethin' that sneaky you-know-who knows Buck'd never stand for—" Her sentence hung unfinished as the *ding-dong* of the welcome bell tinkled to announce entrance of a possible customer. Aunt Em's eyes darted above her pinch-on eyeglasses. "Who's there?" Then, hurrying to the counter, "Oh, good morning, Doctor!"

Expecting to see Maynard (how long had it been?), Rachel found herself looking into a pair of steady deep-sea blue eyes, so direct in their appraisal of her that she felt herself color.

"You must be Mrs. Jones?" he said without waiting for an introduction. "We had no opportunity to meet because of your hurried exit—"

A slight pause gave Rachel an opportunity to do a quick study, remind her that, yes, she had seen him. Where and when eluded her.

Then, remembering her manners, she extended her hand as Aunt Em greeted another customer. "I am sorry, but you have the advantage. Yes, I *am* the wife of the city manager—"

The man took her hand. "It is I who must apologize. I was only admiring you and finding you as charming of face as in public speaking. Excellent summary of local history before the council."

Rachel withdrew her hand. "Thank you," she said coolly, "but I would feel a bit more comfortable if you told me your name."

"I'm Dr. Howard Ames."

Did she imagine a tightening of his smile? The man puzzled her a bit anyway. His manner was both forward and distant. His gray suit looked so new that she could imagine a price tag dangling against the lining of the coat. Certainly no hint of the country practitioner in its long, lean lines. The dark hair, brushed furiously into a pompadour, threatened to break into a natural wave. His features were cameo-perfect—too perfect except that, like his personality, Dr. Ames' skin was weather-bronzed. Not a hint of his working indoors. Yet he looked ready to strip off his jacket and roll up the immaculate white shirt sleeves and prepare for surgery.

Not at all the partner she would have expected for Maynard Killjoy whose manner was abrasive, his eyes habitually hard in what she thought of as a professional gunmetal. Or *was* he? Maybe they *did* belong together. Rachel wondered what bothered her about this man.

"I would like some jelly doughnuts." There was a command in his voice as if he were accustomed to immediate obedience.

"I am not in charge here," Rachel said, purposely adding an extra spoonful of sugar to her voice. If she had expected the doctor to be annoyed, she was surprised. Once again the quick change. His half-closed eyelids in an oblique glance reflected amusement. To hide her embarrassment, she whirled around quickly and found herself facing Willie Mead, a frown beetling his brows below the green sunshade.

"We'll change customers," Aunt Em said to the telegrapher. "Leastwise, I'm s'posin' th' telegram's fer Rachel."

"Why would you go supposing anything, Mrs. Galloway?" The doctor stepped forward. "For Mr. Dunigan, Mr. Mead?"

Willie's head bobbed up and down, his eyes meeting nobody's gaze. "I—he—maybe I'd best hold it here—no, you're right. Guess he did say—"

Howard Ames snatched the yellow envelope from Willie's hand and left without his doughnuts.

"Now, ain't that th' strangest thang? Better check on th' frostin', Dearie. Me—I best be workin' on Nola's dress. Strange though—"

Yes, very strange. "I want to talk with you, Willie, so I'll walk back to the office—"

But he, too was gone.

• • •

Strange, indeed. And stranger events were to come before Preserving Day. The neighborhood children, excited about the up-coming day—marking the last real play-day before school began—clustered almost frantically around Star. They, like David, Saul, Mary Cole and Roland, saw Star as being just what her name implied. Star held all the world's wisdom in an invisible bag and handed it out on special occasions. She was the one who saw "visions"—things that were as invisible as her bag, until she pointed them out. Then, through her eyes, they saw them, too. They would follow her to the ends of the earth.

At this time, Star did not appreciate her following. A promise was a sacred thing. Mother Mine had been too busy to notice; but she, her siblings, and Rowie had doubled their guard since the strange sightings along the river had become more and more frequent. Blest with insight as she was, Star kept watching for the "evil one" to appear since he frightened Rowie.

And he did. It was on the day of the rainbow...

Somewhat like the "Pied Piper," Star whispered to the other children that they must be very, very quiet the moment she spotted a swaying of the willow trees leaning protectively over the river. They were going to play a new game. ("But what could I call it, Mother Mine, and by what rules? Oh God is most good. He answered both questions!" Star confided later.)

Overhead, a black cloud covered the sun's face playfully, dropped three raindrops, then moved away. "Squat," she whispered, "without a word." They obeyed. And immediately there appeared a magnificent rainbow, one which arched the heavens from horizon to horizon with scarves of color. So brilliant were its hues that its red-orange, yellow-green, blue, blue-indigo to violet colors reflected against the trees, through the tall ferns, to paint the very earth around them.

"We are at the end of the rainbow, *niños—sh-h-ssh*! Maybe we will see it, the pot of gold. Not a word—and if we move, we may not see the wee people as they use their magical shovels to find it—"

Wide-eyed with fascination that bordered on fear, they waited. The willows, now still, waited, too. Until, as sudden as the rainbow, a "fairy godmother" slipped through a clump of larkspur in velvet shoes. ("Velvet shoes?" "Yes, *Madre Mia*, because they made no noise," Star would answer to Rachel's question.) But the velvet shoes took her away—until she waved her wand for the elves to hasten with pick and shovel, for already the colors were fading. At that point, Rachel would no longer ask questions until the amazing story was finished.

Elves were larger than even the imaginative Star had envisioned them to be. But they were elves all the same. They were too young to be men. Why did they not wear peaked caps and shoes that curled up at their toes? "Oh," she explained to the children later, "they were in disguise—wearing those masks so they could make an *X* where the treasure was buried and nobody would know their magical powers."

And then there *were* sounds—the first since the game began. With picks and shovels the digging began. And that was when Star began to realize that it was no game! The make-believe creatures had come alive.

Bang! They had found it. Then a pot of gold really *did* exist. But something rang a warning sign. God's Book made no mention of the legendary pot. Wasn't the rainbow His promise that another flood would never wash His world away again?

There were silver flashes in the sun. Flashes as surprising to the treasure seekers as to the girl and her charges who watched noiselessly from their ferny cave. Gold? No, silver buttons or coins, then green bundles. A *swish-swish* that could be oars—yes—and then they stopped and a fat boy who waddled leaned from a canoe which appeared now. With haste the group hoisted a box, not a pot, onto the canoe. The white-haired lady had come back and was waving again. The rainbow faded. The little boat swished away. And woods and shore relapsed into a doze.

Then the dreadful thing! The children, thinking the game had ended, began to clap. And then to run. This they must tell their parents. Well, the damage was done. Star, too, rose to flex her stiff muscles. Instantly a striped-sleeved arm reached out from nowhere. A startled cry from the victim...a scrape of loosened gravel...and the shock of cold water...and the slender girl disappeared...

Now she could paint "Death," Star realized. But only if she survived. If she breathed, little bubbles would tattle. She must hold her breath, make those powerful hands relax their death-grip. How long did it take to die? Could she survive long enough for the water's surface to become smooth, placid? The owner of those talons would want to escape. She could make it. God was looking after her, not the vulture...lie still...play dead...lie *still*. Her body grew limp.

She was not under water for the hazy line of distant hills was visible—purple at the base, then running the chromatic scale of violet till the colors fused. She, why, she was in the midst of the rainbow...floating up...up...up to where God waited to give her a new body...breathe new life into her lungs. She inhaled deeply...

"She's alive," a man's voice muttered as he stroked the thin mahogany wrists, listening to her chest. "That's it, spit it out!" Deftly, he rolled her onto her side and began pumping her small rib cage up and down. Was this how God gave life? Even as water spouted from her pale lips, she found it amusing. How mysterious the ways of God. A dimple in the softly-rounded but determined chin went unnoticed. As did the up-curl of thick jet lashes that lay in heavy fringes on the angelic face. The man was too busy running an experienced hand along the high cheekbones to examine a raw, bleeding cut. This vaguely familiar child—woman—could have a concussion—

A small moan. And then slowly the great dark eyes opened. The man gasped. "Star—Star Jones! Oh, dear God, what have they done?"

Music. There was music. The murmur of water strumming the roots and ferns in its rush to the sea. The garrulous twitter of Cock Robin as he ordered his motley company of feathered cousins to settle in their tree houses, crisscrossing purple shadows warning of coming night. All sights and sounds of music in this strangely-familiar new land . . .

"Lie still. I have patched you up. What happened child? You can trust me. Country doctors are not easily shocked—" Dr. Ames paused when he saw the dazed look fading from his half-drowned little patient, then probed a bit deeper, "but I *must* know how this happened."

"Nothing happened—that I remember. That's how it is when one is a Pied Piper whom other children follow." Star laughed merrily—rare for the child as he knew her. And there was something wrong with the laugh. What was she covering—or whom was she covering *for*? "When leaders approach the hilltop, the other children turn back." The lovely brown eyes closed in concentration. "Or *was* I the Pied Piper? Perchance I—oh, you must remember how a wondrous doorway leading to the land of bright peacocks . . . and flowers put forth a fairer hue open . . . but the doorway in the mountainside swallows them? Or, per chance I was the lame lad left outside. . . . *Verdad*?"

"Yes, I remember. But the boy was able to look within and told all he saw. Now, stop faking—and do the same for me."

"Yes, I will speak—when I see Mother Mine and Dad-dee. I do not wish to fret them. Will you not help me, señor?"

"Yes, yes, of course I will." The doctor's voice carried a hint of frustration. "But, Star, *please* answer me. My questions are important. What or who caused you to fall—and was he the one who also fished you out? Tell me, *por favor, Estrallita*," he implored.

"I do not remember. Do you not believe in God?"

Dr. Ames sighed. Ignoring her question, he murmured, "I wish

I possessed a microscope powerful enough to penetrate that other-world brain, see what it is that you are trying to forget."

He was scooping her into his arms when a woman's cry cut through the still of the late afternoon. Rachel Jones was as near hysteria as one would ever see her....

"Oh, Star—Star, My Darling—what happened? The children made no sense. Why did they leave you?" Her eyes scanned the still figure, saw the bandage, then rested on the bloodstain marking the exact spot where her daughter's head had rested on the shirtfront of the man who held her. Dr. Ames! What was *he* doing here? How did he know?

"You may relax, Mrs. Jones. Nothing broken, no stitches necessary. You are the one who looks in need of a powerful stimulant. The patient is all right, still a bit disoriented, but that will pass— so if you will allow *me* to pass—"

"You are not funny!" Rachel hissed. "How did you know? Why is she dripping wet? Oh, Star, darling, what has this man done to you? Let go of my child!"

"It is all right, Mother Mine," Star murmured weakly. "I fell— only there is something strange about that fall—something I cannot recall. I cannot answer the kind doctor's questions."

"Kind doctor indeed! You still have not told me how you were here," Rachel said accusingly. "I get the feeling you—you knew!"

Anger snapped in the doctor's eyes. "Yes, I knew. But if you are accusing me of being responsible—forget it! I have a son that stayed after the others had run—long enough to know that somebody was here. Brian knows when someone is in need of a doctor—more aware of needs apparently than you—"

Shame washed over Rachel. Why would the man toss a human being into the water then rescue her? Her mind was whirling; but she knew when an apology was called for. "I am not myself—I— am sorry—"

The doctor pushed past her, calling over his shoulder: "Someday you and I must start over, Mrs. Jones—"

"We can start right now by your calling me Rachel—if you will accept my belated appreciation. Star will explain. A mystery is afoot—thank you for letting me know that you are not an accessory. She'll tell."

And she did. In disjointed sentences, her eyes frequently clouding as memories came and went. Only once did the great eyes flare in sudden fear of something unrevealed. "Let me keep it secret," Star urged. (*Even from us, your parents?* But why probe?

Rachel knew with the intuition of a mother that the answer was
"Yes.") It would be years before Rachel knew of Star's sudden
flashback of memory...an instant's impression of a striped
sleeve...then her burial...and resurrection...with something
washed away.

• • •

Real peculiar-like, old-timers would recall. Star Lord Jones
was never the same. More like one uv th' Lord's angels, sent for
His purpose, both His leader and His follower. Made no difference, did it now? Her purpose was of His holy making. (The
legend enlarged.) Why, it was this messenger what drove the
"rats" of sin plumb out. Even th' timin' was right—just two days
afore Preservin' Day. Didn' that give testimony? With rats no
longer gnawin' 'n gnashin' their teeth, good prevailed....

But 'twas uh puzzlement, them spine-ticklin' stories 'bout
children—less'n one took hit t'be children uv God livin' up
yonder. Yep, yep! that had t'be uh prophecy. That story she told
over 'n over ag'in:

But they say that in some far-off land there still lives a tribe of
people who wear dresses that are different from those of their
neighbors, and who speak another language. They are always
happy; they sing merry songs, and they all love to play upon the
pipe. They are suppose to be the children's children of Hamelin
City.

Hamelin City—wharever that was....Who was this Pied
Piper person? This child was so "different."

• • •

Together Rachel and Buck tucked Star into bed. "I don't know
what to make of it," Buck said as they sat down for coffee. "The
other children know nothing. And our Star's still in shock—or
else is withholding something. And that's totally unlike her.
Wow! I made this coffee strong enough to walk—incidentally,
where was Scot? That little animal's never far from their heels.
And he's protective—more bark than bite—still he will bite if he
has to. It had to be somebody he knew—"

"Of course!" Rachel said bitterly. "It was Julius Doogan. Oh,

Buck, I'm at fault—cautioning the children to be on the lookout—I'll never forgive myself—*never!*" She let her head drop on the table, feeling a twinge of pain. So tired, *so tired*—she who so recently was immune to fatigue.

Buck was there instantly. As was Star. "I cannot rest—not when you are troubled over some gruesome matter I am unable to recall, while I need to tell of what I saw but cannot say. There is no memory of earthly things in the grave. But in an underwater grave, I met another self. Now, I know that we must follow Jesus all the way—see? I cannot say . . . I only know that I am new. . . ."

16

Preservin' Day

Nostalgia took Rachel's heart back to the thrill of attending her first Preservin' Day at the home of Yolanda's family. Outwardly, nothing had changed. Today, as then, three-legged black pots were squatting as if to warm their bottoms over the roaring fire. Extra pots, rough benches, rawhide chairs, and culinary wares sat in waiting. And the air was heavy with the brandy-scented, crimson-ripe apples, golden ears of corn, late string beans, and the bittersweet smell of woodsmoke. Vying for attention were the enormous whiteclothed tables already groaning with deep-dish apple pies, baked beans, pitchers of wild honey, pound cakes, chocolate cakes, and cookies of every shape and color. Inside, the roaring woodstove was outdoing itself as it gobbled firewood in exchange for turning out venison roasts stuck with sweet myrtle leaves, clove-spiked hams, sage-dressing-stuffed pheasants, and other mysterious pots; while waiting to brown what looked like thousands of set-to-rise sourdough biscuits. Rachel felt hungry for the first time in months....

And then the vision faded. Things *looked* the same, yes—even the pumping of hands as children and dogs ran wild. But they were vastly different beneath the surface of her thoughts. Over half the faces were unfamiliar, a fact underlined by the number of introductions she acknowledged automatically, hoping that she said the right things.

Only two scenes stood out vividly in her mind afterward. Nola Lee's obvious pride in her first "really nice dress" and Judson's painting her cheeks with compliments (as new to her as the dress). And then, seeing Yolanda's uncertain gesture which took her parents inside. And, (*oh, thank You, Lord*) reaching out to embrace them before the screen door took them from view.

Others saw, too, including Buck. His eyes lighted as he hurried to her side. "It will all work out," he whispered, with a tight squeeze of her hand. "How proud I am of you—admiring glances from all the men which should make me jealous but doesn't. You see, any man is proud of owning the crown jewel! But look out for their mates. Methinks the green eyes of jealousy follow thee, my sweet—and here comes one of them now—"

"Mrs. Ames," he greeted her courteously, "it is my pleasure to present my wife, Rachel—"

"How do you do, Mrs Jones?" a doll-faced young woman blest with a wealth of pale-gold hair said in a voice that went with the face. The full lips (which said with clarity, I-want-my-way-and-allow-nothing-to-stand-in-the-way) smiled slightly without seeming to curve. "I was beginning to think that both you and my husband's partner's wife were only rumors. Certainly you are recluses."

An accusation was certainly no way to pave the way to a friendship. Before returning the greeting with grace, Rachel studied the near-perfect face quickly. One glimpse told her that Mrs. Ames was a spoiled, vain creature. The complexion so creamy-white, the hair so extravagantly poufed and petaled about her small face gave her the appearance of a giant sunflower on a too-slender stem, because of avoiding the sun.

Rachel managed a smile. "Please call me Rachel—and I hope we can be friends. We should have met before—"

"Why?"

Why indeed? Rachel was finding it hard to be courteous.

"Our children are friends—" she began only to be interrupted.

The woman smoothed her white lace blouse then laced exquisitely-manicured fingers through a strand of perfectly-matched pearls as she purred, "Yes, our Brian-Boy has spoken of your overly imaginative daughter. Sometimes the doctor and I wonder if we should allow the association—he is subject to nightmares. Is this typical of her—uh, background?"

Rachel was too taken aback to speak. Which was fine. Aunt Em, who appeared out of nowhere did a far better job than she could have done. She looked ready to stab the insensitive guest with the long-pronged meat fork she held. "Are you sure it is Star's imagination that troubles you 'bout yore Brian-Boy or is it th' color uv her skin? Out here you're gonna hafta learn that we tol'rate diff 'rences—'n I gotta feelin' th' Lord don' take uh shine t'uppety women 'er smart-alecky young'uns!"

The doll-face colored. "How dare you—*you*—"

"Watch it, Mrs. Ames!" Buck's voice was dangerously low. "Mrs. Galloway is a highly-respected charter-member of Lordsburg—drove one of the wagons crossing the mountains over the Applegate Trail. And," he grinned engagingly, "I'm afraid you asked for that."

With a sniff and flirt of her skirts, Brian-Boy's mother was gone.

"Well, I never!" Aunt Em wiped the sweat from her brow. "That Ames woman—guess she ain't got no first name—well, she's out lookin' fer trouble. Uh laugh'd banish that spoiled-child droop uv her lips. An' I'm obliged t'you, Buck, fer shuttin' my mouth. You got a way uv doin' that—a borned leader's more tactful-like than th' likes uv me. That grin you got'll git what'cha want. But I won' 'low my Rachel attacked 'n that nameless woman'd best be knowin'."

Buck smiled again. "I think you made it clear. Her name is Barbette, by the way."

"*Um-hmmm!* I'll wager she's called *Barb*—what waved th' red flag in fronta her highness?"

Buck waved a friendly hand at someone over the clumps of goldenrod in which they were standing. "Probably her husband paid our Rachel a small compliment—guess I'd better help with stoking the fires." He started the direction he had waved then paused. "Have you seen Star—oh, there she is, leading the chase for a butterfly."

"I must keep a watchful eye on Star. I—I'm afraid I let Mrs. Ames distract me. And I must see her husband and thank him—"

The words had slipped out, bringing concerned questions from Aunt Em. Choosing her words carefully, Rachel related the incident, playing it down as much as possible. Emmaline Galloway did not question her, but questions reflected in her eyes. Questions which prompted Rachel to say that Star did not remember the cause of her fall.

Aunt Em nodded. "I best be gettin' back t'packin' jars—no, you don' come—stay 'n mingle. They all wanta meet Rachel Lord Jones. But, Dearie, do be sorta guardin' out fer—fer you-know-who!"

Rachel nodded, trying to hide her feeling of uneasiness, needing to be alone to get control of herself. But privacy was denied her. Aunt Em, having lifted her gingham dress to step over the goldenrod, whirled suddenly. "If 'twas jest uh small incident two days ago—'n I'd stake my good name on our miracle child's tellin th' gospel truth—then why'd yuh be in need uv a doctor?"

This was not the direction Rachel had wanted the talk to take. "He—Dr. Ames was just on hand—I mean, Brian saw her fall and ran for his father—"

Aunt Em frowned. "*Him*? He's uh chip off 'n th' ole block— 'pears innocent as uh choir boy—fittin' now, ain't it with his maw callin' 'im *Brian-Boy*! Well, I'm a-tellin' yuh, he's uh hellion—two-faced as they come—allus lookin' like he'd been scrubbed 'n hung out t'dry. Onct I recollect he *wuz*! He *duz* lissen t'Star 'n hears jest what 'peals t'th'wrong side uv Star's stories. Learnt that uh striped cat cain't let off them foul smells iffen he's picked up by th' tail..."

Others (friends, thank goodness!) gathered to hear the climax. Brian-Boy, thinking it was a cat, so he claimed, took the skunk to *church* to find it a home! Got there and released the animal and ran like a cheetah. Well, there were screams...boys and girls running helter-skelter...and Little Lord Fauntleroy called out innocently: "Let uh spray!" So most of the others got themselves scolded and one layer of skin removed (either through scrubbing or switching) while the *innocent* hypocrite appeared before his parents without blemish—just as spotless and creaseless as ever. Such a *good* child, his mother declared—would another child say, "Let us pray?"

There was a round of laughter, followed by good talks with those Rachel loved. Oh, how good to be among friends...

"Ladies?" a masculine voice broke in, his timid word of address seeming to cast doubt on the title. Rachel saw eyebrows arch in reply.

"Yes, Sir," she said, extending her hand to a stranger whose once-white hair was now streaked with yellow, his once-fair skin red-freckled as if he had measles. His chin lacked stamina and he had trouble removing a wide-brimmed hat in respect (having, she supposed, reached the conclusion that they *were* ladies). "I am Rachel Jones, wife of the city manager. How may we help you?"

The man seemed to relax. "How do you do, Mrs. Jones? You're the one I need to speak with. I—I am Sheriff Brimmerton," he pointed to a heavy tin star on his hatband as if he doubted his own status as well. Surely it would identify him, although it looked more like a lead sinker than the emblem it was. "I—I am retired—but am appointed to this office until there can be some decisions—"

"I understand," Rachel managed to say, "I will be glad to talk with you—but first allow me to introduce the other ladies. You will be working with their husbands."

As she called their names, they nodded and turned away one by one. And then it struck her: *What was the man doing here?* How silly that her heart should pound. Why, of course he *should* become acquainted. But—

"I have a feeling," she managed to get the words out in what was almost a gasp, "you have come to inquire about—what happened—to our daughter. Only—I am the one who—who needs to know—if you have brought news—"

"Yes and no. That is, what I have is testimony from others, my best source being Dr. Ames—and his son, who, so the story goes, is somewhat unreliable." Mr. Brimmerton shook his head. "Shame, a real shame neglecting children, letting them grow up like noxious weeds—"

"Neglecting? Brian appears to have the best—"

They shouldn't be discussing other people's faults, Rachel thought. But she purposely welcomed the detour of the conversation because her pulse rapped out so painfully in wild tattoo that she would never be able to hear the man's words. And listen she must.

"What *is* the best, Mrs. Jones? Sure, he's got schooling, spoiling, and a father looking after his teeth—but what about his heart? I'm thinking it aches for love. Anyway, he's got a deep-down need for a good example, being cut from the same bale of cotton—"

Cotton? The man must be from the South. Not that it mattered. Well, yes, it did, somewhat. Law enforcement was next to godliness there. This man would keep probing in his own peculiar way. As he was doing now.

"Well, bless Pat! Here comes our man Johnny-on-the-spot. Good to see you, Doctor. Interests me that you were able to get away while Dr. Killjoy failed to make it—and these being his in-laws—"

Dr. Ames ignored the comment. He also neglected a greeting. "I understand that both of you wish to speak with me? Make it brief please as I wish to see the Jones girl—"

Something inside Rachel flared. "Her name is Star," she said coldly.

"A fact established quite some time ago. Your question?"

Rachel could not bring herself to express her appreciation in the face of his rudeness. "Proceed, Sheriff," she said politely.

Sheriff Brimmerton took his time getting out his notebook and pencil. "Where did you say you saw the canoe?"

So he had seen it, too?

"I didn't say, but for your information, I've seen it several times—as has my son. He has made up some pretty fancy tales about robbers, thieves, and pirates. Discount those due to—well, never mind, I doubt that the canoe had anything to do with Star's—er, fall."

"Fall, Doctor—I got the impression you said she was pushed."

"Did I say that?" the doctor's face reddened and he appeared flustered. Then, shrugging, he said, "Either way, she was pushed—and please refrain from asking by whom. My patient either did not know or is afraid to tell."

"Star is not afraid of anything. And rest assured she will not lie." Rachel interrupted furiously. "You are the one who mentioned pushing!"

Howard Ames' handsome face crinkled with a smile. As if they were alone, he addressed Rachel: "All right, I've managed to get off on the wrong foot again. Forgive me, Mrs. Jones—Rachel—"

"Touching scene. Now, may we get on with this?"

Dr. Ames responded to the sheriff. "Yes, let's. You're about to inquire if the same person rescued her. The answer is a flat *no*. Now, save time by not asking who either party was. I failed to take along my field glasses, the bushes were thick, and her life was at stake. Now, no more questions. I want to see your daughter, Rachel."

"I will accompany you—"

Rachel interrupted the sheriff. "As will I—I do not want her upset—any more than you do," she added courteously to the doctor. "Let's just approach the children casually—listen, then—"

The men were already striding toward the clump of children seated casually, talking animatedly, while devouring an enormous platter of drumsticks. Dear Aunt Em. Of course, she would see to it that children were taken care of first instead of making them wait until adults had done away with all but bony necks and those silly feet "scratchers." The situation was perfect. The children went on with their conversation, unaware that adults were near.

"So that is the end of the story as the Bible tells it. It is a nice story, yes? Helping others is very *importante*. I think that is what God meant that we should learn. It means we love—"

Star placed a bone on her tin plate and wiped her mouth daintily with her handkerchief. "It is well that we all be Good Samaritans."

Saul leaned forward. "Why did the story end there, Star?"

"Yeah," David chimed in, "that's what my Gran'pa David Saul says. He's the one who named us, you know, that makes us his namesakes—and he always wonders too. What happened to that poor old man the robbers beat up?"

"Who says he was *old*?" Brian Ames' eyes sparkled with the weaving of a new plot. "Maybe he was big and strong like Sampson and got even—beat 'em all up—or," he sobered, "did he appreciate that Good Samaritan?"

"I like to think it changed his life," Star said slowly. A strange look, entirely foreign to Rachel carried her far, far away. Of course, one could not always read the special child's mind. She was still as hard to hang on to as a handful of smoke. "I wonder if the man he ministered to changed the shape of his life as I do with my paints—and became a new man?" She paused deep in concentration.

"Can't bad people do good things?" the little girl called Sarah asked. "Or good ones do bad things?" Questions came from all directions. But Star did not answer. Did she even hear? She was in another world.

Somehow the talk turned to animals. Was a giraffe good or bad? Must be good. God gave him such a long neck he could poke his head clear into heaven. Giraffes in heaven? That long neck wasn't for looking—it was for stretching so he could eat, huh, Star? He never *said* kind words 'cause teacher read a book 'bout giraffes having no voice. True, but *people* could be Good Samaritans without all that talk. They could just go around "gir--affing" . . .

"Glad th' Good Lord did'n put two uv ever' kind uv *humans* in His ark, them giraffin' ones. Yep, this ole world'd be one unholy place, all th' yappin' 'n scrappin'—wonder who'd eat who, thar bein' Wicked Samaritans well as Good—"

Brother Davey!

"Davey-Love—come gimme uh hand, will'ya?"

The man who, small in stature but pure of heart, responded to his Emmy-Gal with a twinkle in his eye. But not before witnessing a startling turn of events.

The quick exchange of words interrupted the children. They looked toward the Galloways and then turned to the trio which had waited before interrupting. Something seemed to frighten them and they scampered away.

"Good," Dr. Ames said under his breath. Then he turned to Star. "Let me see your throat, Dear," he said gently.

Rachel expected Star to open her mouth. Instead, she raised her head as if anticipating his next move. But Rachel had not. Why was he rubbing her throat with practiced hands? "Scratches," he said of the purple lines circling her neck. Rachel gasped. *How on earth—*

"What do you make of it?" Mr. Brimmerton asked in a low voice. "Oh, hello, Mead. May we have some privacy?"

Willie Mead! How did he get away from the telegraph office? He could leave it with his apprentice, of course—

Star's eyes opened in horror, focusing on his face—then on the striped sleeves of his shirt.

"Why did you push me?"

•   •   •

The rest of the day passed in a white haze for Rachel as if she were under an anesthetic, numbing her pain but also robbing her of her senses. No amount of coaxing, she recalled later, brought further explanation from Star. "Let her alone!" the words must have been Rachel's, although it sounded unfamiliar to her own ears. And there was something unnatural about Star. Too pale, but functioning, she spoke when spoken to—seeming to have forgotten the accusation. Star vaguely reminding Rachel of the cuckoo clock Buck had bought—a lovely thing with all kinds of carved wood, but housing a dumb bird at best, hopping out periodically to announce what the grandfather clock already knew. A nonessential comment about time. So why did these men keep applauding for more? Were they happy now? Didn't they know that the door had opened once and now the mute bird had hopped back inside? That it may have forgotten the time? Or that just maybe the little bird had died? Somebody had *tried* to kill it . . . *Where was Buck*? She needed him. . . .

Once, she caught sight of Yolanda. She was all smiles and wild roses bloomed on her cheeks. They waved their oh-so-much-to-tell-you smile then went on finishing the day. And then she saw two of the Lee boys. *Two?* Abe, the one who had stayed home while the others wandered away to spend their "portion of good" meted out by the father. So this one—Bart—*Bart*, yes, must be the prodigal. But he had not come home! Instead, he was moving stealthily among the late-afternoon shadows in the grove behind the house as if searching for something or someone. Something warned of danger. But Rachel had no proof, no reason to sound an alarm. Or did she? Wasn't that Julius Doogan motioning to the boy? His back was to her. Anyway, what would she say? "Announcing the arrival of Mr. Jules Dunigan, reliable citizen?" Oh, nothing made sense—*nothing* . . .

And now the caravan was heading home with wagons loaded for winter meals, dried and sacked, sealed and stacked. Thank goodness Rachel's head was clearing. She and Buck could talk. Only talk was denied them. Children and dogs ran alongside the wagons, weaving in and out, definitely *not* "giraffing," Rachel remembered with a smile. Somehow above the thunderous noise the reverend managed to shout: "Let us give praise for this day!" What could be more beautiful than the blended voices joined in hymns rising above the evergreens en route to heaven? From its lair behind the mountains the sun sent good-night shafts of rose-violet high into the evening sky. Lights twinkled in scattered cabins.

Peaceful? Not quite. Why was Star's head drooping on Buck's shoulder while the other children still played?

17

Just What If...

Yolanda leaned forward as far as she could bend. "Did you ever wonder what might have happened had you taken a different trail where the road forked? Just what if..."

Her voice was strained, Rachel observed. And it took little imagination to be sure that her ears were, too. She was right.

Mrs. Maxton trundled in with the tea-cart. "Time for madam's afternoon tea," she said with studied casualness. "I laid out service for two—hearing another voice."

"That was nice of you," Rachel said. The woman did not meet her eyes as she poured the tea. Yolanda was right. There was something strange about the housekeeper Maynard had employed.

"I will pour—may we have some privacy?" Yolanda reached for a cup.

"But Dr. Killjoy said—"

"Dr. Killjoy is not here," Yolanda reminded her coolly. "Please close the door behind you."

When the *whirrr* of wheels said there could be no eavesdropping, Yolanda's eyes flashed. "'You must stay as quiet as possible'," she mimicked in a high falsetto. "'Take your nourishment like a good child,'—my word! She's a spy and a mischief-maker, thinking I'm totally without a modicum of intelligence. Don't you see it, her acting like I'm helpless? Fancies herself a doctor, as well—a doctor who cures with food invariably. As if one could cure ailments of the heart, soul, and body with pickles and cake. I'm *sick* of food—sick of being waited on, spied on—"

Rachel attempted a laugh, seeing a delicate bloodvessel beating wildly on Yolanda's right temple. "Don't be too hard on her. She just might be for real. We are not to judge, you know—"

"'Lest we be judged!'" Yolanda hurled back. "I *am* being judged—judged, convicted, and serving time—"

"You *are* being difficult, Yo. Lean back and relax. You look like a startled bird, poised, ready for flight. Aren't you going to offer me a slice of that lemon cake?"

"Sorry," Yolanda said, shoving the cake across the tea-cart. "Ready for flight—*me*? I couldn't make it off the ground!" She set her cup back on the tray with a clatter, then grinned in appreciation of her feeble attempt at humor.

Rachel's laugh was one of relief. "There's my Yolanda-of-yesteryears—I thought you'd forgotten how to smile. Now, try to realize that other people's minds spin off course, too. We all have problems. And, Darling, I did *not* come here to talk about your domestic affairs or even your personal affairs—oops! the wrong word. But we never had to tiptoe before, so let's not start now. I was going with Buck to a meeting, but begged off—important as it is. You know that Haute's back with all the legal ramifications of setting up our own government—you're not listening! So, let's catch up and talk—*really* talk. It has been two weeks since Preserving Day. A lot has happened. So what different turn were you talking about? Get it out of your system!"

Yolanda sighed. "It doesn't matter. You wouldn't understand—but thanks for getting me back on course like you always do—*did* anyway."

"Has our relationship changed?"

"No—well, yes. You haven't loved and lost as I have. My heart feels like it's been crumpled up and tossed aside—"

"Stop it, Yolanda! You're about to say I always win, life never touches me—don't deny it, I've heard it all before. Let me remind you of something," she said, trying to control her own blood pressure and her irritation, "Try and remember my losses—my own *husband*, the man I loved more than life—and then the dear General who tried to mend my heart and who, bless his dear soul, left enough money for carrying on Cole's dreams of building the church, getting a school, continuing our town. But now—oh, Darling," she pleaded, "Try and see what God has done for us. How silly to waste a moment on wallowing in the past. He sent us other mates whom we promised to love and cherish—gave us beautiful children. Oh, what's the use? End of lecture! I want to hear about your family. You *did* tell them?"

There were tears in Yolanda's eyes. Tears which Rachel ignored, while biting her lip to keep from apologizing. She mustn't—not now.

"Yes—yes, I told them everything. They were wonderful, Rachel, just wonderful," Yolanda's eyes lighted with affection and her manner became animated. "None of it seemed new. I'd forgotten that my father would have heard about—J–Julius at the council meeting. He is a nonviolent man, but his attitude scared me—says he'd take the law in his own hands if—if this Jules Dunigan ever sets a foot on his property or ours—"

"Did he know the man had been both places?" The words were out before Rachel realized she was going to say them.

A look of horror crossed Yolanda's face. "You—you saw him there?"

"I'm sorry I mentioned it—but, yes, Yo, he was there. However, your father did not see him. I doubt that anybody spotted him slinking around except me. You know that he sticks with the newer folk—"

"Then why was he there?"

"I can't be sure," Rachel evaded, hoping that withholding was not the same as lying. "I get the feeling that he's still recruiting our young boys to do his dirty work. He did that for awhile, you know. Any more signs of him around here?"

"All the time. I am terrified but am learning to live with it—"

"Good girl."

Yes, she was. Yolanda surprised her by saying almost playfully, "Next you'll be ordering me to roll over or shake hands." Then the sift of sunlight disappeared behind the dark cloud of her mind. "Did you know that—that this woman," her dark head jerked toward the kitchen as she whispered, "and the Dunigan woman at Welcome Stranger are *sisters*?"

No wonder Yolanda was scared! Julius' tracks could mean that he was gleaning information from Mrs. Maxton. She would know of the activities through Dr. Killjoy. He would have knowledge of the closed meetings of the council. Providing, of course, that Maynard cautioned the woman to be on the lookout for one Julius Doogan, now Jules Dunigan.

"How much contact does Maynard have with your house-keeper?"

"It's more like what does *she* tell *him*?" But for the first time a question came to her dark eyes. "Of course, I guess it could be a mutual exchange—then—oh, I am confused. But don't give me that I-told-you-so look saying I'm to go running to my doctor-huband!" Her voice was bitter. "There's more! He's seeing his partner's wife, a reason for divorce—only there's this child within me—"

"Yolanda—I don't believe it. I've met Barbette and thoroughly disliked her—but, with all his peculiar ways, I am unable to believe *that* of him. But I am relieved that you have thought of the unborn child—and praise the Lord that you have given up ideas of—"

She was unable to get the words out. Yolanda finished the thought for her. "Destroying the baby? I was too cowardly to go through with it. I never meant to have a surgeon doing something dangerous and illegal—just scrub floors—force a miscarriage—but (tears were streaming down her face) I—I felt movement. And then I came to realize that either way it would come out *murder*. Oh, Rachel, pray that God will forgive me—even though I want no part of—of a child fathered by—"

It was then that Rachel leaped from her chair, almost upsetting the cart in her leap to kneel, pull Yolanda to her, and say, "Oh, Lord, thank You! Thank You that love is stronger then death—"

Someday, Rachel decided, she would tell Yolanda the details of Star's identification...that it might not be exact...and that there was more to the mystery that Star couldn't remember, except in her dreams. But Yolanda had had too much excitement already for one day.

Later, of course, she would remember that certainly she should have asked Yolanda how she came by her information about Mrs. Maxton's being a sister to Mrs. or Miss (she was unable to recall whether she knew the title or the given name of the blonde woman). And about the impossible, untidy relationship with Barbette Ames—

But a sudden entrance of their husbands interrupted. Buck rushed to Rachel and pulled her to her feet. She could feel the pounding of his heart as he drew her gently to him. "What's wrong, Darling? Who made you cry? Oh, Rachel—"

From that position she was unable to see Maynard Killjoy's face. But she heard him say in a low command, "Lean back, Yolanda—breathe deeply—that's it—I want to check your pulse after this scrap. What on earth were the two of you doing—having a cake fight or trying to bust up all the china?"

Yolanda laughed. Actually laughed. And then they all did. Had they lost their minds? If so, Rachel hoped that they would never regain them. What if—? Never mind. A miracle—a funny one—had happened....

18

Heart of the Matter

October had burned its way into November before school began. There had been delay because of what some grumblingly referred to as "separation of church and state." Now, come to think on it, which really took precedence? There were monies available from Colby's will—put aside for building on to the school and the church (couldn't the pipe organ and those honest-to-goodness temple bells for the "main church" wait?). Children's minds shouldn't be idle—regular devil's workshops—all because volunteers were busy with city affairs. Tension ran high, tempers flared, until they reached the "Great Compromise" which City Manager Buckley Jones led men to think was their own idea. No sense in being a bunch of mindless blackbirds caught in a net and finally brought down by some farmer's gun—all because every blooming critter tried to fly his own way. Sure they could work together, dividing their time between adding on more rooms to the school and working on enlarging the church.

Then the twittery Little Miss Muffet hired to aid Miss Annie, the scholarly "hickory-stick" spinster who'd been around since creation added on the west wing of the world, up and married a performer in a traveling medicine show. So another delay until a teacher of Miss Annie's liking could be found. Some joke, his name being Bonaparte Bixby—what with his black hair whacked to a Napoleonic point on his forehead. Well, Cal Merriweather's razor could fix that . . . but the drooping shoulders and one eye that, like his tie, always drifted to the left, the trustees shrugged, could be tolerated if he could pass inspection by the tightly-corseted despot he'd be working with. Strange, wasn't it just? that

102

Young Bixby sort of swaggered in looking like the cat that swallowed the canary instead of cowering? The woman took one look, walked around him and ordered: "Staighten those shoulders and wipe that Chessy-cat grin off your mouth, else you won't last out the first day!" The cat disgorged the canary.

So tomorrow school would begin.

"Brilliant leaves are God's signature to summer and it is almost erased. We must hurry and gather letters," Star told the children who tagged her heels as Scot tagged theirs. "Think of each leaf as a love letter. But we must search nearby. That we must remember, for we are commanded to obey our parents. Yes?"

"Yes," countless voices echoed. "Oh, look—here is a crimson one!" Saul called out in victory. "Red is to remind us of His Blood!"

"No, please," David said. "It makes me sad that the world was so bad, Jesus had to die."

"Be not sad, Dear Brother Mine," Star comforted, reaching for a golden leaf. "God sent His Son because He loved us most tenderly."

Wading through the head-high ferns, wild grape vines, and the tangle of laurel and manzanita, the children searched through a jungle. Leaves . . . leaves . . . there *had* to be leaves for the classrooms tomorrow. Their search became almost frenzied. Laughter ran out as each spotted an especially brilliant limb where leaves continued clinging to the parent trees. "It's like buried treasure!"

Buried treasure. "That was my warning," she was to tell her mother later. "I remembered then. The canoe. The buried rainbow. The treasure of coins. The fall . . . no, the push . . . the Good Samaritan . . ."

But it was too late. There was a shot, followed by Scot's howl of pain, and then bedlam. The disoriented children ran all directions in search of their beloved friend. Men and boys appeared from just everywhere. Helpers surely. "Oh, please help us find our dog. He is suffering much pain—" Star pleaded.

But they were bad men. Men who said terrible words, such as the evil one would speak—only he was not there. Who *was* there? Boys, young boys, with faces very white who ran—oh, now Star remembered—like her father ran when Indians attacked their wagon train. To desert those in need of help was most dreadful.

But they were scared, those boys. Else why would they cover their faces? "And I was scared, too, Mother Mine. Is there a difference in being most scared and being a coward? I was scared because our Scot was alone and weeping blood as crimson as the bleeding leaves...and the other children were running near the water where we should not be...and there *was* danger."

No, she did not recognize faces—well—(slowly) there was one. A man who looked like Ichabod Crane, the schoolmaster, only he carried no rod for rapping palms—just a shovel. But his eyes rolled around like those of a snapping turtle. Did that happen to older men? Or only to the unkind ones?

Brian had frightened them all by confronting the man. "What have you done with our dog, you beast? You shot him and I'm going after the sheriff. He knows what to do with outlaws."

The stranger ran at Brian, and Star was certain that he, like Elisha, would call out the she-bears to devour the children who tormented him and they would be swallowed whole. Instead, he screamed: "I will bury him, just as I buried that stupid, no-good wooly, barking dog—"

"Go—go to school, all of you, *niños—por favor!*" Star's plea sent them running and crying their little hearts out about their loss.

Then God told her, Star would go on to say, that the man had no real power. It took a *good* man to rebuke mockers. There would be no she-bears. They must be calm...the leaves must be taken to school before they wilted away...and God would direct her to their Scot...and he would have a nice funeral....

That's when the beautiful lady appeared again—yes, Star had seen her before—and she had a sweet voice. She would let no harm come to them. *If* they obeyed their leader. The lady watched as they did her bidding, smiling bravely, but looking uneasy. Then she faded from sight. A vision?

"I must find our *perro*, dear God. Lead me and I will follow Thee anywhere..." she had begged.

A faint whine. And then the wounded little creature crawled to Star's feet and collapsed. Somehow she managed to pick him up and wrap him. It was necessary to make use of the shawl of many colors Grandma Em had woven. But a loving heart knows of sacrifice...

Star wished she could place Scot in the hands of Auntie Yo's doctor. But he was most busy with another patient, a life-size doll really. It would be nice to give Mary Cole so beautiful a big doll. But one must not do such unseemly things. It was forbidden...wasn't it?

Mary Cole, David, and Saul were meek at dinner. A sure sign of trouble. The way they kept casting little sidelong glances at their older sister as she told the parents that their future lay in her hands.

"Tomorrow's schoolday, dear old golden rule day," Buck said, pretending nothing was abnormal. "So it's off to bed *early*. You look tired just thinking about it. I will fill in for Star, hear your prayers, and read your favorite story—"

There were no arguments tonight, no wheedling, just relief. Rachel, too, was relieved, but confused. She and Buck must get to the heart of the matter. . . .

19

Black, White, or Inbetween?

Star told her story well. Poor child. She surely must feel she was the key witness in a court trial—giving her testimonial without the aid of an attorney. Buck sat quietly, leaving all questioning to Rachel as if preparing to cross-examine. If so, it would be an emotional scene. She had never seen his face so dark, so angry.

"This man—the Ichabod Crane as you described him—" Rachel began in what she planned to make her last question. "Had you seen him before?" At a shake of Star's dark head, sending little shock-waves of brilliance from the blue-black hair fanning her face, Rachel herself said slowly, "I have seen such a person—let's see, first making a purchase at Aunt Em's Eatery—then speaking with William Mead."

"I do not know. They acted like a flock of lost sheep—belonging together, men and boys, but lost all the same. They had no leader." Then suddenly something seemed to click in the young mind. "I know what was so strange. They were not a flock. They were an *army*. At first I thought perhaps they played a game—that the gleam the sunbeams found came from pop-guns. But no! They were weapons—and one shot our doggie—oh, tell me Scot will be all right!" A sob caught in her throat.

"Don't cry, Baby." Buck reached out fatherly hands and took Star's small, dark ones in his own. "You are as cold as ice, Sweetheart."

How could any man be so angry yet so comforting? Only Buck. Rachel, her own vocal chords tied in knots rendering her unable to speak, wondered what her husband would say next.

"Of course, your Scot-dog will make it, Star. You were wise to take him to Dr. Killjoy—"

"Dr. Ames," Star corrected. "Uncle Maynard was busy. At first, I thought he held a Persian kitten. But it was the beautiful fur collar of the doll-lady he held—it does not seem right, does it, *Dad-dee?*"

Buck inhaled sharply, the deep crease between his troubled eyes asking: *Why must parents be expected to know all the answers?*

"She is not his wife," Star persisted. "God joined him to Auntie Yo. The mystery lady was holding fast. Who could she be?"

Buck appeared to have reached a decision. "Mrs. Ames!" he burst out. Then, trying to control his voice, "But we do not know the circumstances—so we must not judge—"

Star did not hear. Her mind had drifted to shadowed valleys where none other could follow. "The mystery lady is Brian's mother?" she whispered as if talking to an invisible person other than herself, "I understand . . . she possesses strange powers over men . . . can open doors to which others have no key . . . and her mission here is secret . . . unholy . . ."

So Yolanda had grounds for her accusations. Rachel caught her lips sharply between her teeth. *What will I do now, Lord? Apologize to my friend, admit I was wrong in saying she was giving way to her imagination-complex? But wouldn't that be tale-bearing—compounding problems?*

The million Lilliputian lumps of ice coursing through her veins melted. Swallowing her heart which had clamored so painfully in her chest, she looked directly at Buck. Their eyes met and held. As always, they communicated without words.

Better to know the enemy. They must beg deeper. Their "buried treasure" lay in wickedness. Somehow, with the help of the Lord, they must destroy it—before it destroyed them. Just how this all tied together neither of them had an inkling—except that it did!

• • •

Rachel paused to look through the ruffled kitchen windows as she hurriedly set the coffee to perking and bacon to frying on the cooperative wood range. Good that there was no wind. The beast had a way of being contrary when the wind blew from the north, snorting down the flue and filling the lungs with blinding smoke.

But today was perfect outside the window. Beauty! Beauty everywhere. Only a few clouds blotched the faultless sky. A flame of crimson in the east foretold a sunrise against which a few robins, wings made gold reflected by the light, agreed with the crowing rooster that morning was nigh. It seemed impossible to imagine evil defiling such beauty.

"Lovely." Buck's hands were on her shoulders, tenderly. "Lovely out there—and in here. I wish," his voice grew husky, "that this day were finished—that we were alone—"

His mood ran shoulder-to-shoulder with her own, sending the blood throbbing through her veins. The house was still—momentarily, just long enough for Rachel to turn to him and exclaim girlishly, "Why, Mr. City Manager!" and Buck to whisper, "Now, don't be coy!" And then the house filled with joyous laughter. Today was the wonderful "first day"!

Rachel walked to school with the children. She was spared conversation by their chattering. There was much to turn over and over in her mind and many decisions to make. It was frightening that no line of demarcation seemed to exist anymore between black and white. Or was most of it in between? How did one recognize the enemy anymore? Somebody—it *had* to be Julius Doogan, even though there had been not one false step—was recruiting and *training* an army. That was not news. The terrifying thing was that "friends" were enlisting along with enemies. . . .

20

"Spreading the Word!"

Rachel had remained at home in peaceful bliss for too long, she supposed. It had served to heal her mind, body, and spirit of the years of bruising and battering, but the healing took its toll. Left scar tissue in the process. When the spirit wihin her giving heart said quietly, "Arise, take up your bed and walk!" she obeyed, knowing that the desire to be active triggered her natural sense of adventure. Now she was realizing that for everything she paid dearly. A portion of the cost was becoming a stranger, staggering back but still blinking in new-found light. She must become reacquainted.

The realization became more vivid as she spoke confidentially with Miss Annie in the room Star was to occupy, now garlanded with brilliant leaves. She had met the teacher before but scarcely recalled what the lady was like. Rachel found her to be understanding and gentle in spite of her reputation of being a tyrant, while sensing that there would be no hesitation to live up to that reputation if need be.

"Miss Annie, I know this is a busy day," Rachel smiled, "But it is wise that we understand about certain matters—"

Miss Annie patted the hand Rachel had extended. "I think I do, My Dear. But I welcome your suggestions. You refer to the situation of possible danger. News travels, but how can I help with your children?"

"All the children," Rachel began slowly, only to end up explaining a few details about Star. Miss Annie kept nodding. All would be well. Rachel left smiling, a burden lifted.

One thought of the brief conversatation was new. One which lingered as she hurried to Aunt Em's Eatery. Was Miss Annie right in suggesting that perhaps it was time to get the word out in the open, let the suspects know that citizens of Lordsburg were onto their wiles? Instead of doing the tiptoe, why not give them a war dance? Maybe, she said with a sly twinkle, even exaggerate? The woman was wise, so—

Before Rachel reached the Galloways, her nostrils picked up the tantalizing scent of pickling spices combined with cider vinegar. Green tomato relish—something Aunt Em always made as she and the frost tried to outwit the almanac. It was uncanny how Aunt Em always won. Tomorrow there would be frost. *Poor Richard's Almanac* said so.

Aunt Em was mending. Biting off a thread, she waved Rachel in. "Come in, come in, Dearie. I declare, that man can bust off more buttons. Set yourself down 'n we'll visit uh spell—oh, push my thimble over, Dearie, an' pour us some coffee. Hafta make haste while th' sun shines 'n that means savin' all th' steps I can— gotta corn on my big toe 'n my rheumatiz's warnin' uv uh change. Bad time I picked out t'add pickles fer sale—but, oh, Dearie, Davey-Love, bless 'im, is a-puttin' in uh pump. Right there on th' back porch. Can you believe it—hand-pumpin' water in without all them trips t'th' river with buckets? 'Course," she reached for another button, "this means I hafta be at my man's beck 'n call— 'n cain't keep watch as good. But I kin tell you there's been lots uv goin's on—did I hear 'im holler? Oh, is th' relish stuck?"

"Stay put, Aunt Em. I'll check!" Rachel sprang from the cane-bottom chair, gave the relish a twirl with the wooden spoon then hurried out to check on Brother Davey's howls.

He was jumping up and down, thumb of his right hand gripped with the left. "Consarn that hammer—allus actin' up— 'specially when I'm a-needin' hit most. Plumb pulverizing my finger 'n me wantin' this pump installed afore boardin' up th' attic. Yuh knowed Miz Annie wuz a-gonna board with me 'n Emmy-Gal? Folks she's been stayin' with decided on goan' back t'Kansas. Ain't that witless?"

"I really *am* behind—no, I had no idea they were friends."

Brother Davey grunted. "Wimmen! Beggin' pardon, Rachel. But they're blest with short mem'ries. My Emmy-Gal's got a way with more'n uh needle. She fix't th' rip 'twixt 'em—sompin' 'bout who'd play th' new orgin. Sorta compromised, that bein' th' word—agreed, y'know one'd play hit one Sunday, t'other th' next, takin' turns at weddin's 'n fun'rals—"

Rachel smiled, a vision of who could out-talk whom if the Galloways ever engaged in a battle of words. That would never happen. Aunt Em, as her superior height and well-cushioned frame would indicate, mothered her short-of-stature but long-on-words husband, always letting him feel he was in charge. Brother Davey had the advantage anyway. Time had robbed him of his hearing while proving the law of gravity by pulling his body toward earth. He made use of an ear trumpet which he used only to hear his own voice, admittedly. "Bein' a peacemaker, I put that gumpy thing t'rest when others git argumental. Serves t'end uh senseless argument, yuh understand."

Yes, everybody understood.

The thumb seemingly healed, the carpenter now picked up his tools and proceeded to hammer and talk. Oh, this newfangled gadget would be pleasing his good wife who deserved the best. Why, it cost beyond four dollars when he could've purchased a two-dollar pump model had he been a cheap-like husband . . . but this one was "garn'teed" . . . fitted with top-cap . . . iron cylinder . . . and "oh, by jiminy, what uh handle—fitted fer uh woman's hand like uh glove!"

Rachel indulged him by allowing him to talk. It brought him happiness, set him dancing like a rubber ball. But she was to pay for the delay . . .

"Thank you, dear sweet Rachel," Aunt Em, who had set to work frosting sweet rolls, frying ham, and baking biscuits, wiped away an unwelcome tear, "he's gettin' on."

"Brother Davey will *never* grow old—he's too spirited—"

" 'N too devilish!"

The two burst into laughter. And without a word Rachel set to helping Aunt Em prepare for the noon rush. They talked as they worked, coming straight to the point: "Yolanda?" Aunt Em parried as if dreading her turn.

Rachel caught her up in short phrases, including the heartless shooting of the dog. That led her into a trap. At mention of the doctor, she paused—unwilling to share gossip until she could think it through.

"Go ahead," Aunt Em said quietly as she laid out silverware. "I think I know. Is it about that Ames woman?"

"Yes. Do you believe it?"

"I would believe anything of her—but we hafta consider th' source."

"Star?" Rachel gasped.

"Oh, *no*—that despicable darlin' she calls Brian-Boy. He's got th' mind uv a adult when it comes t'spreadin' tales. Still 'n all, we dunno now, do we? As th' sayin' goes, 'Little fires grow great with a little wind'—but does Yolanda know?"

"She *believes*. Her marriage hangs by a thread, Aunt Em. She seems to hate Maynard anyway—doesn't want his child." Rachel turned palms up in despair. "I—I honestly don't know how much is real. Surely you remember how difficult it was for her to face reality—"

"An' 'twas her husband brought her back. Life's uh puzzle."

At the sound of footsteps, Aunt Em stopped. But in quick whispers, Rachel told of Miss Annie's suggestion that they be more aggressive. Wonderful plan! Maybe that lying tongue of young Ames would help!

The footsteps were those of the sheriff. He opened the door gallantly and, removing his wide-brimmed hat, bowed comically. "I need to speak with you, Mrs. Jones, ask some questions. I am not exactly satisfied with answers—"

"Please—not now," Rachel declined. "I must pick up the dog and am late already."

He intended to hold her captive, force her to say words she was unwilling to say. With a sort of desperation, she ducked beneath the arm barring her way—attempting to make the move appear playful. "Another time—"

"But the dog? My sakes, woman! Don't you ever stop to breathe?"

"Seldom," she said lightly, hastening away. *The dog!* Why on earth had she made another slip of the tongue? Didn't she know they were playing with fire? That there was an enemy, perhaps an army of enemies, in their midst and caution was essential? She stopped with a jerk as a rumble of distant thunder echoed along the canyon. The jolt was as surprising as her sudden thought. Did this man know more than his off-hand manner indicated? As Buck said, one grew suspicious.

Back at Aunt Em's she had acted flippant. Now, she was painfully aware that she was as alone as Robinson Crusoe. Alone and in need of her man Friday. But Buck was at an afternoon council meeting. Just a brief one, he had promised, so they had arranged that he would meet the children at school and she would pay Scot's bail. They had laughed. It was no longer funny. Lifting her skirts, she ran the short distance to the office of Killjoy and Ames.

Howard Ames opened the door before there was time to knock, almost as if he had rushed to get there before his colleague. Rachel, as always, was struck by his finely-chiseled good looks, the deep blue of his intelligent eyes which were now focused on her. "Good as new—your puppy-dog. Spunky little critter. Who would do such a heinous act?"

"I wish I knew, Doctor—"

"Howard, remember? We decided on a first-name basis—Rachel."

Rachel nodded numbly. "Yes, Doc—Howard. And if you will name your fee—"

Howard waved away the idea. "My pleasure. I know you're in a rush, what with a storm brewing. But *please* shed any light you can on Star—I'm afraid the storm hanging over Lordsburg is more threatening than anything nature can produce. Can she unlock her mind? I feel I'm close to an answer, then something whisks her into another world. I want to help. You believe that, don't you?"

Another rumble of thunder, closer this time. "Yes," she said quickly, finding that it was true. "And I promise to help—but something is blocking her mind, Howard. Star is no ordinary child. I really must go." Feeling a sense of urgency to get home—and there was that stretch of woods between her and safety—why did she hesitate? "She *sees*, but the vision floats away. If only I knew why—"

"It's the man who kept her from drowning she's seeing. Let's not dismiss her identification of the striped-sleeved man—"

"Mead?" A whisper was all she could manage. Surely not . . . yet . . .

A desperate howl. And then Scot was all over her, whimpering and licking with a frenzied tongue of welcome. The splint on his back leg and bandaged shoulder meant nothing in his delight. Laughing while trying to dodge the warm tongue, Rachel gathered the still-whimpering Scotty into her arms and ran, hurling a "Thank you" over her shoulder.

The wind had increased in volume. It tore at Rachel's stole, finally whipped it from her shoulders and hurled it back the way she had come. With a maddening display of temperament, dark clouds blotted out the last fire-opal rays the sun had left as a path for the half-moon. Whisking the clouds back and forth the wind, as if eager to puff out all light, heaved mightily and drew the heavy clouds together in a black drape, bringing on a premature darkness. Blinded, Rachel realized she had become disoriented, taken the wrong trail. She had to be approaching the river. Else why was she compelled to stumble from boulder to boulder? The panic which the wind had spread in the treetops was no greater than that in her heart. Was it the panic or the drop in temperature that caused her to shake so violently?

Lost. She was hopelessly lost. Even Scot knew. His whimpers had changed to sounds of warning as the trees swished, murmured, and groaned in agony above them. *Stand still. Close your eyes. Think!*

Rachel obeyed her own command. When she opened her eyes, directly ahead there was a ghostly blur of white moving stealthily alongside what must be the riverbank. And then a blinding flash. Lightening? No, lightening would never follow such a foolish path, swinging back and forth, leaving a dizzying reflection in the water. She was too frightened to move. The treasure . . . the Dunigan woman . . . and *danger* . . .

In such a setting, it came as no surprise when a gloved hand reached out and grasped her free one. "Hold on! And watch your step, you little idiot!" The words were a hoarse-whispered command.

The dark figure whirled her around and, gripping tightly, forced her footsteps away from the slippery rocks and onto the soft cushion of pine needles and sward. Safety. But they must not leave! Even though her heart beat like a defective sewing machine—

"I could shake you like a rat. All that saves you is being female!"

Sheriff Brimmerton! "You dared follow me—"

"Squat down and shut up! It's risky, but we have to chance it— then we'll have some real facts when we go spreading the news. Get down!"

Cramped as she was and praying that Scot would not howl made minutes become days. And at last it happened. First, paralyzing Rachel, then revealing truths so shocking that her mind was unable to accept them.

The light again. Not signaling, searching! Surely the assembly of men—so many more than she had expected—must have spotted them. She must not move a muscle, even breathe. An eternity seemed to pass. And then, oh, praise the Lord!—the light turned its beams back to the canoe. And men were everywhere at once. Lifting heavy boxes, cursing their weights, and at last unfastening ropes, prying open the lids. But what were the fiercely gleaming objects? Not money—

"What—" she dared whisper, realizing that her voice carried because the wind had stopped without warning.

"Sh-h-h!" Sheriff Brimmerton warned. "It's contraband!"

Contraband. Weapons. Guns . . . bullets . . . a regular arsenal—

And there her shock gave way to another far greater. Bart! Bart Lee! And then the incredible—*all* the brothers, Judson and Nola's sons, so prayerfully brought up—

With no thought of fear for her safety, Rachel sprang up and, in spite of the Sheriff's effort to restrain her, raced mindlessly toward home. Buck must know *now*—then the Lees. Oh, how could she follow through with the agreement to spread the news? Choking back hysterical sobs Rachel ran as she had never run before. Until she fell—

Immediately, she felt herself being picked up, set on her feet.

"Why, Mrs. Jones! Tut, tut—how undignified for the future mayor!"

Julius Doogan! Why was he always around when trouble raged? How did he know when she knew nothing of today's council decisions? *Mayor?*

Fear turned to confusion and then anger. "Let me pass!"

"Without a 'Thank you'? Well, our next meeting—"

"There will *be* no next meeting!"

"Oh, yes, Your Honor, there will be—depend on it!" There was a dark threat in his tone. "So spread the news about *that.*"

21

Healing

Lordsburg rang with a symphony of sawing and hammering. Growth created problems in organization. On the other hand, each group of new arrivals brought men with needed skills. Now if only the two factions could solve some existing problems and draw closer to God and each other. Well, nobody could say that the solid citizens were not trying.

Could they be trying too hard? Pushing too fast? "Could be, just could be," Buck agreed when he saw the folly of going public with posters and "Wanted" signs covering the walls of the new post office. The news spread like wildfire that the now-incorporated city would no longer tolerate the intimidation of its peace-loving community. Once begun, rumors became warnings that citizens were on the lookout for violators of the laws of the land, whether created by the government or within Lordsburg. It all began with Miss Annie's suggestion. And even before Rachel could get home, she had locked horns with new facts. The news beat the city manager to his meeting, hitting him full-face and without preparation.

Returning home before Rachel, he had prepared himself for a report. When the hour grew late and the storm gathered strength, he and the impatient children had decided to meet her. Relieved when they met, he had gathered her close, said a meal waited, such as it was—probably was a burnt offering—as soon as she could towel herself dry. Too exhausted to correct his thinking that the storm was responsible for her shaking, she let him set the food on the table, too weak to object. Not that she could be heard above the commotion Scot's homecoming created. It was best to let Buck talk. Drained as she was, she knew he had news.

It was hard to concentrate but she caught the essentials of the council's actions. There was agreement on almost all matters. Brimmerton wanted to stay on, if it was their pleasure (strange that he made no appearance, just sent an application by Mead). Not strange at all, but Rachel was too exhausted to attempt an explanation. A deputy would assist. Also remaining would be Judge Hathaway...James Haute as city attorney, his voice droned on. Council members would remain...election next year...and the most important decisions were that they would have help in tracking down the rumored army (*It's not a rumor*, Rachel's heart cried out, but she was struck dumb). Undercover government men to work on the robbery. Star's experience was essential to the solution of the mystery—if only she could piece it together. His voice drifted away then came back clearly to say, "*You* are to be mayor protem, the office to be filled by election next year. But the year is nearing an end—and Rachel, an election now would be dangerous. Rumor has it that Dunigan has gathered a following (*and an army, Buck!*). They are circulating a petition..."

Rachel nodded numbly. So that was why Julius Doogan *alias* Jules Dunigan— or was it the other way around? had hissed out his warning.

Sadly, the Reverend Luke Elmo announced that he could no longer serve as chaplain but had a young minister in mind he hoped their church would find acceptable—"different but fundamental, believes in healing under certain conditions." Would Rachel allow Reverend Luke to stay with them until he could find a home? "Think it over, Darling," Buck had said with concern. "I have worn you out—what could I be thinking of? You must rest." *Yes, yes, she must!* But still Buck detained her. Brother Davey brought an invitation to a quilting bee, get the ladies together to talk and plan...Miss Annie having announced her plan for making everybody detectives...could be dangerous...but the Ames boy was already acting as a junior Paul Revere. And the story would enlarge with every telling, Rachel had wanted to say. *Later...later...*

Buck let her sleep late. Rachel awoke with a start. The sun, having driven last night's storm over the camel's hump of mountains, now concentrated on patches of frost it had yet to conquer. The unmistakable smell of coffee filled the house, where the accusing sun was magnifying every molecule of dust.

"When are you going to do your dusting?" Rachel said with a luxurious stretch and yawn when Buck opened the door a crack, only to have it pushed open with a bang as Scot leaped onto the bed, ran circles, then ran back to report to the man-of-the-house, splints still in place.

"Down, boy! Now to answer, Your Honor, let's see, would a week from next Tuesday be acceptable for the dusting?"

Dear Buck, dear wonderful Buck. Rachel knew without asking that he had fed the children and seen them off to school. "I'm afraid I'm not much of a housekeeper these days." There was no apology. Dust would always be around. It all began with Adam. And, no way would she go back to the days when she was a perfectionist. She had needed the peace, the quiet. But it was good to be needed again, to be involved.

Involved. It all came back to her then. The situation had taken on a sensitivity that required her to choose her words with utmost delicacy—even with her own husband. Sleep had robbed her of the opportunity to think things through. They had always been so open. And now she felt cautious, somewhat as if she were unpacking fragile crystal.

"Something wrong?" Buck sat down on her side of the bed.

Wrong? "Well—I feel a need to say, 'I love you, Buck Jones'!"

"You make beautiful music, Rachel Jones!" Buck brushed her forehead with a kiss. "Hungry?"

"As the saying goes, 'I could eat a horse'!"

"Sorry—fresh out of horseflesh. Will flapjacks do?"

"Hear that sound? That's me running!"

Minutes later, they sat silent as Rachel finished her second cup of coffee. How was she to begin sharing a situation which put such a burden on her heart? How could she betray either side?

Buck made it easy. A sense of relief spread over her as he looked out over one section of their apple orchard where the late fall apples, so red one could believe they had captured all the red fires of the summer sunrises, begged to become pies. Beyond, the orchard unselfishly shared the rich soil with the ancient stand of timber—evergreens, whose needled branches snared a passing breeze. "I've been thinking—wondering how they," he nodded at the scene, "can live together in harmony, the old and the new, and we human beings are unable to do so? Maybe we ignore God's plan—try to plant bananas where they can't survive and watch them die."

Rachel surprised herself by laughing. "Know anybody who died?"

"Did the Creator tell Nature more than He told us? Nature seems to know what's best. Mortals try to force togetherness without thinking it through. We know-it-alls anyway—"

"Darling, you are no know-it-all! And you are not a *tree.* Otherwise, you'd have a wooden head!" Feeling more secure and drawing the warm, woolly robe Buck and the children had given her for her birthday about her, Rachel pulled her chair next to his, and, slipping her arm about him comfortingly, rested her head against the warmth of his upper arm. That way, although her questions remained unanswered, she was able to relate every detail of the frightening discovery and repeat her short encounter with the man calling himself Jules Dunigan word for word.

Buck listened without comment, although she could feel a mixture of emotions fighting for right-of-way.

When Buck dropped his head in his hands with a slight moan, Rachel knew he was deeply troubled. "You could have been killed," he said at last. There was no inflection in his voice, just acceptance of something too great to bear. The truth was that his mind had gone blank, refused to allow the full impact of it all to sink in. Now was not the time to confront him with her questions, Rachel thought wisely.

She waited for full impact to come. The waiting was not long. But when it came, it came with a jolt. Of all the questions she might have imagined, it would never have been this.

"I want to ask you something, Darling." His lips curved into an attempted smile. Not very successful. But his eyes were no longer dazed. And his voice was clear. "Grab hold of your heart and think before you speak. It's touchy. When you finally said 'Yes, Buck, I will marry you,' did you honestly think I could bring you the peace I promised?"

"Yes."

"Then I have failed you. If you had one regret—what would it be?"

"That I did not say 'Yes' sooner."

"But there is something wrong—did I take the wrong approach? Should I back off? Oh, Sweetheart, what do *you* want to do?"

"I want to do what my husband thinks is wise."

Buck inhaled deeply. "I thank you from the bottom of my heart, but it's no answer—"

"It was no proper question! You are in charge. Husbands always are, you know. It's not up to me to lead. I'm to follow—but now I am afraid I am the one who took over—" Rachel stopped.

Realizing that the critical point had come, she tried to lighten the moment by changing to another tactic. "Well, I'm stuck with you—therefore, your decisions." She gave him a playful jab in the ribs. No smile—more a look of concern.

"What is it, Rachel? Why do you hesitate? We *have* to talk."

The blood drained out of her body. "Oh, Buck, what are we going to do?" she gasped. "Word has it that names are being whispered—and that names will be made public—"

"Wasn't that more or less the plan—wise or unwise?"

"But don't you see? We will be doing untold damage. Think of what we are doing to Yolanda's family—without warning—"

That was when he said that he, too, was having second thoughts. "But—God help us—we have to follow through—not playing favorites. There is no stopping it now. But this I promise, Judson Lee will know in advance—somehow. I will, as you say, take the lead. Furthermore, I will see to it that we will *not* point an accusing finger at those we only suspect. There must be positive identification."

"That means—oh, Buck—that I must testify against the boys—"

Buck kissed her palm, helped her rise and pulled her to him. "I'm afraid that's it. There were no other witnesses. God will stand by. We will get through this, Rachel. Have you ever known Him to go back on His promises? It is the *Lord* who will lead—*not* your husband!"

True. Tears, too long held back, streamed from Rachel's eyes. And then she felt the warmth of Buck's tears against her cheek. The words of Aunt Em came back to comfort her. "I got me no use fer no man what cain't cry. Them's tears is uh sign uv strength—not weakness!"

Strength. One's strength was made perfect in time of weakness, Paul said, promising a healing of the spirit. Rachel felt the spirit within her enlarge. Not perfect, but "pressing toward the mark."

She was suddenly glad that the young minister the Reverend Elmo mentioned leaned heavily on healing.

Her mind had wandered. It came as a surprise that Buck's mind had taken the same path. "The Ames boy says Star has met Patrick O'Grady, Reverend Luke's *protégé*—and plans to seek counsel. Strange she made no mention of it."

22

Waiting
for a Miracle

Lordsburg was to learn the benefits of delay. The government could not be rushed. Postponement after postponement of the council meeting allowed tempers to cool, investigations to proceed more rationally, and bonuses nobody would have hoped for.

Certainly there was no delay in activity. Changes moved at the pace of runaway horses, unhampered by heavily loaded wagons. The Galloways plastered the walls of the Eatery with "fade-proof" paper about as wild as the runaway horses, repainted the Shaker furniture, and hung curtains in a wild abandon of designs ranging from flying geese to hearts and watermelons. Miss Annie needed beauty around her. The fact that the clutter of poorly crafted folk-art was phony made no difference. To Aunt Em, who had seen so much of death and disaster, endless stretches of nothingness except new graves, it was all beautiful. And somehow it managed to be. For, mixed with the near-comical tastelessness of it all, there mingled a priceless collection of stoneware and pewter, always filled with great bouquets of Oregon's beauty and homemade breads, fresh vegetables—and history-in-the-making. With pride, the industrious pair swung a ladder for a stairway to the attic. Of course, the good woman would have to hike her skirts and step "high, wide, and handsome." But she was a rugged soul. And, well, a real gentleman would close his eyes. Miss Annie moved in.

"Sech good timin'," Aunt Em declared. "Jes right fer th' quiltin' bee—chance t'show off our pump while a-pumpin' others fer news!"

It was thrilling to see so many women fill up the Galloway quarters. All brought food galore. And all brought fabric scraps as bright as the flamboyant decor around their working area. Aunt Em had brought the quilting frames from the attic. It had been a long time since Rachel had seen her so spry. "Look at all the new folks—come outta curiosity I'm a-guessin'," she whispered to Rachel. "My word, Rachel, take a gander. Bless Pat if it ain't thet Barb Doctor Ames calls a wife, here t'spy les'sen I miss my guess—"

No guessing about it. She was right. Barbette was all ears without joining in the flow of talk. Dressed "fit t'kill," according to Aunt Em's way of putting it. The get-together was a "roarin' success" in Brother Davey's report to the husbands. "No need t'pump 'em. Women spilled their insides. Jest wait 'til I get me uh chance t'tell them bull-headed husbands their wives know uh heap mor'n they do!" It was probably true judging by the bits of conversation threading through the crowd, mingled with peculiar-like strangers uprooting the ground like they were drilling for oil—mostly at night—and, yes, they could name names— that is, of some. Aunt Em took over, instructing them to hold their tongues. "Here is whut t'do 'n how t'do hit—"

Rachel missed the rest. She had spotted Nola Lee tethering her horse and making an effort to get out of the ancient buggy with some degree of grace. She wore the dress Aunt Em made and carried a large box. Quilt scraps probably. Wrong guess. Nola turned bright eyes to Rachel who had hurried out to lift it and help her from the buggy.

"Guess what! It's a secret you'll keep, but I can't wait to tell you the contents—a layette Emmaline and me are making for my Yolanda. Jud stopped by to see her—and Buck's there, too. It pleases me mightily."

Rachel was glad she'd chosen to wear the lacy collar Nola had made for her and Yolanda. Mrs. Lee touched it appreciatively, then frowned.

The two had reached the door. "Rachel honey, somehow I—I feel uneasy. If you see fit—well, it's a heap to ask, but would you be able to get away, sort of check on the men and Yo? I promise to be along shortly, but—" she hesitated then burst out, "of all the strange places to be looking in on, one never thinks of it lurking right under your doorstop. Will you—?"

Rachel nodded without telling her that had been her plan.

Without a backward glance, she bounded toward the doctors' offices.

Outside the doors, she paused to get her breath. What she overheard broke her heart. Yolanda was sobbing softly. "I—I feel responsible, Paw. Being your eldest, I should have set a better example—"

"Now, now, Lassie," her father defended, "you was always a good daughter—and still be. What ye be doin' back yonder be resultin' from needin' me'n yore maw—foolish but forgot in me heart. But, begory! th' scoundrel best not be showin' up here-abouts—but ye be in no ways responsible for yore brothers' sins. Not ye girls—"

"Oh, I'm sorry—I'm sorry," Yolanda's voice was muffled as if her face had found comfort against her father's woolen plaidie. Judson Lee, the undemonstrative! "I wish you could have been spared all this, my dear father. Rumors that the contraband authorities are investigating—and other things—had reached me, but I hoped they would prove unfounded. I ignored Mrs. Maxton and her prying. You see, I am blind to faults of my own family—I can't bear to see you hurt—don't cry, Paw—please—you break my heart. I've never see you break—"

Judson Lee weeping? Then his rich, Irish voice changed timbre. "Me, I be thankin' ye, gal—knowin' whatever comes, yore hasty heart's done pledged to be standin' by in trouble. And, begory! trouble's comin' fer them offsprings o'mine! Th' likes o'me longs t'pluck out them freckles by th' roots—one by one. Aye, indeed, Buck, I want 'em exposed! An' they be boun' t'apolo-gize in public ever' bloomin' one—then come home an' earn their board 'n keep. I be knowin' they been misguided—which just be provin' 'em weaklin's. They're a-gonna git some muscle—'n seek th' Good Lord's blessins. I be thankin' ye, Buck. Be ye feelin' better, Daughter? We be boun' 'n determined on gittin' 'em back in th' fold—but ye be takin' care—'cause o'th' little 'un...."

Judson urged an early meeting of the council. "I can under-stand your wanting to settle this in your family," Buck said. "And God alone knows how completely I agree with that—it's the least we can do, but it's impossible."

He was explaining when Rachel slipped away. First, there was the government to contend with. Then the men who would become the city officials. And (gently) Jud must remember that his sons must be found... other mysteries to ravel, piece by piece, flushing the culprits out in the open...forcing this explosive situation to make sense. If only other citizens would be as cooperative as the Lees, they would use the delays to be a boon to the entire cause. Straws would pile into a solid stack of conviction.

She hurried to the school to meet the children. Seeing Nola from a distance, Rachel dodged behind the telegraph office in order not to distract her. How thankful she was that God had lovingly preserved a remnant of the Lee family, bringing them together, readying them to welcome the prodigal sons—which, no matter how gruff his tactics, Judson Lee would do. Already the process had begun. A second glance had shown that Callie was with her mother. Of course! Miss Annie would have had to leave a substitute in her place....

But, she realized, that second glance revealed something else. Something which she had suspected and now knew for sure. Willie Mead was part of the missing puzzle. Star was right. The man wearing the brown-striped shirt was talking with Jules Dunigan. Talking? More like conspiring. He wanted to destroy the evidence, protect himself from the child's accusing finger. Although she felt surprisingly calm, Rachel quickened her steps. Star knew too much...she was doomed to die...*he was the one who had tried to drown her*!

Only it wasn't going to happen. A plan formulated in her mind, one which she would discuss with only a few—dangerous, but essential.

• • •

November came and went, celebrated by another quilting bee at the Galloways. The day was unseasonably warm—warm enough to allow the overflow of people to eat out-of-doors, putting the settlers and the newcomers together in a growing understanding. The men barbecued an overfed porker (declaring that the meat would spoil in such weather if there were leftovers, which there were not!) while the ladies began a new quilt. What would they do with *two* quilts? "Never mind, there'll come a need," Aunt Em assured them.

Yolanda did not come. It was too near her "confinement." Maynard refused to leave her. Good sign, Rachel thought with a smile. Barbette Ames was there, listening and holding her tongue. Her restless eyes met Rachel's only to drop to her new suede shoes. But Rachel, watching from the corner of her eyes, saw that the woman's eyes continued to search the group. Looking for Maynard—that is, *if* the ugly story was true. When Barbette's gaze caught sight of her husband, she turned her back, her eyes sparkling with something akin to anger.

Events unfurled with incredible speed after the quilting bee. And there was seldom time to pause and take stock. The Reverend Luke moved in with the Jones family and adapted so readily that it was hard to realize he hadn't always been around. He was custodian of a great deal of information, but confined his revelations only to facts. Suspicions, true or false, one kept to one's self. He had a blind spot where his flock was concerned. He pledged, however, to hold nothing back. His new headquarters put him in the right position to be on the lookout for evil-doers, as did frequent visits with members of the congregation.

"What Lordsburg really needs is an old-time revival, one that will shake the rafters of heaven. I'll propose it at the deacons' meeting, though, like the city council, time after time it's postponed."

Before Rachel's mental vision events fell into place. Yes, what Lordsburg needed was a miracle. But God performed them in many ways and she was not convinced that meantime they should all play dead.

Neither was Sheriff Brimmerton. Knowing he could depend on her, the weak-chinned man confided what he referred to as his "guessings." With newfound authority, he had visited every crack and cranny without finding real evidence. At least, he'd learned those to distrust. Best keep those he had doubts about in ignorance. Take that Mrs. Maxton and her addiction to gossip. It was hard telling what that woman was up to. And that little witch, Barbette Ames—well, Rachel would be pardoning his language, but if there were a house of ill-fame in Lordsburg, he could picture her there. There *was* no such place, of course— never would be. But there *was* one new building, rather a room 'way back in the willows behind Welcome Strangers place— foundation laid before new regulations restricting building without permits. "There's something in that barber's hands that sets men's tongues to wagging. Talk is that something's going on in that lean-to." He leaned a bit forward. "Talk has it that they— those under suspicion—are using it for contraband hauled in for storage. I wish I could deputize *you* to snoop a bit. But we could never pull it off. 'Twouldn't be acceptable for a woman to enter. Wait—I think I got me a thought. You know, they tighten up when a big official like me walks in—knowin' I won' hesitate to investigate every stranger. But what if—" Quickly, he outlined a plan.

Sheriff Brimmerton's plan matched her own. Crazy. Dangerous. But—Star had been dragged into the whole evil plot innocently, helplessly. But for a miracle she would be all the way under. *God, give me the courage.*

"Tomorrow, Sheriff," Rachel said.

23

Truth
Has Many Faces

Rachel examined her reflection in the bedroom mirror. "That will have to do," she murmured. "Surely if I am unable to recognize *myself*, others can do no better."

She took a second look and gasped like a fish, hooked and gaping for water. She curbed the hysterical desire to laugh. This was no time for her irresistible sense of humor to surface. Not when the hard throb of her pulses warned of danger. How could she have agreed to this? Even now, although the house was quiet, she could imagine curious eyes peering through the window. Straightening her shoulders and wiping the senseless grin from her face, Rachel affected a swagger and walked out the front door.

Minutes later she entered Calvin Merriweather's barbershop, plopped down casually, picked up a three-day-old newspaper, and covered her face. Nobody seemed to take notice. These men were regulars, accustomed to all kinds of garbs, accents, and behavior. "Howdy, pilgrim," one ventured. Rachel nodded and went on with her newspaper while rowdy talk and the odor of stale tobacco smoke, socks in need of laundering, and bay rum robbed her lungs of oxygen. The drum of her heart gradually slowed its tempo, allowing her to listen. Nobody suspected a customer, even that ridiculous-looking creature badly in need of a haircut—could be a she-woman garbed in a slouch hat and soiled bib-overalls who dared invade men's domain? Why, 'twas nigh as bad as entering a saloon...

Listen...listen! Rachel commanded herself as the conversation split in a dozen directions and broke into meaningless phrases: "Cain't put much stock in hearsay, still sumpin's goin' on et th' Welcome Stranger place . . . Yep, yep, plain as th' nose on yore face . . . Whadda ya mean, boats unloadin' . . . that mealy-mouthed sheriff's smarter'n uh body'd thank . . . gang . . . reg'lar army, armed 'n trained . . . Me, I cain't feel comfort in puttin' off gittin' thet council a-goin' . . . lotsa goin' on we got uh right t'know . . . peculiar-like wimmen 'pearin' t'know mor'n men . . . th' buxom blonde woman, too skeered uv her shadder t'be involved . . . still . . . Whatta yuh mean Dunigan? 'Y he's got uh sounder mind than th' rest o'th' heny-husbands here'bouts . . . shudda been 'pointed mayor . . . 'course ye could'n' find fault with Miz Jones . . . good background 'n brain 'nuf t' let 'er man take keer uv bizness . . . does make a body wonder, thet funny-thinkin' girl they got theirselves . . . knows uh hep, else is uh soothsayer like unto Agnes Grant, anybody else been here long enough t'recall that witch 'ceptin' me . . . Truth wears many faces . . ."

The conversation switched to crops, sawmills, and mining then back to new building. Then again to the problems at hand. What about the new doctor's wife, wasn't she a looker? Consensus was beautiful but dumb. "Dumb like uh fox!" one man took issue. "She's in on sumpin' 'n goes th' rounds with ever' male she can grab in th' dark uv th' moon—" the insinuating voice dropped to a whisper, undoubtedly too shoddy to be spoken aloud as it set off a round of guffaws.

One of the men spat, the tobacco-tainted secretion missing the spittoon and landing on the floor beside Rachel's foot in an ever-widening brown froth. She mustn't be sick. She *mustn't*. Shifting her eyes, she was grateful when talk resumed.

"Heard anything more about the Jones girl's accusations? Couldn't be so—could it? I mean her pointing a finger at Mead?"

"Nobody wants t'talk about it. But if you be askin' me, I'm a-thinkin' Miz Annie 'n that new preacher knows uh heap—"

When was *he* going to show his face? Could be he—funny they didn't so much as know his name—going to take the pulpit from the reverend? Talk had it that the young man just could be one of the secret agents—yeah, you know the ones not even revealed to the council. Or, 'course, not wanting to start a new suspicion (but weren't they called on both by the council and the Good Book to be on the lookout, sly as an adder), well, that preacher-boy could—just *could*—be one of the betrayers.

There was a gasp that circled the room. It sank into Rachel's heart when the man to her right said. "My stars 'n garters, men! I seen that chile go inside th' church hours ago during books time—'n she ain't come out—"

How could she escape without drawing attention? She must get out. *Now!* Maybe the dark cloud covering the sun and creating sudden shadows in the crowded shop was a God-given advantage. Somewhere there was a slight movement. Conversation stopped. Rachel dared let her eyes travel an inch above the newspaper toward the fly-specked mirror and there she saw a dimly reflected man's figure against the doorway to the shadowy hall. He was bent slightly over as if listening. The reflection vanished like a spirit caught up in the mist of the cloud.

"So *he's* in on this. Who'd a-thunk it?" one white-faced man, obviously scared out of his wits, blurted. The others sat as if starched. One was whispering that this must be kept among themselves. Mum was the word.

Biding her time, though her adrenaline urged her to race out to the church, Rachel looked at her pocket watch, tossed the paper to the floor, and sauntered out. Just another customer tired of waiting.

Dodging the window, she broke into a run as if pursued by demons—which she was.

Frantically, she jerked open the church-house door. Voices! Oh, praise the Lord! One of them was Star's . . .

24

The Realm
of the Dream World

Panting, Rachel felt her way down the narrow hall with only the voices for a guide. There were several doors—hand-hewn and yet unpainted—which had recently replaced faded cretonne curtains to divide Sunday-school rooms. She was tempted to dodge into one of them. But no! Star's safety was by far more important. Were there exits between the rooms? That would afford passage. Unable to recall, she tiptoed past them. The sound of footsteps behind her continued. It was like shadows after the object itself had disappeared. . . .

And then all was quiet—except for the low-pitched words of a man and the Christmas-bell tinkle of Star's silvery-voiced questions.

"Do you not believe the words of Jesus—that He can heal?"

"Yes," tentatively her answer came. "I believe—"

"In the laying on of hands?"

"Can you heal my mind—or is it only the body?" Star persisted.

Rachel sensed the young minister's hesitation, saw in her mind's eye the pucker of the brow she would not recognize.

"*I* cannot heal you, Star—no mortal can lay claim to that. But let me be quick to add that some persons, gifted by our Lord, possess a certain gift which cannot be explained—that of receiving a power beyond the flesh, a healing power—through the hands—"

"To believers?"

"Oh, Star, *Star!* Where do such questions come from?"

"Jesus," Star's answer was instantaneous. "I have great faith He wants me to use. But I need healing. I am in great need, *Padre*—you must help me push open the gate, help me *see* again."

"You are asking that God bring back memory of who pulled you from the water? That takes a great deal of faith. Faith in what people call 'faith healers' and faith on the part of the one seeking to be healed—and then something more, a certain attitude that sets man in tune with God. I realize, my dear Star, that I'm speaking to you as I would an adult, which somehow you are (he hesitated) and it *has* to be God-given. But I—I warn you that our kind of thinking is dangerous—that it leads to rejection. I have faced rejection and all but burned at stake—"

Then, excitedly, "You *have* helped it happen then?"

The minister groaned. "Life would have been simpler if I hadn't."

"*Please*, God knows those around us have a need to know the man's name. Doctors have tried, but He asks for more before He can use me."

"All right!" There was determination in the young man's voice. "Just kneel, pray, and let God lead. Yes, my hand is on your head—"

One minute . . . two . . . three . . .

Star broke the silence with something akin to a shout of near-victory in a child's game. "I saw . . . it was like a dream . . . a warm feeling in my hands. Not a healing power—am I saying it right, *por favor*? It is—*como se dice*?—how can I say what I do not know? I know—*I see* in my dreams—and the power God placed in my fingers, not my tongue. Oh, my heart is singing and dancing within me!" Star's voice was filled with elation which went beyond Rachel's understanding. And then it stopped. "Do you believe in dreams?"

"I know something happened," he said humbly. "Call it a dream. Who can know the mind of God? Do I believe in dreams? I have no answer. The only explanation is what I think—and remember that novelty thinking is not always truth—but I see slumber as a playground without supervision, allowed to fill up with unruly fancies and little imps the mind has no time for during the light of day. Somehow, when we drift off into the netherworld of sleep, we struggle to find truth."

"Tonight's dream will bring it—and I shall draw what I see— you know, like the handwriting on the wall—call it our miracle!"

"Star—wait—I witnessed something—something I am unable to explain. But I felt it, too. No, *wait*, listen to me! Remember that

Jesus always cautioned those He healed to tell nobody. For now, our miracle is incomplete—and I beg you that it remain between you, me, and God. But," his voice dropped lower yet, as if he were talking to himself, "you and I shall always share a special bond. Now go in peace. Oh, my goodness! I lost all count of time. Is there somebody with you?"

"Of course—"

Never mind if Star referred to the Lord's Spirit or a companion, she must not know of Rachel's presence. Quietly she backed away and, with her back against the wall, turned the doorknob, and eased into the shadowy hall—only to have a hand clamped over her mouth.

"Don't scream—we're not alone. I hereby deputize you—" Sheriff Brimmerton thrust something metallic and sharp-pointed into her hand. A star. Her only weapon. This she absorbed just before bedlam broke loose.

One of the doors opened then closed. But the sheriff was too quick for the man who emerged. With the importance of a pouter pigeon, he puffed his chest, and thrust a gun barrel in the ribs of the intruder.

"There's a mistake—let me explain!"

Doctor Ames? Unbelievable . . .

There was a scuffle during which two of the other doors burst open at the same time. One of the sparring trio left the door through which he exited open a crack, just enough to reveal facial features. Brimmerton yanked the one nearer to him and bumped his head against the doctor's with a clatter designed to leave a headache. "But—but—you don't understand—Mr.—what's-your-name? I—I followed, yes—but," one eye was shifting to the left. "Just let go—I'll explain—"

"Fat chance! Another step and you're a goner!"

Sure, Bonaparte Bixby. Probably here to accompany Star—but who knew? This was no time for explaining—the third man was heading for the door. But Rachel was too quick for him. Emerging from the wall, she threw her body forward. Aim for more than you can achieve, Michelangelo had advised. A second leap and she had a point of the star square between his shoulder blades.

"Don't move a muscle, Julius Doogan. Rattlers like you get their heads blown off! Now, get those hands in the air!"

Was the voice really hers?

"Why, Your Honor," he exclaimed with an attempt at bravado—but taking no chances, he lifted his hands. "You don't understand—"

"Enough!" Rachel ground out. "Three times we've heard that in the last minute. Not one of you is entitled to be here. Don't look around," she warned, jabbing a little harder.

His head, about to turn, jerked back in place. "Of course, I could say that you were not supposed to be in a men's barbershop either—"

How could he have known that? Unless—

"Hold'em, Deputy—while I rope 'em like a chain gang. Go get your daughter. These fourth-class citizens can tell it to the judge."

Forgetting her clothing, Rachel hurried to find Star, questions whirling in her mind. Which of the three had the men in the barbershop meant by: "So he's one of them?" Bixby, Dr. Ames, Doogan—or (surely not!) the sheriff himself? She, like Star, teetered on the realm of a dream....

25

"This Is the Man!"

Buck and the other children were waiting at the front door when Rachel and Star, swinging hands but not talking, hurried up the walk where only straw-flowers remained. "We must make a winter bouquet."

Nobody heard Rachel's mindless comment. Star was still in deep thought. And the rest of the family was doubled up in laughter.

"This, my children, is your mother!"

Buck's straight-faced introduction sent them into another fit of laughter.

"Do not laugh at Mother Mine. She and I have been on a long journey. We are weary. 'To sleep, perchance to dream,' is this not how Shakespeare said it?"

They sobered. Something troubled their beloved Star.

"Something like that," David said solemnly. "Mr. Bixby pays more attention to *McBeth*, 'Sleep that knits up the ravell'd sleave of care'—"

"*Him*—Brian says he can't spell, calls him Napoleon—" Saul interrupted.

"That's the way they spelled when William Shakespeare wrote," Mary Cole defended. But Brian's right. He's a no-good teacher—can't even parse a noun—just asks questions and questions and questions about all of us. None of his business, huh, Daddy Buck? Brian's the only one who answers—told him something awful—there are two kinds of awful and this was *awful-awful*—about Uncle Maynard and Dr. Ames' wife—he's not coming to Rowie's birthday party either—"

"Whoa, Dobbin! Slow it down a little. Who's not going to the party?" Buck asked as if it made a difference.

"Brian—'Brian-Boy,'" Mary Cole made a clownish attempt to imitate Barbette's baby-talk. "Wanta know why? His mother won't let him play with us, says Star's strange—different—"

"We're *all* different," Buck interrupted. "Did you think God made a paper-doll pattern from Adam and Eve?" His voice was light. His eyes were not. "Now, if you will let your mother pass—"

Yes, oh, yes, Rachel's heart pleaded. But it was Star who answered. "I do not mind being different—I expect rejection by those who do not understand and think I lead others astray. I *dream...*"

Would she share a dream with them? *Please*, Star. They loved her.... *Wheedlers all!*

As they trailed after her, Buck called: "Not so fast! You are not to listen to Brian—what's more, do *not* answer impertinent questions. It is nobody else's business what takes place in our home, and," his tone took on an unusual cloak of anger, "that includes your teachers!"

Standing at attention, arms crossed, and motionless as always when scolded even by a tone of voice, the four of them looked like a shelf of blank-faced Buddhas. "At ease," Buck said, smiling in spite of himself. They saluted and marched away, all chattering like magpies. Brian and Mr. Bixby got into this *awful*-awful fight.... Brian told him he needed his tongue split like *his* Napoleon, the crow...then he could talk more...and he called Brian a bad name...(one of them whispered the word and then they rounded the bend of the stairs). *What was it all about?*

"Now, Mrs. Jones," Buck turned to his wife, "it is time you gave account." A grin twitched at the corners of his mouth. "Why are you in this garb? I want the whole story."

"Oh, Buck," Rachel murmured helplessly, "I wish you hadn't asked."

Buck's face filled with concern. "Oh, darling, something *has* happened. Come here—no, don't say you must change, the children will give us little time—and it's time for the reverend—"

"But—but I mustn't talk about it. Star promised *she* wouldn't and I shouldn't either—"

Buck cut short her feeble objections by sweeping her up in his arms and sat down on the nearest rocker. Pulling her head against his shoulder, he rubbed his chin against her forehead. "Husband and wife are of one flesh. There is nothing we cannot discuss. I love you."

In spite of her fatigue, Rachel half-giggled. "Mr. Jones! Are you wheedling like your offspring?"

Then, without hesitation, she related events of the day. "Don't scold me—I know it was dangerous—but I would lay down my life for Star. God has given us a part of Himself—not to love more than we love the other children—but to nourish, allow Him to direct. Now I know how Mary must have felt. What can it all mean?"

Buck drew her closer. "We will know more when the council meets. Yes, the date is set at long last. All the persons we have waited so long for will be here to complete making us into a city proper. The entire community will be included. There will be an installation—and somehow we must work out a plan of identification of those who are trying to destroy us. Some we know—or think we do—but there must be proper evidence. As to the new minister—"

"Yes?" The reverend had entered the hall. "Oh, I beg your pardon."

"It is quite all right, *Padre*, sir," Star welcomed. "You and I— you, too, *Dad-dee*—we shall talk while Mother Mine dresses. Do you believe in dreams?"

Luke Elmo ran his fingers through his wind-blown silver hair. "You do come to the point, don't you now? We have accounts all the way through God's Word, including Revelation. Dreams— how can I apply them to today's world—except to say that helpless in the impartial lap of slumber sometimes the heart remembers what the mind forgets."

Star nodded. "And healing?"

"Again, I can only quote God's Word. Healing is a gift, not intended for all, I suppose—at least, according to Paul. By the way, my replacement is better versed than I and hopes to be invited to deliver a message—after the deacons' meeting— which I understand is to take place after the council meeting, right, Buck? And, oh, something more, there is an evangelist down the road apiece who would like to hold an all-church revival here—say, in the springtime. He is a believer in healing by faith—the pouring on of oil instead of swallowing pills. Forgive me for going into this— I feel a little uncomfortable getting into this area—"

He excused himself to wash up and Rachel hurried to change and get dinner underway, realizing that she was more confused then ever.

• • •

On the day of the council meeting, Rachel stopped by to see Yolanda. Aunt Em was there, frosting Rowie's birthday cake and scolding good-naturedly. "It's more'n you should oughta be doin', what with th' wee one due—let's say Christmas! Rachel, dearie, take uh look at th' layette me'n Nola stitched up fer th' newborn. Calls fer a real celebration 'cause both uv us is wantin' a girl—her holdin' out fer uh namesake. How 'bout (she deliberately paused to wipe frosting from the knife and lick it from her finger with an "Umm—m-m") ticklin' yore tongue with Emmaline Nola? Davey-Love's laid claim t'two 'grandsons'.''

Yolanda smiled, seeming more at peace with herself. "I should offer refreshments, but I'm hungrier for news—can't we talk?" Quickly the three of them caught each other up on the news— friendly, warm, but guarded—each obviously holding something back. The visit ended with a disturbing revelation from Yolanda. "Rowie's so excited, planned a treasure hunt with Star in lead. This is his first birthday party, you know. What's wrong, Rachel?"

A straight-forward answer was best. "Star will be unable to do that, Yo. She—she for some reason has asked to attend the meeting—and to sit by the new minister. Without her—and, well even *with* her, I wonder if it is wise. The children being allowed to roam—"

Yolanda's seemingly insouciance vanished like a light smashed to earth—leaving her world in darkness. Her lips were white, her voice a mere whisper: "Oh, Rachel, if it were anybody on earth but you I'd say you wanted to frighten me, but why would you do that?"

"I wouldn't!"

Yolanda slumped back into the deep-cushioned chair, breathing heavily. "I can't disappoint him—I just can't. Oh, please can't you—*won't* you try to change her mind?"

"No, and I am not in a position to explain—oh, Darling, I'm sorry."

Aunt Em cleared her throat. "Now, relax th' both uv you. I'll stay—ain't no law sayin' my presence is needed. Tell you what— I'll bring th' other cake planned t'feed them men 'n Rachel, you can brang over th' new officers fer uh sorta joint celebration—"

Soft waves of pink eddied to Yolanda's hairline, but whatever light had flickered briefly within her troubled heart had died.

What can I do, Lord? What can I say? When I, too, am filled to overflowing with apprehension? Rachel longed to offer her regrets, say Mary Cole, David, and Saul would be unable to attend . . . but already Brian would be missing . . .

With great effort, she forced a smile. "You're like a tonic, Aunt Em—what a wonderful offer! Until tonight then!" With a little fingertip kiss blown over her shoulder, Rachel hurried out.

● ● ●

She had a hard time deciding what to wear. A hot bath had failed to relax her. And now Rachel found herself incapable of making the simplest of decisions. Her black silk? No, too funeralish. The red linen suit? Too bright, even flashy for the occasion. The navy tunic would have to do. No jewelry. But she could make use of the lovely collar Nola Lee had made with such care.

Lee. Thought of Yolanda's family set her heart pounding so hard it shook her entire body. Would Judson follow through with his plans, march his sons down the aisle. She could think no further . . .

The meeting was even more difficult. Painfully aware that Star sat in back of the hall, dark lashes sweeping her cheeks as if caught in the web of slumber, Rachel saw the slender hands moving across what appeared to be a paper big enough for a page used for chart-class.

Concentrate. She must concentrate. Forcing her eyes to ramble from where she sat at the long, up-front table to the audience, she saw the ever-enlarging audience through a haze. Members of the original council, present and accounted for, including Judson. But, dully she noted, the boys were not with him. Strangers . . . so many strangers . . . dignitaries no doubt, here in an official capacity. For a brief moment, she awakened from near-slumber to feel pleasure in seeing that those making the long trek West with her and Cole in their youthful migration were here *en masse*—both men and their wives. She waved a small royal left-to-right greeting to the Farnals, O'Gradys, Burnsides, Sanders. Then her eyes focused on the entrance of the Honorable Judge J. Quentin Hathaway who would preside after Buck's introduction, followed by City Attorney James Haute, head high but left shoulder slanting far below the right to accommodate a brief case so large it surely must contain rocks gathered from all over Oregon! Reverend Luke joined Star and her remarkably handsome companion. Solemnly the two ministers shook hands. Star did not seem to notice.

Rachel continued to watch the enlarging parade intently, knowing exactly the one person she hoped to see. Star was safe here. But what about the other children? She shuddered, thinking of the treasure hunt. Buck noted and, although deep in conversation with the judge, thoughtfully laid his suit coat around her shoulders.

Perhaps she murmured appreciation. Perhaps not. She was in too much shock at the sight of the two doctors entering together to recall. And what was this? The China doll, wearing a black velvet dress, too tight about her hips, tripped down the aisle, fingering a necklace nobody else in the hall could afford, wedged herself between Maynard and her husband. Barbette Ames! Rachel experienced an unholy urge to leave her chair and choke her! How glad she was to have chosen the simple dress that would not embarrass the other women...

And then all such thoughts dissipated. Julius Doogan (all right, Jules Dunigan!), followed by the buxom, kind-faced lady called Miz Lily, entered. He nodded to a knot of men Rachel felt were those whose conversation she had tapped. Willie Mead joined the group casually. Sheriff Brimmerton, arms crossed, stood alone in a shadowy corner. His eyes darted from Doogan to Rachel, narrowing a bit as he turned palms up in a released-because-of-lack-of-evidence gesture. The teacher was conspicuously absent. Shouldn't he be interested in city affairs?

A rap of the gavel and the meeting was in progress. "Hear ye, hear ye," Buck smiled, "court is now in session." There was a round of laughter, understanding that Judge Hathaway sat straight as a ramrod at the table. "Before turning the meeting over to His Honor, may I take a minute to present Lordsburg's first mayor, my wife, Rachel Lord Jones?"

There was a deafening applause. And then the unexpected. One by one those present rose to their feet in standing ovation.

Oh, Cole! Are you seeing this up there? What you dreamed has come true for us all....

There were tears in her eyes when Rachel, with more humility than one ordinarily saw in the eyes of a person in her position smiled. She stood to acknowledge the high compliment with a small bow but was too overcome to speak. Tears sparkled in the eyes of the onlookers. Buck saw and saved the moment by standing, too—then removing his coat from her shoulders. The small gesture was touching, revealing more than the onlookers had known about a relationship which set an example all could strive for.

"My dear, your reputation—fine indeed—does not do you justice," the judge whispered as he accepted the gavel from the city manager.

In an incredibly short time, the well-organized meeting was nearing the end. The by-laws ... the repeating of plans for needed changes ... the naming of leaders who, like Rachel, would finish out the year ... then elections to follow. Why not allow present council members to remain? Nods of approval. And why not appoint original settlers to serve as members of the law enforcement? Again, agreement.

"There is one matter the officers appointed must discuss in executive council. Be patient with us as we plan a strategy in identifying and bringing before the grand jury certain suspects and examine carefully all evidence. Let us assure you that each person attending tonight will be a part of the procedure—reporting any suspicious acts as outlined in the by-laws. You will be assisted by the government, those men in uniform—and a number of plainclothesmen whose names will never be made public," Judge Hathaway explained. "Before the benediction, is there anyone who has a word to say?"

There was surprise in Buck's eyes when Rachel rose. "It is my pleasure to invite those who will be serving you to share refreshments at the home of Dr. and Mrs. Maynard Killjoy—"

The sentence went unfinished, interrupted by a small cry and Star's racing forward to hold up a finished drawing. "This is the man!" Julius Doogan! and then, "He pulled me from the water!"

26

Treasures—
Then Tragedy

The meeting had begun at four o'clock. Now pink swans-down clouds gleamed like paper cut-out ships against a sunset sea of sky. Twilight was approaching. The treasure hunt would have begun. Still, Rachel felt an irresistible urge to run. Why—when Star's "seeing fingers" drawing had cleared Julius, or should have. It had served only to shock and confuse Rachel's mind. She simply did not like the man. Neither did she trust him. Once again he had won however. Managed somehow to become a hero instead of a villain. The pattern was not new. And that was what troubled her. Star's crayons had turned the world upside down, dividing *thinking* of Lordsburg newcomers from *knowing* the settlers. But knowing was not enough...there had to be hard evidence...the proof.

Had she been too hasty in her departure? Probably, but with good reason. There were others—menacing threats until apprehended. Others who had a leader. Armed and dangerous. And how would she distinguish between them and the undercover agents whom she would never know? Buck had nodded reluctantly at her attempt to explain that she must finish preparations for the reception. The ministers wished to talk further with Star and would accompany her to the Killjoys' home. But something was wrong. Rachel felt it. Apprehension turned to downright fear as the last remnants of the sunset died away and she reached a shadow-lined street. *Someone is following me,* she whispered to herself.

She was right.

At the door of the Killjoy house, there was no choice but to turn and face her stalker. In the fading light she saw a small figure. The thin face looked even thinner, dominated as it was by thick-lensed glasses which enlarged his eyes. An owlet was the only word she could think of. But when he spoke, she gasped. "Miss Rachel—"

"Brian! I didn't recognize you with the glasses—oh, Darling, you should not be here!"

"I—I know," he whispered, fingering a large paper bag and glancing over his shoulder nervously. He cleared his throat and told his mission while tears, magnified into rivers, filled his eyes behind the glasses.

"I—I couldn't come but," Brian's voice registered little hope, "oh, Miss Rachel—won't you let me leave these? They—they're for the treasure hunt—"

As if to prove it, the child opened the sack to reveal an assortment of awkwardly-wrapped items, obviously prepared in haste. Never in her life had Rachel so pitied a child. The child who had everything but the love of a mother. No matter what her honey-dipped words dripped from the painted-doll lips, they were as false as the rest of her. At that moment every molecule of respect Rachel had held for Barbette Ames died. The shallow creature did not possess a woman's greatest gift—love for her child. Rachel had allowed her that virtue until now.

Brian was waiting hopefully while Rachel's heart turned over and over. What could she do with Jesus' "least of these"? When he lifted his head, his eyes registering defeat, Brian's glasses plunged downward and dropped to the boardwalk before he could recover them. Quickly, he knelt and began to feel for them. He—why, the child was almost blind! But not half as blind as his fickle mother, Rachel thought, as she reached down to retrieve the glasses. "Come in, Darling—come on, I cannot allow you to be out alone—"

Aunt Em opened the door. Her eyes narrowed at sight of "that lyin' little imp" and then took in the situation without an explanation. "Come in, Sweetheart," she murmured, gathering Brian close to her side while casting a warning glance at Yolanda. Small wonder the poor, neglected bit of flesh boasted and contrived stories—

Then there was an ear-splitting blend of voices. The children were screaming, "Brian, Brian, she let you come—just the right time—"

The three women wiped their eyes while the children looked on, then shrugged. Adults were funny, always crying when they were happy. Why not make them happier? So their noise resumed with renewed vigor. So vigorous that nobody heard the scuffle in the kitchen. And only Rachel realized that Mrs. Maxton had entered, placed a warning finger to ashen lips, and inclined her head toward the door behind her.

And then there was a click from the other side, locking them out of the kitchen. This was no time for speculation . . . to wonder what Mrs. Maxton's role really was . . . to try guessing who had locked the back exit. No time even to imagine what would happen next. One word dominated Rachel's mind—*escape!* They were trapped if an unseen hand barred the front door.

Aunt Em went back to the long-ago days on the trail. One reacted and thought later when it came to saving human lives. "Quiet!" she whispered. "We gotta be quieter'n mice, sneak up on th' hiders uv treasure . . . stop th' foolishness *now!* First rule is we gotta spy. Second rule—*come* on! git goin' t'th' door . . . line up 'n march straight to th' Eatery whar we pick up uh map Star drawed . . . she'll be joinin' us . . ."

Shivering with excitement, the children had tiptoed forward without a whisper, caught up in the exciting game. Gone! They were now gone. Wise or unwise, they were out of the house. The adults must take their chances here. Yolanda was in no condition to be alarmed. And certainly not to travel. Rachel, having regained a measure of composure, followed the example of Emmaline Galloway, reacting with remembered skill. Once again, she was second-in-command in the caravan moving West.

When Mrs. Maxton made ready to whisper an explanation, Rachel shot her a dart of warning. And when Yolanda gasped, "What happened? They can't be out there alone! I'm going for them—how could I have stood here and let this happen—" Rachel was armed as she was on the trail.

"There's no need for panic, Yo. The men will be along—and we must hurry with preparation. Get hold of yourself. Take the knife and slice the cake in advance. Mrs. Maxton, I can smell the coffee—good for you—so why not turn the lights a little lower and—" she said with enough emphasis to communicate the need of a weapon, "do please stoke the fire with the largest of those pokers. The wind is picking up—"

Like puppets the two other women moved as if Rachel held the strings. A strange silence fell, allowing the three of them a sort of understanding without understanding at all. Just functioning, playing a game, the rules of which none of them knew.

Outside, the wind whistled and whined and sobbed—occasionally pausing to wipe its eyes, allowing Rachel's straining ears to pick up the swish-swish of oars and the scraping of metal. And something else, a sound she was unable to identify. At the questioning look in the eyes of the other two women, Rachel forced a smile. "The treasure hunt has begun!" she whispered—meaning it both ways. Something was going on.

She tiptoed to the window, opening the drape farthest from the low-burning lamps a crack no wider than a hairline. But one glimpse revealed a world flooded with moonlight. And men. Men everywhere.

The showdown was at hand—whatever it was. Inside, the game must end. "Get back," she ordered. "Then don't move—"

And the beginning of a terrible tragedy began. Someone threw the front door open. Window panes collapsed as axes struck the glass. And the kitchen doorknob was turning. The women were surrounded...

27

Victory—
and Defeat

Questioned later, Rachel had to struggle to recall which happened first. Scenes ran together like a too-thin wash of color a painter would discard. In her mind, it all happened at once. She would simply have to sort out events, remembering clearly those in which she was the key figure and inserting—no, superimposing—the others. Possible or not, it all happened simultaneously. Which was near the truth. Shakespeare's *Comedy of Errors* which ended in temporary victories, then new beginnings which ended in defeat. It was the middle of the tragedy which blurred.

The door to the kitchen, so cautiously moving at first, now swung open with startling speed. *One...two...three, four, five...* the great clock was striking. Rachel realized vaguely that she was counting the men pushing into the living room, not the mellow chimes of the clock, because the gong had stopped and her count continued.

And then stopped. There were 11. There had to be as there were 11 of the Lee boys. "Bart! we've been through this before—drop those guns, *all* of you."

There was a blurred vision of the shame-faced boy letting go of his weapon, the others followed his lead. It happened in a split-second, too fast for her to count. And then somebody rushed forward just as two shots rang out. *Oh, dear God, no!*

Before her brain could register the full impact of seeing a body drop to the floor, she realized that thuds behind her were other persons....

Mrs. Maxton stood at the front door, swinging her poker with the force of a hurricane. *Left, right,—whang! Bang!* Each swing

145

brought down two men, falling forward with a cry of rage and pain. Between swings, the woman lifted the poker, allowing some to pass—only to swing again with—of all things—a roar of laughter from the newest arrival whose head she spared. How did she know the sheep from the goats?

"Good work!" the man Rachel recognized as the head revenue officer introduced at the meeting (wondering then, as she wondered now, why they were included in the government crew). Two of his assistants, wearing silly grins on their faces (imagine a woman's out-foxing them!), began pulling bodies out of the path of others yet to come, while dodging the two-at-one-blow swings of the poker.

Yolanda, her face drained of color, pressed her enlarged body against a chair for support. Then, with the fury of a wildcat, she charged at her victim, a man who had stood unnoticed by Rachel in the bedlam. Mrs. Maxton snatched the butcher knife from her hand without breaking the rhythm of her hard swings. "Thank you, Officer!" she responded, finding time—goodness knows how—to notch a stick of firewood at each strike. "Grab the man Mrs. Killjoy's about to slaughter—too good for him (*wham*!)—deserves a trial (*bam*!) "Sorry, Sheriff, one out of 12 is not too bad!"

"What th'—?" Sheriff Brimmerton, hat crushed, brim covering his eyes from the skull-crushing blow was trying to regain his dignity while leaping toward Yolanda who had sprung against the man who had stood with a mocking look on his triumphant face, while continuing to hold his gun in feigned innocence. Too late—Yolanda was scratching, clawing, and screaming her pent-up rage. "You demon! You two-face *murderer*!"

Rachel was coming to. Her head cleared. *Julius Doogan!*

"Rachel, Rachel darling—are you all right?" Buck's welcome voice was filled with concern. But he took no time to look her way. He and Howard were rushing toward the victim of one of the shots.

"Maynard!" both men registered shock as they knelt beside Yolanda's husband. "Come on, partner, let me examine you!" Howard commanded.

"Never mind me—just a flesh wound—check on my wife—"

Rachel went into action. Unfortunately, Yolanda had not finished her job. Jerking a lace panel from the window, Rachel threw it as a net over the bloody face of honorable-citizen Jules Dunigan. His curses filled the room with evil—evil which followed him wherever he went—

"Got him!" Sheriff Brimmerton said, jerking Jules Dunigan to his feet.

Rachel turned quickly. And then she was sick. Yolanda had dropped beside her husband. Helpless, both lay in a pool of blood...

"Take care of Yolanda—the baby—" Dr. Killjoy, still on his face, the red circle enlarging below his shoulders, indicating where the bullet had entered and lodged, lay motionless, while trying to move.

"Lie still!" Howard Ames commanded, beginning to tear away his shirt.

"*Lie still?* When your wife's about to give birth—"

Dr. Ames mumbled something unintelligible which sounded suspiciously like "I should have—*lie still!*"

Maynard tried to get up, only to fall back with a moan. "We'll have to operate—and don't worry about Yolanda—Mrs. Galloway's coming—best midwife this side of the Rockies—" Howard said soothingly.

Aunt Em! Where were the children?

Rachel jerked her head to see her entering, the second cake in her hand. She was dangerously near dropping it, what with two masked men fighting for right-of-way with a screaming, hysterical Barbette. "Where is my child? You kidnapped him—I'll have you arrested—stop pushing me, you low-lifes—and *you*, you old crone, clear the way. Oh, Maynard, what have they done to you—get out of my way!" she screeched, giving Aunt Em a shove.

"Grab th' gal—she'll spill 'er insides. Queen uv th' Bootleggers—"

"Not before I spill yours, buddy!" With one stroke, Mrs. Maxton disposed of the two black crows. "*Now*, Mrs. Galloway!"

As Barbette made a wild dash forward, interest focused on another woman's husband. Aunt Em screamed out, "Praise th' Lord fer this opportunity!" and flung the cake she carried into the face of Barb with such force the doll-face was buried in frosting. Spitting and mumbling, Barbette Ames choked, "Ho-ward ... what kind—kind of man (she called him an unmentionable word which cast reflections on his birth) are you—letting such—a witch—do this!"

"Sit down and shut up!" Howard Ames commanded as he and Buck gently eased Maynard onto a folding stretcher. "Get hold of that trollop bearing my name, boys!" Ames motioned to the Lees now standing against the wall with their father in charge. Judson nodded and they bore the stretcher to one of the bedrooms, while Emmaline Galloway rushed to kneel beside Yolanda. Rachel hurried forward to assist.

"Nobody needs tell you what to do. We've gotta git this precious baby delivered. In th' bedroom joinin' th' father's ud be best—"

Sheets . . . boiling water . . . scissors. Rachel knew the routine. But first, "Oh, Aunt Em—the children? Alone—"

"Never no mind, Dearie." And to Yolanda, "Open yore purty eyes, Sweetie—that's it, breathe gently—don' be pushin' yet." She wiped the beads of sweat from Yolanda's pain-twisted forehead and leaned forward to hear a labored word, "Rowie?"

"Relax, th' both uv yuh," Aunt Em soothed. "Davey-Love's in charge, 'long with Callie 'n Patrick 'n Scot, o'course, th' tail-waggin' guard dog!"

"*Patrick?*" Rachel was halfway into the kitchen.

"Th' new preacher—oh, 'n thet new teacher—they all discovered th' treasure with Miz Lily's help. Breathe shallow, Yo, Darlin'—Rachel, Dearie, what's a-holdin' yuh? Oh, Star's with Brother Patrick—"

Head awhirl, Rachel's hands moved as fast as her thoughts. *Treasure? Patrick* (so that was his name? Rachel found that important somehow) . . . *Boneparte Bixby?* (that solved his whereabouts, but which side did he represent?) . . . and *Miz Lily*! She almost dropped the kettle with shock. *Oh, dear God, let us get this baby into the world safely, then we will talk all this over!*

Five minutes later, Dr. Ames rushed in to help with lifting Yolanda and laid her gently on the bed, leaving the door ajar as Maynard had requested. "I want to hear the first cry," he said reverently, "even if I can't feel bodily—I can feel with my heart. Oh, how helpless I feel—how useless—"

"How can a father be useless?" Rachel's eyes brimmed with tears as she heard Buck's question. And then his chuckle. "Lie still until Howard can get back to diagnose further—and I'll tell you about the birds and the bees!"

She longed to rush into the other room, thrust herself upon his lap, and be held close as she laughed uncontrollably at the comedy of it all . . . the terror . . . then weep with him at the terrible tragedy . . . formulate a million questions . . . then take him by the hand and drag him away in search of their children. Did Buck know the real truth about Miz Lily, who she was and *what* she was? And then her mind took another direction. What had the two masked men meant by the "Queen of the Bootleggers"? Was the fickle woman capable of leadership—even the wrong kind? Did that explain the presence of the Revenue officers?

It must, for the officers had gagged the screaming, clawing Barbette and were roping her to the enlarging string of men. "We'll take them all in for questioning—on suspicion of being involved in the train robbery, transporting of contraband—and, of course, rum-running. Not that we've rounded 'em all up—got to find the river-rats and the pussy cat in charge."

"Not a-tall are we through," one of his helpers nodded agreement as he pulled the guns from men on the floor. "Wouldn't you think the citizens would've suspected something?"

"They're good, God-fearing folks, looking only for the good in mankind. Here, hog-tie this one," the Revenue officer in charge said, letting go of the rope held between his teeth to reach for wire to finish the job.

His helper took over. "Guess they didn't have no awareness of the hooch. Is Clauson out there searching? What did these innocents as you make 'em out as being, think we officers were here for—our health?" He grinned at his own attempt at wit, wet a finger, and polished his metal insignia with pride. Then, rising, "What about the Lees? We don't know yet who fired the shot, so?"

"Shots—two of them," his superior officer corrected.

It was Judson who interrupted. "Leave 'em in my charge, I beg. "Twould plum kill their maw—'n I be swearin' we'll stand responsible if perchance they should escape, which they won't! They're good boys—"

In the other room Yolanda screamed. "*Oh, what could I have had my mind on, Lord?*" Rachel gasped. Then grabbing the instruments Dr. Ames called for, sterilized and ready, she concentrated on her lifelong friend.

Yolanda grabbed her hand, "We'll save the baby for you, darling—we *will*—"

"Not for me—for Maynard—no, both of us. If I don't make it—" she paused to scream as Rachel soothed her brow as if she were a child, then continued, "If I don't—oh, Doctor, help me—tell Maynard—tell him I'm sorry—" Yolanda's voice trailed off, "for *everything...*"

"You'll make it!" Maynard's voice yelled from the other room. "I love you, Yolanda!" His voice filled with agony, "I—I couldn't tell you then—but I can now—oh, God in heaven, help me! There *was* a reason. But it—it wasn't worth it—oh, Yolanda *Darling*."

Dry sobs told the story of a contrite heart—the iron tears shed by the broken man who has never cried before . . .

"Well, what have we here? A perfect baby girl! Take over, Mrs. Galloway," Howard Ames, face tired but filled with a sort of glory, said, wiping his hands on the towel Rachel handed to him. "I have to get back to Papa Bird!"

"Well, hello there, Emmaline!" Aunt Em grabbed the wee bundle and hurried to the kitchen for its first bath. The lusty wail announced to the world that the Killjoy baby's lungs were as perfect as her face—and objected with all her seven pounds to what "Grandma Em" called her "christening thee, Emmaline!"

"*Nola* Emmaline," Yolanda whispered weakly, as Rachel sponged her, changed the sweat-soaked pillow and said, "Rest, Darling—sleep—"

"He's babbling like a wild man," Buck reported to the doctor when he entered.

"Settle down, old chap," Howard chuckled as he jerked the cover from Maynard's naked back—then gasped. "The area's blue—lead poisoning. Pre-gangrene—I don't need to tell you that loss of blood means the soft tissue is dying. Prepare for surgery—bullet's got to come out."

"Not before I see my daughter!" Maynard was adamant.

"One peek while I scrub—*Rachel!*"

Rachel rushed in, holding the tiny, fat-cheeked piece of humanity as close to Maynard as his position allowed. He was too overcome to comment, but his wet lashes spelled *miracle*. "Proceed, Doc, and tell Yo—"

"She's asleep. Let's save your life for your family!"

In an incredibly short time, Dr. Maynard Killjoy had joined them in slumber . . .

Hand-in-hand, Rachel and Buck tiptoed out, awed by the miracle. But they must find their own children. *Oh, how had it all begun? And why?*

Only God knows the ending from the beginning. And once again He proved it. Unbelievably, the Reverend Luke rushed in, followed by the greatest miracle of all as far as the Joneses were concerned. In an endless line they came—their children . . . Rowie . . . all for the party . . . the reverend in charge.

"And now, folks, how about that birthday cake?"

28

A Speedy Trial

Making the whole series of events blend into one plot took time. Rachel wondered if, even then, there would remain some unknowns. She must rest, calm down, be patient. And, most important—as wife, mother, and mayor—she must trust the Lord to melt the billions of Lilliputian ice-barbs again bombarding her heart, allowing her to think objectively—and with compassion born of bringing together rules set down for her in God's Word and the laws of the land, else how could justice with mercy be achieved? One step at a time...remembering each scene, if possible...going back to the beginning....

The beginning, according to her formula, was the memorable evening of Roland's birthday.

With mother and child snuggled together, the proud father (a miraculously changed man) made as comfortable as possible, and the triumphant law enforcement officers proudly marching all suspects they were able to corner to jail (refusing bail until weighing evidence), the long day was at end. (How wrong Rachel was in her hopeful thinking.)

Feeling ridiculously lighthearted now, however, she all but skipped along beside her husband after making a quiet exit from the Killjoys. The children, each with a story to tell, all talked at once while Scot made senseless circles around them, barking as if to verify their words.

"Hold it! Silence, all of you," Buck laughed. "One at a time—"

"That'll be Scot—he was the real hero!" Mary Cole began. "He grabbed the man's leg, tore his breeches—oh, it was funny!"

"Be quiet, Mary Cole—didn't you hear Daddy? He has no idea what you're talking about—"

"Right, David," Buck said calmly. "Go back to the beginning. Star, you were in charge of the treasure hunt. Only," he said thoughtfully, "I understood the adults called it off."

"Brian—it was Brian—it was his birthday, too—" Saul's words tumbled over each other in his excitement. "He ran ahead toward the funny light—you know the one Mr. Lee calls St. Elmo's fire—said it really *was* a jack-o'-lantern bobbing out there in the river—you'd think his mother knew his birthday—but at the river—"

"The river—you went *there!*" Rachel's light mood vanished as the iron hand of fear immobilized her. She stopped in a patch of moonlight just before they entered the stretch of shadowy woods. The bushes at her left had rustled. No doubt about it. Not by the wind—the brisk breeze had stopped to take a breath. It was a *human* sound, filled with ghostly whispers, stifled snickers, and warnings. Well, what had she thought? That it was all over? "Not that we've rounded 'em all up...river-rats...pussycat in charge..." The pines had set the words of the officers to music. Watched—they were being watched—maybe stalked. Quickly, Rachel took a double-step to catch up with the family, removing her face from the shaft of moonlight.

"Brian—where *is* Brian?" Rachel's question was probably out of context. Only a moment had passed, but she had no idea of what she had missed.

"With his dad, opening all his presents—holy smoke, I never saw so many—and he'll get to stay with Rowie, 'cause Dr. Ames'll be watching out for the new baby. How soon can she—Nola Em—eat cake?"

Depend on Saul to take them all on a detour, make them smile.

"Mrs. Maxton will be there, too," Mary Cole blurted out. "I mean *Agent* Maxton—did you know she was one, Mother?"

"I suspected as much—" Rachel said slowly, shaking her head to clear it. "I guess I knew for sure tonight."

"We didn't—" all were talking together again. "Watching Brian's mother...She's real mean...I don't like her...She's mean to Brian...And tonight something super-awful happened...She—she's no lady—did you hear what she said?... Sure, told the man with the biggest star, well, to go that bad place...Said she'd *escape*...Oh, it's exciting being junior detectives like us..."

Buck laughed. "We want to hear more about this tomorrow. But, for now, junior detectives need rest so they can carry out orders. Soooo, order number one is—"

"Ah, Daddy, do we have to?"

"Yep, you do. Good officers obey, secret code is B-E-D." Saul yawned in spite of himself....

Rachel slept fitfully in spite of Buck's tender praise of her courage as she cuddled against his loving arm. If only...she... had heard Star's...story...

• • •

The dream awakened her. In it, she was attempting to man a large ship, alone, lost, with no idea what made up the great outmoded vessel's cargo. It was another century, one which she did not understand, so what could the crude map spread before her mean? "Yo, ho! 'n uh bottle o'rum!" Lusty attempt at song invaded her ears as if to shake her awake. But deeper and deeper she sank...or was the great sea-going voyager tilting as if to drown her? And then she saw them—so many in number that in their victorious climb aboard, they were running her aground. Pirates! Swarming over the leeward side, cutlasses in hand, strange-looking guns dangling from their wide sashes. Stripped to the waist, wearing only petticoat breeches, they leeringly advanced upon her, their dirty faces enlarging in close-ups. Horrible blur that the nightmare was, Rachel could almost—but not quite—identify the pirates, even with their disguises of stringy hair, golden earrings, and knives dangling at their sides. Rats, afraid of the sinking ship, were running everywhere—leaping overboard. And then a woman! She was unable to see the face, but the voice she knew. Pussycat... "Queen of the Rum-Runners"...*Barbette Ames*...

Sweat-soaked and clutching her pillow as though it were a life raft, Rachel awoke and looked out on the real world—a world frost had visited during the night to fringe the tips of every tree. And now the golden disk of sun slipped over the eastern hills to cast a layer of bronze over all, as if adding the final touch to endless clumps of Christmas trees. Where were the pirates—and the leader? *The name*...she must remember the woman...

She jumped as Buck eased the door open to ask, "Awake, Sweetheart?" Wordlessly, she reached out to him, almost upsetting the two cups of coffee he brought. "Wide awake and sloppy!" Laughing, they wiped up the spilled coffee.

He summarized Star's version of the evening before. Brian wandered, unobserved, toward the lights "so blinding he was near hypnotized, like following the eyes of evil." Brother Davey saw and, without taking proper caution, ran screaming through the brush yelling, "Git thee behind me, Satan!" and vowed that was what happened! His ranting alerted the men—

What men?

Oh, those holed up in the building near-hidden in the button-willows where the cache of guns was stored and with it—spirits. The twins, hearing the word, were carried away—*spirits* meaning evil forces, instead of liquor—so they bounded out to solve the mystery. The masked men chased them and would have done them harm—perhaps kidnapped them, even (God forbid!) taken their very lives. Except that pup all had thought lovable but witless, specializing in chewing up shoes, went into action. He grabbed at their pant legs, biting into their flesh, fortunately leaving a trail of blood. Yes, Scot followed the trail but lost it at the water's edge. *But* the bootleggers had a sophisticated organization—foolproof, obviously aided and abetted by local residents. A well-organized spy system, ready and waiting to conceal all evidence, letting the dummies who'd sell their grandmothers for a dime make a getaway before law-enforcement officers could spot the trouble.

"It's against the law!" Rachel cried out. "Remember how hard you and Cole worked at keeping Lordsburg clean, making it worthy of its name? Where is their sense of *values*?"

"More coffee, Darling?"

When Rachel shook her head, Buck frowned and studied her question. "I guess the word is archaic—no, that's unfair. They're misguided, blinded—all of them—into thinking they'll get away with it, somehow not realizing that it will catch up with them and their households. New-world law breakers we're up against."

Rachel shuddered, thoughts too lurid for comfort. "Buck, I'm frightened. Why, these traitors are merrily and cockily flouting the laws in our faces—no better than old country rum-smuggling *pirates*—"

Buck broke into her colorful imagining with the first belly-laugh Rachel had heard from him for ages. And suddenly it felt good to laugh at herself. It was the dream, of course. And yet, her mind took wing, flying back to Star's conversation with Patrick. It was a dream which restored her memory, identified Julius Doogan—while, she thought bitterly, clearing him. How much strength could one put in dreams?

She jumped as her own dream came back clearly, Barbette dominating the scene. The mention of her name last night merged with the woman in the dream—"Pussycat" . . . "Queen of the Rum-Runners . . ."

Buck broke into her thoughts. "Try and rest a little today—investigations begin tonight." At her look of surprise he nodded. "They are entitled to a fair and speedy trial. We have to know who's caught in the web—them or us."

29

No Black
in a Rainbow

Grim of face, the Grand Jury sat listening to the judge explain their duties. Strictly a fact-finding committee, Judge J. Quentin Hathaway emphasized, squinting slightly as he checked his notes, then adjusted his glasses. Plans were, he said, that until a more efficient method could be arranged, members of the council would serve. A few had been excused as they were here to serve as witnesses; others, because of "extenuating circumstances."

The judge cleared his throat. "It is rare, gentlemen, when we allow a child, even one as mature as Star Jones, to be present. But the young lady may be of help—so, may I remind you, men, to guard your language, a young lady is in your midst. May I remind you also that this is strictly a fact-finding committee—not a trial?"

Rachel wished she could turn around and see who was in the audience. It would be awkward, of course, as both she and Buck had surrendered their chairs at the table in order to serve as witnesses.

To the surprise of all, Jules Dunigan was called first. "Just what am I charged with?" he demanded with such force that one would think he was in charge. Rachel felt the same sickish sensation she always experienced when the crafty turncoat spoke. How did he have the *nerve*?

"Several," Judge Hathaway growled. "Somebody is in charge of the conspiracy here and questions have been raised—no comments at this point," he ordered Julius Doogan (he would always be that to Rachel, no matter what higher courts had ruled). "Just answer the questions."

James Haute had come forward when Rachel's mind brought her back to the hall. "You have the right to an attorney," he said after reading Jules Dunigan his rights.

"I have no need for one and if I did it would not be you!"

"So noted," the judge said tersely. "In which case I deem it proper to call witnesses to the stand— some of whom may very well be charged themselves—"

Rachel's face whitened with anxiety when the Lee boys were summoned first. Obviously, the young men were scared out of their wits. Otherwise, why would 11 shy, non-talkative boys be babbling all at once? They knew nothing of his activities... they worked for somebody, yes... but they didn't know who... needed money... knew nothing of other people's involvement... did target practice and did some digging... didn't even know they were trespassing at Superstition Mountain... somebody who told somebody else said there were treasures... and it would be "finders, keepers"... then somehow they got separated... and they even stopped working together...

The judge brought down his gavel—hard. "Order! Do you mean to say you never so much as met this man?"

Abe spoke up immediately. "I never took part—I never left home. But, yes, my brothers know him. He's Julius Doogan, an outlaw—"

"Then be seated. It's Jules Dunigan who is suspected."

"But we never worked for him—this Dunigan er Doogan neither," one of the boys denied vehemently. "We dropped our guns when Miz Rachel ordered us to—all uv us did, Your Honor—"

"The accused," who had sat cool and collected with the hint of a sneer on his hateful face, leaped forward in fury. "Liar, liar!" he screamed. "One of the dummies on the far right aimed and fired at me—wouldn't have missed either if Dr. Killjoy hadn't tried to save me—"

Several men rushed to restrain the man gone mad as the gavel pounded harder and harder on the table. Ignoring the judge's repeated words of "Order—order in the court!" Judson Lee's voice rose above the din of angry shouts. He had risen to stand beside his chair.

"Of *course* they be good shots—all me boys!" Judson's Irish voice boomed. "They learnt at home fer huntin'—we be allowed t'bear arms in our own homes! But fer killin' purposes, me misguided boys had uh master teacher. *That criminal!*" He pointed a shaking finger at Julius who was struggling to free himself while filling the courtroom with oaths. "Shooting an innocent man in the back—"

The judge was trying to call a recess. But the unbelievable happened. "*Judge!* Hear me out—listen to me—cite me for contempt—whatever my fate, this *has* to be contradicted! This is a blatant lie! The shot entered from the front! And," his voice rose another octave, "I would kill Julius Doogan—Jules Dunigan—or any of his other aliases—if I didn't mind getting my hands dirty! Because of him a new father lies paralyzed—probably for life. Get this man out of my sight—"

And then Dr. Howard Ames bent over and gave way to dry sobs.

• • •

Everything went out of focus again when Rachel tried to recall the sequence of events. Everything happened at once, people rushing forward (changing personalities as one hurriedly changes clothing). "Lynch 'im!" The chant came from an unsavory group she had no time to recognize—if ever she had seen them before. "He ain't worth savin'—betrayed us—git uh rope! No, wait, they ain't never been no hangin' uv wimmen, but they's allus uh first time. Git th' harlot from behind bars—"

The sheriff and his deputies were trying to elbow their way through the angry mob, one of them yelling, "Use restraint, comrades—remember your training in crowd control. Night sticks instead of guns!" The ashen faces of government men bobbed up and down like corks. Pushing...push...pushing...everybody pushing toward the front.

Brother Davey trying to take command: "Hear ye, hear ye—oh, fools that thou art! Cain't yuh see I got news?" But only those closest, Rachel included, heard. And they were helpless in the mob.

Yet still they came. Aunt Em demanded the floor. Someone behind her said she'd better *vamoose*, else she'd be *on* it, face down. Mrs. Maxton—*Mrs. Maxton*? Yes, hands doubled into fists, gave her lungs a workout. "Why would I be hired on to protect Yo—I mean Mrs. Killjoy—excepting for this flour-faced crook? Gag him—stuff out his blasphemy—"

Boneparte Bixby...then Calvin Merriweather trying to explain the mystery character eavesdropping at his barbershop. "First we knew *he* was one of them!" To no avail Mr. Culpepper, who had closed his hardware store, tried to verify the identification. Then, Miz Lily, her softly-lined face as white as her name implied, tried vainly to reach the man she took care of—her Jules. Oh, how sad, how pathetic, this wilted flower...

Only one even stood out, as well it should—proving once more that "a little child shall lead them." *Star!* And soon the silver-spoon voice rang out.

Looking like a sun-bronzed angel in her white, blue-sashed dress, which swept the top of the table where Patrick had placed her, she raised a near-lifesized drawing above her head. Composed and with a look of foreverness, Star turned from left to right then back, the magnificent rainbow catching and holding the lamplight. The colors shimmered, reflecting on faces in the hysterical throng. All talk stopped, and all who saw were transfixed, motionless, as if frozen in time.

"I saw the underneath side beneath the water, all colors of the spectrum which God placed in white. Everything was so clear, so perfect when brushed by the guardian angel He sends. Mr. Mead pushed me. Mr. Dunigan pulled me from the depths—but only because God sent me a guardian angel. Dr. Ames came. I now remember. *Comprehende?* Love will conquer evil—when we know there is no black in the rainbow!"

30

Fear, the Beginning of Wisdom

The investigation resumed. Long, grueling hours of it. And Rachel sat through it all. Sunrise. Sunset. Had she ever been so tired? Buck grew concerned and begged her to rest. "Not until this is settled—that is, as far as we can take it." She was the mayor. But she was the mother, too, and, his eyes devouring her with admiration for all she was, *his wife*. But Rachel shook her head, although her mirror reflected a colorless mask of determination with blue flames burning in dry eye sockets. Buck understood, of course. As city manager, he was even more deeply involved. Evidence against Julius Doogan was piling up. The name, Jules Dunigan, was gone from lips of former admirers. Any jury would convict him, but the judge was squeezing him dry in an effort to find out who the followers were. He was indicted and ordered shackled for the safety of them all. And it was essential, Judge Hathaway confided to the the jury, that they find out just what part Barbette Ames played...just how Miz Lily came into the picture...and what Dr. Ames knew. He read off list after list of names and ordered them all rounded up.

On one night in particular, Rachel felt on the verge of collapse and asked to be excused early. "*Both* of you," the judge said gruffly as he examined their faces. "You look risen from the dead before the Lord called!" Perish the image...but if one had strength to see...

"Oh, what a night! Or, is it because we're together—alone?"

"Both, I think. Listen!" She snuggled against his warm body when he removed his jacket, wrapped it about her shoulders, and pulled her to him tenderly as they walked home slowly.

The river understood. Its voice dropped to a whisper. The moon's one eye beamed upon them benevolently. The stars blinked shrewdly. The air was damp but sweet with the fragrance of evergreens. And from their private stretch of woods came the plaintive call of a night-bird seeking its mate. Rachel stilled her turbid thoughts, and gave herself totally to the beauty of the stolen moment.

One moment was all they had. The next moment something stirred as it moved by the wind—but there was no wind. Tuned in to every clue as they were, Rachel and Buck stopped. With her heart in her throat Rachel trailed the bushes with her eyes. The moonlight held, helping her see something which could have gone unnoticed. The outline of a man or boy stepping onto the trail uncertainly. She squeezed Buck's hand, but the outline had backed into the shadows. Did she recognize him? There was something familiar and yet—

Then some intangible something in the gangling motion served as a spark to her memory. Now she understood exactly how Star had felt. Now she knew beyond any doubt, if ever she had had one, that the child was right. For it was the same spark within herself which set afire a powder trail to her own memory. The shadow which had vanished so quickly was that of the boy-apprentice training with Willie Mead. Why had he come? He would do them no harm. Quickly her heart changed tempo—too quickly to share with her husband. The boy was afraid.

"Come out—" she called, wishing she could recall his name. "We are Mr. and Mrs. Jones—you are safe with us."

The boy edged from his hiding place, looking gaunt and frightened. And then he swayed. Buck took in the situation more quickly than Rachel had. "What happened to that arm, Britches?" Rachel then saw to her amazement what accounted for his weakness. One sleeve of his white shirt had been shredded. The openings disclosed an ugly knife-furrowed gash beginning at the shoulder and reaching almost to the wrist. And she had never known the human body held that much blood.

"You have to see a doctor—now!" Buck said in a tone that left no room for argument. But the youth was desperate enough to try.

"No—no, *please*! You don't understand—they'll kill me good—"

The panic in the young eyes touched Rachel's heart. But Buck was already binding the arm to shut off the flow of blood. She smiled at Britches to give him encouragement. "You can tell us what happened while we travel. Dr. Ames will be at the Killjoys—that's close."

"The handkerchief-tourniquet should arrest the bleeding. That will have to do—there's no time to waste," Buck said with a worried look into the chalky face. "Lean on me—and, Rachel, can you support the injured arm, hold it at body level if possible?"

"Of course!" she said, feeling faint but continuing to smile as if transporting blood-soaked arms while marching down the street were a part of her daily schedule. *Distract him . . . keep him talking, hoping to keep him awake instead of passing out from loss of blood.* "Now tell us what happened to you, Britches!"

He closed his eyes but began talking in a ragged whisper:

"I done a dumb thing—along came this big boat—first time ever I see one this big. A man spotted me and ast if I wanted to see inside. Yes—a mistake, a trap—I knew soon as I walked th' plank—but, but—*how much fu'ther?*" Britches gasped.

"Turning here. I see a light in the window. Hang on, pal."

Buck's calm voice seemed to reassure him. "Th' crew was s'posed to be loadin' th' canoes with guns 'n bottles—but got fightin' over holdin' out loot fer theirselves so the big guy—that's what they called their leader—would'n know. They plumb forgot me—so I tried runnin'—but this one man caught me—slashed me up and throwed me overboard." He paused to cough. The awful ordeal, the shock of the cold water, and the loss of blood were taking their toll. "Never would'a made it 'cept I follered th' light guidin' th' canoes—oh, but I—I gotta tell yuh they was pickin' up messages meant fer us—gotta receivin' set 'board—I got th' messages—th' names—I—know—" Britches' bleached face sagged against Rachel's shoulder and his body went limp, just as Howard Ames opened the door.

"Lay him on the kitchen table," Ames ordered. "My bag?"

"Right here, sir." Mrs. Maxton's expertise at 'overhearing' came into play. "Water's boiling—bandages here—"

The patient rallied slightly. Enough to say, "I . . . hafta . . . tell . . . Mead's . . ."

The doctor plunged a needle into the injured arm. The boy was asleep instantly. "You'd better leave the room, Rachel. Buck will help—"

It was a wafer-thin Yolanda in a downy white robe transforming her shadowy self into a snow queen, who touched Rachel's elbow, guided her to an oversize green velvet settee. Rachel dropped into one corner gratefully and with a small laugh of surrender, Yolanda sank down in the other.

"We have never been able to function without each other, even tonight it takes two of us to make one. . . . Oh, here you are Mrs.

Maxton. I was about to ask," Yolanda said as she turned to Rachel. "Mrs. Maxton's the only person I know who meets one's needs before they're expressed."

"I know that you both need to be put to bed!" The woman sighed. "But I guess hot tea will have to do. The water was hot—"

As she set the steaming cups before them, Rachel wondered just what to make of her. Yolanda's exaggerated description and her modified behavior did not coincide. But nothing made sense. Even as she carefully spooned sugar into the tea and answered Yolanda's questions, her mind was asking questions of its own. Was this lad conscious enough to retain and decode the little dots and dashes of the receiver set? It had seemed important to him. And what had he wanted to tell them that was so important? He had made mention of his employer. At that point, Howard had stopped him with an injection. To ease the pain—or (*Stop it, Rachel!*) to silence him? So this was an evening of rest? What a quaint thought! The courtroom was more restful....

"The children are with Aunt Em and Brother Davey, I'm supposing?"

Mention of the children aroused her. "Yes, and I'm guessing Rowie is, too? We're so grateful for Reverend Luke during this crisis—always with them—" Rachel came back to the *now* with Yolanda's question.

"As is the bodyguard." *Who said fear was the beginning of wisdom?*

"Bodyguard?" Rachel was startled—and then amused. The tea had relaxed her and she was able to smile. "Ironic, isn't it? I've absolutely lived in that courtroom—all the while coveting time to stop by and bring you news. Now here, under strange circumstances, its *you* filling *me* in on the outside world."

As if complimented, Yolanda's brown eyes sparkled. "There's more—did you know that Miss Annie's taking a room at Aunt Em's Eatery?" Reading surprise in Rachel's face, she rambled on quickly, undoubtedly to disclose all she could before being ordered to bed. "And the reverend's going to make his headquarters at the Welcome Stranger—be running it temporarily. Miz Lily plans on a spare room, you know, as soon as the government takes away all that evidence—let's not talk about *that*! Miss Lily's coming here—she's a registered nurse, you know, until Maynard can walk and the baby's stronger. Her sister—yes, she and Mrs. Maxton *are* sisters. She—Mrs. Maxton, I mean—will help with Brian until we see what happens to the body-snatcher woman who's married to Howard. I offered to keep the child, but his father can't bear to be parted—"

Rachel's head spun dizzily. She was glad when Dr. Ames entered with a report.

31

The Right Bait!

This morning there was the smell of rain in the air. Dark clouds, then a brisk breeze whipped at her skirts and roughened her hair, but Rachel almost welcomed the oncoming storm. The air needed clearing, both weatherwise and in her mind. She had been in turmoil for so long, particularly since Britches became an important link. Some of the problems were on hold, but others needed help that the Galloways could give, while delighting in "playin' hit dumb," as Aunt Em phrased it, if others probed.

Rachel and Buck had remained at the Ameses' long enough to learn the boy's condition then, at their insistence, to see Maynard and the baby. Invited, Rachel had explained that she thought both father and daughter would be sleeping. To the surprise of all, Maynard was a good patient. Unbelievable, given his attitude in the past. Unbelievable—and unexplainable by Yolanda. She only basked in the sunshine of "having my husband back since—" The whispered confidence went no further, broken by the entrance of Howard and Buck.

The doctor's report was guarded. "Hemorrhaging's under control. Good job you two did getting the lad here in time. Of course, he's weak, somewhat irrational—we'll ignore his babbling, Buck." Was there warning in his voice? "What took so long was the tying together and suturing—probably wise to hold him here for observation—if that is all right, Mrs. Killjoy?" Yolanda nodded. "Mrs. Maxton has agreed to remain until—" Dr. Ames stopped and busied himself with writing out instructions. He left, leaving a million questions unasked and unanswered. It was as if Lordsburg were in no crisis. Or that this boy was uninvolved, and Rachel's mind had gone multidirectional, that it was perfectly natural that a boy would sustain such a life-threatening wound. She shook her head to clear it then went in to see Yolanda's husband and their "prize."

And prize Baby Nola Em was indeed. "I have never seen a more perfect child," Rachel said, her admiration sincere. The chubby darling with a question-mark curl looped by a narrow pink ribbon yawned and stuck a dimpled fist in her mouth.

"She made sure I was here," Maynard declared. "Pull the baby closer, Darling, so I can show how she grips my finger—strong, I tell you!"

Yolanda pushed the hooded bassinet with her knee until it touched Maynard's hand. "Destined to be a lady weight lifter," she smiled. But Rachel noticed that the slight movement caused beads of perspiration to form on Yo's forehead. "Are you all right?" she whispered in Yolanda's ear as the men talked about babies in general. Yolanda crooked a finger toward the door and they tiptoed out.

"Fine—I just tire easily. It's Maynard I'm worried about. He's not recovering, Rachel—just thinks he is. Howard's not squaring with him yet. Part of the bullet's lodged against the spine—it'll take a specialist to determine if anything can be—be done. But," she brightened, "his spirits are sky-high—and we're platonic lovers—now. Some day," she dreamed on, "we will—well, be back to normal." She stopped, pink-cheeked. "Oh, I wish we could talk longer—about his strange conduct allowing that awful woman to cling like poison ivy. It was all a ploy—couldn't even tell *me* officials were setting a trap. It worked and—"

Once more, they were interrupted. "We'd better go before we all fall on our faces. The reverend will have put our small fry to bed ..."

Buck was right.

• • •

Now, with nothing settled in her mind, Rachel was nearing Aunt Em's Eatery. Good thing. The sky had darkened enough to set a rooster crowing in the distance. And was that thunder? Or the sound of a steam engine? Quickly she glanced at the white-crested river and imagined the children's pirate story repeated. That accounted for the flash of white surely.

When Aunt Em opened the door, the wind all but pushed Rachel inside. An affectionate round of greetings ... the usual hospitable offer of food . . . and they all burst out talking at once. It seemed urgent that they compare notes. The clouds turned green. The lamp cast an eerie glow.

Rachel gave a quick run-down on the trial, most of which the Galloways knew, then bombarded them with questions. Was it all true, she asked, after giving an account of Britches' sudden appearance, about Mrs. Maxton, Miz Lily—and did they know more than she knew about Maynard's assignment with officials—or had they heard?

"Whew!" Aunt Em laughed, although a frown furrowed her forehead. Yuh gotta give old minds uh spell t'think fast as yuh talk, Dearie—lessen we're relivin' the Stormin' uv th' Bastille Tower. We ain't releasin' prisoners—we're roundin' 'em up."

"But, yep, hit's uh fact 'bout Mrs. Maxton—'n all th' housin' 'rangements. 'N me'n Emmy-Gal here's preparin'—'cause we," Brother Davey raised his cane and banged the table for emphasis, "laid down th' law—"

"Stop bangin' th' furniture, Davey-Love. Yuh ain't Moses no more'n th' table's uh rock. Wanna set water gushin' all over th' floor from thet pump yuh flooded us with? No time fer repairin' damages agin—"

"Can you trust Miz Lily—I mean, who and what is the woman?"

"Mrs. Maxton's sister fer one thang," Aunt Em began, only to be interrupted by her husband. "She knows thet a'ready," Brother Davey broke in—but Miz Lily Dunigan's—try swallerin' this—is uh crook named Julius Doogan's aunt. Th' scum took on her name—in court, mind yuh!"

Rachel tried swallowing it and choked. "And yet you *trust* her? What about the lights? Everybody was convinced she was signaling her brother—only he turned out to be a nephew. She *was* the one?"

"Wuz fer uh spell," the little man butted in, "trustin' 'im, tryin' t'make uh man uv 'im. Then she learnt th' truth—"

"But they continued to flash." Rachel's voice was little more than a whisper. "I find it all confusing. The lights. The woman, who was it?"

"Would yuh be believin' 'twas Miss Annie drest up like her— tollin' 'em in whilst we entered th' buildin' 'n found all th' evidence—with Miz Lily's help—"

Aunt Em talked on, but Rachel did not hear. So everybody in Lordsburg knew but her—and maybe Buck? She must have spoken her thoughts.

"Had t'reserve uh few credible witnesses 'cause yer gonna be makin' some mighty weighty decisions. 'Course th' two uv yuh'd be fair 'n square no matter how th' cookie crumbles—keep Cole's dream alive."

They all jumped when an explosion of thunder split the world in half. For a moment Rachel thought there were screams then dismissed the idea, crediting the sound to the whine of the wind.

"Close, 'tweren't hit? Musta struck uh tree. Think we're 'bout t'hit bottom on roundin' up these here tainted souls?" Brother Davey said hopefully, obviously hoping to play hero when he took the witness stand.

"No!" Rachel said flatly. "I think we're only scratching the surface. Britches could be of some help—unless fear holds him back."

The thought aroused Brother Dave's ire. "That shortstop! That saplin'd hafta fert'lize 'is face afore growin' uh beard!"

"Now, now, Davey-Love," Aunt Em soothed. "Think back on yer fishin' days. Recall whut yuh done when yuh hooked uh undersized fish?"

"Throwed 'im back—an' thet's whut—"

"Now, Davey-Love, you did'n' allus toss 'im back. Yuh used him fer bait!"

A deluge of rain drowned any answer he may have made. And with it a desperate pounding on the door. Without waiting for an invitation, Miz Lily, in a hooded black slicker, all but fell inside. Aunt Em saw the woman's frenzied expression and took no notice of the puddles of water dripping from the rain gear onto her carpet. "What on earth?"

"Come!" the woman panted. "Quick—something awful's happened—canoes capsized—men drowning—oh, help—*help!*"

Taking no time for wraps, the three of them rushed into the blinding storm to follow Miz Lily. It was a life-and-death matter—of that Rachel was sure. That thought gave her courage to push against the wind with all her strength. Half-blinded by the rain, she tried to make out the crazily-tilted object far down river. A phantom ship? How silly! Nevertheless, Rachel found herself shaking all over. The drenching rain had soaked her to the skin. Small wonder she was so cold. Pushing her dripping hair aside and squinting, she was sure that around the black object great oily pools were spreading closer to shore only to be swallowed up by the raging current. And then—*oh, dear God, no!*—the body of a man whirling in circles for a moment before disappearing forever in the rush of the water to join the sea. The horror of the scene mingled with the stifling smell of oil fumes made her lightheaded, made her wonder if she imagined it all. And then reality struck home, spawning a panic to spiral counterclockwise in her numbed brain. Valiantly, she fought for self-possession. *Tell me not to be afraid, Lord. Guide me...*

Catching her lower lip between clenched teeth, she bit hard. Her throbbing pulses skipped a beat then slowly began to beat rhythmically. She had prayed for strength. It came, enabling Rachel to look down, seeing exactly what she expected. A capsized canoe near shore, dipping impishly in the shallow water which lay almost motionless. And bodies...men waving...frenzied...growing weaker. If they weren't rescued at once, they would drown. Or, perish the thought, if they were caught in an undertow....No! she would not think of such tragedy.

Only a moment had passed. To Rachel, it was an eternity. Glancing around quickly, she spotted her companions. Aunt Em had had presence of mind enough to bring a lantern. How she managed to light it in this downpour was one of heaven's miracles. But she was turning its feeble light, swinging it to signal the helpless men that help had come. Miz Lily had found an oar. And what was this? Brother Davey with a pitchfork? Never mind why—

"Can you reach the boat—bring it to shore?" Rachel's case of nerves had ended and here *she* was, issuing orders to experts. It made no difference. "Aunt Em, hold the lantern higher—we'll have to get it upright—drag the men in and get them ashore!"

Aunt Em aimed the feeble beam at the canoe, so near and yet so far—bobbing, skidding, and prancing like a skittish horse—and tried to scream. Rachel caught only a "No!" of protest. But Miz Lily had gone, Brother Davey close at her heels, and Rachel stumbled blindly behind.

The rest was blotted out in her memory. The oaring, the seasickness she felt. All of it, except her wild desire to laugh in the face of tragedy at Brother Davey's triumphant yells, "Praise th' Lord, 'n drag this 'un up, Rachel! I got me a'nother by the rump with this here pitchfork!"

And then they were all ashore. And somebody was giving orders amid the bedlam, "That's it, folks! You've got guts—pardon, ladies—courage and a God-given spirit of the law. All right, men—here we go. We'll be holding you for witnesses—they're blue with cold, Miz Lily."

Brimmerton!

Aunt Em swung the lantern toward her cafe. But Miz Lily cupped her hands to her mouth and called, "The storage house, Brother Davey—I'll care for them. I'm a trained nurse."

More bait, Rachel thought foolishly.

32

End of the
Long, Dark Night—
and Then?

"Oh my darling—don't you *ever* do such a wonderfully-foolish thing again! I was worried sick but unable to find where you were—what you were doing—" Buck, his voice thick with emotion, obviously not trusting himself to continue, left his thoughts unfinished.

Rachel reached across the table to grip both his hands. "Look who's talking! I couldn't find you either and demand a report. We have both cultivated suspicious minds, I guess," she teased. Then, glancing at his drawn face, she changed tactics. "I'm very sorry, there was no way to contact you, Sweetheart. And let me promise that it won't happen again. I've had enough excitement in the last 24 hours to stamp out the fire of adventure. It was an emergency, believe me—and I just happened to be on hand—"

"It was providence" Buck said soberly. "You saved lives—but almost lost your own. It's just that I couldn't bear it if anything happened to you—"

"I know—oh, don't I know how you feel! Let's have coffee before we both have a long cry—it's stopped perking."

Buck nodded as he poured the coffee absently. Then, for an instant, he closed his eyes as though gathering courage to make a confession of his own. Instead, he said, "Tell me the outcome, Rachel."

They must be in court in less than an hour. A summary would have to do. "The drowning men ran into the net like a school of fish. How Sheriff Brimmerton and his posse knew I've no idea—"

"I had them searching for you and they suspected the rest,"

Buck interposed. Warmed by the coffee, he appeared more relaxed. "Thank God they found you!—Now, go ahead."

"The men were scared to death. And who can blame them? They've been operating outside the law and then they betrayed their leader and plotted an escape. Criminals they are—but I can hardly help feeling sorry for them. They'll make no attempt to escape. They're too smart to show their faces, knowing they're safer under the protection of the long arm of the law than out there."

"Will they testify against Doogan? He *is* the leader, right?"

Rachel nodded. "To save their skins—not because of remorse."

Buck took a man-sized gulp of coffee. "Go easier for them."

She nodded again. "Brimmerton's taking no chances, of course. He has illusions of aggrandizement, although—" Rachel let go of the laugh she had stifled during the terrible ordeal, "Brother Davey insists that a pitchfork's more powerful than a gun, a four-pronged implement being the weapon Satan uses!"

Buck joined her laughter then inquired about evidence of the treasure. Rachel wondered how she could have forgotten that the government's search for the money and the men involved in the train robbery were the root of all this nightmare. "I'm guessing it sank in the river's current—" she said slowly, "or that it could have been secured to the raft and is on its way to the ocean— providing this was, in reality, its burial place."

"It was," Buck assured her. "And probably still is—meaning that there may be more." Again he hesitated, then, measuring his words carefully, said, "Rachel, you need all the information you can carry with you today—although some of what I'm about to tell you will have to remain secret even after the trial."

The world stopped turning, the silence between them so thick Rachel felt she could slice it. Surely the beating of her heart must be audible. To hide her sense of premonition, she managed to say lightly, "Don't tell me *you* are a secret agent."

"You know better than that. I'm not qualified. You know I withhold nothing from you. This concerns what I was doing last night—you asked, you know—it's too complicated to explain in full, and there's too little time. You've noticed the change in Yolanda, of course. I've no idea how she has explained it to you, so I'll simply say that Maynard *is* one of the agents—was even before this thing reached gigantic proportions. You've spoken so often about his being—well, different. He's a good choice you know, his profession demanding secrecy of sorts, doctor-patient confidentiality. And he is required to report gunshot wounds, among other things. You can understand that he is qualified."

Yes, suddenly she could.

"His cover is blown now. He's never given much thought to all the recent happenings—getting himself shot, Britches dumped on him—everything at once. But he had planned to terminate his connection with the government anyhow—realizing that it had come between him and his marriage. There was nothing between him and Barbette, as you may know. He knew she was using him—spying for Doogan—"

"Doogan? All that flirting to *spy*. Why that conniving she-beast! But you mean Howard put up with it—didn't care—"

"Both. He knew the plot and that she was giving out information in exchange, reporting to *him*—"

"Howard! He's an agent, too?" Rachel gasped. Buck was right, it *was* complicated. When he nodded, Rachel was unable to ask if Howard, too, would be withdrawing from his service to the government. When at last she could speak, she put the question into words.

Buck shook his head. "He's a born adventurer, as well as being a fine doctor. Mum is the word, of course. The judge will not let this be revealed at the trial. We *have* to go, honey." Buck was reaching for his hat.

"Wait! I'll get my coat. But, Buck, I have to know about Britches."

"Of course—how could I have forgotten? Here, let me help you with that top button. Britches is a sensible boy—frightened of course, afraid we didn't believe his story. Maynard told him that Dr. Ames taking him in and shielding him, should be proof enough. Convinced, the boy finished what he tried to say before the injection took effect. By the way, I saw the look of suspicion you gave Ames—and, yes, he timed it both because Britches was in need of immediate attention and because he wanted to silence him without revealing his role in this tangled web. Ready? I'll continue with this as we trot to the trial—trials, I should say."

Outside, the breath of the morning was sweet after last night's storm. Rachel inhaled deeply as hand-in-hand they hurried through the blue-satin morning.

"Britches wanted us to know about the stack of undelivered messages. Willie Mead had withheld incriminating telegrams— Jules Dunigan was one and the same as Julius Doogan, James Durand, Joe Dodson—and on and on. The boy transcribed the dots and dashes, got suspicious, and was prepared to deliver them to me. You know the rest, except that Willie was nowhere to be found. We found the decoded messages in his boots and filed them with the judge as exhibits which won't be presented until Doogan realizes he's doomed and spills his insides. Let's hurry."

Rachel's head was whirling. She wished the day were over, that she and Buck could turn out the lights, snuggle by the window watching the moon through the clots of shadow in their private forest. Not talking, just reviewing the day's outcome . . . thinking . . . thinking . . . thinking. Relieved, at peace, as frost—delicate and sweet as summer's frothy-white border of baby's breath—silvered the ferny rim of the river, waiting for the violet dawn as it stole over the eastern treetops heralding the end of months of long, dark nights . . .

• • •

The hearings (for some) and the trials and sentencings (for others) moved like clockwork. After all, the groundwork was laid carefully, the witnesses prepared, and, unless something went awry, the leader identified. Julius Doogan, still cool and arrogant, had laughed in the face of the law. He would make fools of these simple people, his behavior said. There would be no need of an attorney. Little did he know of the drama which was about to unfold before him. . . .

Rachel had performed the difficult task of pulling the white kasha frock over her head without ruffling a hair and showed no signs of the stress and sleeplessness she had endured for so long. Inwardly, she was drugged with drowsiness . . . wishing she and Buck could fling themselves onto their bed . . . grope sleepily for the fleecy afghan Aunt Em had knitted them for Christmas . . . punch a shared pillow to fit two close-together heads . . . let go completely . . . and catch 40 winks . . . at peace with the world. Well, after today . . . so, head erect, she directed her mind to stay alert, even though her vision was blurred, unable to focus so as to differentiate, amid that wild sea of faces of spectators, between those of the accused and those who prepared themselves to testify.

The judge might have been carved of stone as he brought down the gavel, his china teeth glistening, his face without expression. "We will dispose of 'the least of these,'" he announced without prelude.

"Disposing of formality, I call the Lee brothers to approach the bench—and, Judson, you and Nola—if she chooses—may accompany your family."

"Th' boys' mother is with our daughter, Your Honor—both o'th' good women be prayin' their hearts out, they be—"

The boys shuffled forward, their faces no longer white or their heads bent with shame. Obviously, they had been disciplined in a manner which prepared them to face the world, express their regrets—hoping for leniency, but prepared to face whatever punishment was meted out by judge or jury. They had sinned, sought forgiveness—and now must confess.

Rachel was prepared to testify in their behalf, tell of the incident at Superstition Mountain, their part in the shooting, and their clean background. It was unnecessary.

Judge Hathaway removed his glasses, wiped them, and told the family to step closer—away from the audience's hearing distance, but close to those at the table. "I have all the evidence documented. I am prepared to release you to your parents' care since this is your first offense—*providing* you are in church Sunday!"

"They will be, me boys," Judson declared. The boys turned to Mr. Lee. Then father and sons, true to the return of the Prodigal Son, fell upon one another's neck and wept. It was a touching scene.

Julius Doogan forgot his role and, although guarded on either side, screamed out an obscenity. "Some judge. Forget this kangaroo court! You let those ignoramuses go—knowing—" Sheriff Brimmerton yanked a foot-wide bandanna from his pocket and stuffed it in the prisoner's mouth as a temporary gag. Doogan chewed out the remainder of his accusation, "knowin'," he sputtered "they shot Dr. Killjoy!"

"Order! Restrain this madman," the judge ordered. "You are aware that such outbursts only go against your cause. It has been shown already that the shot came from your gun. The shell is among the exhibits."

Judge Hathaway, undisturbed, glanced toward the back of the over-crowded hall and responded to a signal given, too quick for the human eye except by the one it was intended for. Wiping his glasses, he said over the muted whisperings:

"Ladies and gentlemen, under the unusual circumstances, and certainly with consent of the parents, I now wish to call children—together with all adults within the school who have guarded them, guided them, and taught them the value of bridling their tongues as they cooperated in practicing the privileges of a working democracy while holding sacred *e pluribus unum*—the seal on our coins—'one of many.' Reverend Luke, we praise our Creator for leading our nation's hope of tomorrow's generation—our children—to know the value of 'In God We Trust.' Neither must we overlook your younger colleagues and helpers."

Rachel and Buck looked at one another in surprise, which quickly turned to pride—pride such as they had never known before. Star, who surely must be the largest star in the ever-enlarging flag, led the group, a luminous shine in her flashing dark eyes. How many, Rachel wondered afterward, followed? Children first. Followed by...Miss Annie...Callie (Oh, how proud the face of Callie's father!)...Young Brother Pat... "Teacher" Bixby...and, bringing up the rear, the Reverend Luke Elmo...

It was all a dream. It had to be. The drowsiness had come back, drugging her with the longing to shut it all out in her mind. While her heart said something quite different...propping her eyelids open...letting her hear every word even while she saw "through a glass darkly."

Little Star hesitated a moment, seeking her father's eyes questioningly. Buck nodded. The judge saw the exchange and encouraged her gently. "Take your time, little one—you have nothing to fear."

"Your Honor, I do not seek revenge. Like Paul, I do not wish to behave unseemly—or seek my own. I do not rejoice in iniquity—but rejoice in truth. It is through love that I believe and hope all things that are good in God's eyes. I will not swear falsely..."

The house was hushed in order to hear the cymbal-like tinkle of the small witness's voice. "God created me different—I see everything in rainbows. They are my tonic, stronger than a medicine. There is healing in God's wings. They let me see the good in those who would do me harm. It was in the rainbow, beneath the water, that I was changed...and, how can I say it? I hoped that the two men would be changed—the man who pushed me in, my enemy, and the one who rescued me," Star paused. "for no *amigo* was he—"

Star stopped, a faraway look in her eyes. And Rachel took note of her slipping back into her native tongue. That means she was disturbed, not sure how to proceed.

The judge leaned forward. "What changed your mind, my child?"

"I lost my memory. *Los padres—*"

"The ministers?"

"*Si*, the ministers—and Dr. Ames. The doctor saw the man who saved me—he—" Star was near tears, "tried to choke me," she gulped. "The Reverend and Brother Pat healed me, made me remember, through the power of the Great Physician—" Star choked before resuming. "The man knew that I had seen too much. He dared not let me live."

"There is more as the story goes on, but I can see that you are weary," the judge said. "One thing more, then you may rest—think carefully, *Is the man in this room?*"

Exhausted, Star could only point sadly at Julius Doogan.

Doogan's face was livid. He all but foamed at the mouth as he tried to scream, with the bandana hampering his speech. "Th-at half-breed—th'ly'n' tr-tramp—many t-times—I—sav-ed'er—can—can't—p-p-prove—"

The gavel came down hard. "One more outburst from you and you will be removed from the room! You deserve no trial—but law demands it. Now, behave as if you were human, about which there is some doubt. *Not another word!*"

The rest of the children's testimonials were a childish jumble which brought a smile to the eyes of the sober judge. That they were sincere he could have no doubt. How Julius Doogan had threatened them, attempted to bribe them into silence, dogged their footsteps, spied on them *everywhere* including the school, even when they "had to go," and "Oh, My Honor—*Your* Honor, we were 'specially careful 'round the river because of strange lights—other men—and then the pirate ship so loaded with gold she sunk...so we *know* there's a pot of gold at the end of the rainbow—"

The adults accompanying them verified their words and gave testimonials of their own. None of the evidence surprised Rachel—not even when a brave-hearted soul, one of the more recent settlers, she supposed, wearing a tent-like dress which failed to disguise her size and shape (somewhat like a beached whale) interrupted to declare that she *knew* Julius Doogan—and his Aunt Lily in another city.

Judge Hathaway thanked her politely then tactfully asked that members of the audience remain as they were unless called before him.

Rachel must have given in to her fatigue and dozed. Imagining the organ-toned boom: *one, two, three, four* . . . of the grandfather clock at the stair-landing, followed by the wee-bird-chirping echo as the little hop in and out of the cuckoo took place, she jerked erect and checked the pin-on enameled watch on her white waist-top. Four hours had passed? Unbelievable! Nobody had noticed, for they were hearing what she already knew. But her eyes widened with dismay when Barbette Ames, flaunted herself up the aisle as if she, not the judge, should be addressed as "Your Honor." The heavily-rouged cheeks did not quite hide the chalkiness and her vivid lips suggested strain. But the ends of a delicate green scarf floated mistily behind her like gauzy wings (as she undoubtedly planned). And there was a hint of appeal in her eyes (wide-open to effect innocence), entirely foreign to her nature. So this was the game the brazen woman—*chameleon*, really, changing hues like the old-world lizard—Barbette would play? Would it work to confuse the judge or jury as it had the spectators? The room, so mild before she entered, now seemed to vibrate.

And then Rachel's heart began to pound. She had spotted the defendant's husband's entering. *And* Yolanda!

Wheels of all sizes spun rapidly in Rachel's head. How much could Dr. Ames reveal without disclosing that his work as a secret agent must be kept under wraps? And Yolanda must have come in place of her husband. But who would watch after Maynard and the baby? Both were helpless. All wheels increased speed. Why, Miz Lily...

Howard strode unobtrusively to James Haute. The attorney nodded and rose. "Your Honor, in view of new evidence, may I ask a recess?"

"Long overdue anyway. Court will reconvene in 15 minutes, and you, Mrs. Ames, may be seated."

"You may call me Barbette." Her voice was sickeningly sweet. A cake with a second layer of rich frosting. So sure was she that the "new evidence" would clear her... show her to be the maligned, neglected wife... the perfect mother...

But she had taken one step too far. The judge's eyes were frosty.

The next scene, vitally important as it was, seemed to take place in the twinkling of an eye. Brother Davey importantly escorted the men he had helped rescue directly to the judge. Without permission, the cocky little man crowed: "Now, yer honer, me'n these men'er castin' our pearls before them swine— do we hafta string 'em up fer yuh?"

The judge overlooked the breach of order and invited James Haute to explain the new evidence. The attorney wiggled his moustache, waxed to curl upward in matching question marks, from side to side, making him look like a bright-eyed mouse. But there the resemblance ended. Nothing mousy about his manner as he presented the men and summarized their roles. And he had instructed them well. Their manner was quiet, but not timid— and certainly not without color as one spokesman said, meeting the judge's eyes squarely:

"We transported the gold we unearthed to the buildin' the leaders prepared like th' preacher here says—"

"Leaders plural? There were several?"

"Two, Yer Majesty—Honor, Sir—beggin' pardon—an' all fer th' love uv mammon, I'm a-mind t'think th' Good Book calls it—"

Judge Hathaway leaned forward. "Who were the leaders? We want to get to them first."

"But, Your Honor," another interrupted, "that's not all—we ain't finished. You see, we—we knew that pair was 'bout t'be caught—and we wanted our share of th' loot—lots uv it, some even dumped. So we helped ourselves—th' leaders bein' dishon-est'ern us, never payin' off—"

"What!" Julius Doogan's voice was that of a madman. Some-how he had dislodged the bandanna and his words filled the building. "You dirty rats! You were supposed to clear me and Barbette—"

Barbette was no longer the pathetic child-wife. She was a tigress, untamed, in a jungle, starving for wealth as other man-eating beasts are starving for flesh. "You've spoiled everything. You idiots were not to involve *me* no matter what my husband—" Seeing what she had said, the wild-faced woman clapped her hand over her mouth—too late. Then, "You can prove nothing— *nothing*. I have a right to an attorney—"

James Haute, anticipating her next move, merely shook his head without moving a hair from his oiled hair and turned palms up in refusal. Her raucous stream of oaths was stemmed with a stroke of the gavel which shook the building.

"There will be order or I shall have this hall of justice cleared!"

In the pin-drop silence, James Haute whispered something in the judge's ear. He nodded and the attorney turned toward the door. There were some who vowed to their grandchildren that "th' smart law-man rubbed uh magic lamp..." Brother Davey would have loved the tale because either way he had a long figure standing beside the attorney with the speed of a genie. One could almost hear, "Yes, Master?"

But the lad, Britches, said no such thing. Clean-faced, cheeks pink from a fresh shave (perhaps his first), the telegrapher's apprentice stood tall and straight. "Your Honor, I served with William Mead, as you probably know. Mr. Mead has disappeared, holdin' these in Morse code." He handed the decoded messages to the judge. "You see, Sir, accordin' to the dates, they were withheld purposely. But such decisions are not to be made by me—"

The face of the judge, bland and objective until now, twisted with anger. "He *dared* delay *these*? When they were for immediate delivery!"

RECORDS CONFIRM TRAIN ROBBERY STOP TRANSPORTING ARMS STOP RUM-RUNNING STOP CONTACT THIS NUMBER IMMEDIATELY FOR IMPORTANT INFO TO FEDERAL AGENTS YOUR AREA

"Then the secret code follows. All right, men, close in!"

Men popped up like asparagus spears from every direction, some in uniform; others, in plainclothes, their movements as out of focus as a sliding-lantern show. Handcuffing Julius Doogan and Barbette Ames (or was her name Doogan, Dunigan? It was all so confusing). The woman, shocked, white, babbled incoherently, her eyes evil slits.

"He—he—did it all—money, all for money—promising—lying—" Wild-eyed, Barbette looked at the man she called her husband. "He's tricky—a no-good, threatening me—if I didn't marry respectably—"

"Liar! Liar!" Julius Doogan raged. "Ask Ames—" while trying to wrench free.

"That is another matter," one of the men said calmly. "We have proof enough without getting into the matter of bigamy. It is up to the government to decide your fate—"

"Give me a moment," Barbette cried out pitiously, changing tactics as she was being led away. "Oh, help me, Howard. I did it all for you." Seeing the doctor's noncommittal face held out no hope, she began screaming again. "You fiend! You married *me* for money. You hypocrite! Daddy will be here tomorrow to bail me out—"

"If 'Daddy' shows up, he'll find you en route to Washington, D.C.," the plainclothesman said roughly. "Bribery will only serve to incriminate him. Let's go!"

Barbette played her final domino. "I'll sue for false arrest. And, you," her wild eyes focused on Howard Ames, "will not take *my* Brian-Boy! *You are not his father!*"

Julius, gagged and being pushed from the room, tried to make himself heard. "That—that minx d–dares—c–call *me*—th'—th' father—of—of that—that disgusting lyin' kid—I—"

The judge's voice rose above the bedlam as he pounded on the table.

And then, like a bolt of lightning a white-faced Brian rushed to the judge. His sobs touched the weary man's heart. "It's not true—it's not true—I hate her—she's not my mother—oh, Daddy—where are you—tell them she's lying—"

Rachel's composure dissolved into disjointed thoughts. Hadn't the reverend taken the children home? Then how did Brian reappear? It was obvious that Howard had not expected this. Miz Lily...?

Dropping her head down on the table, she tried to concentrate, aware only that Buck—dear, wonderful Buck—had taken her hand.

"Cry out your heartache, child" the judge was saying, stunned by surprise himself. "Dr. Ames—"

But Howard was already by Brian's side, laying a tender hand on his head, then leaning down to draw him close, a dry sob catching in his throat. "Your Honor—I am out of order—and must guard my words. But Barbette (he tried to conceal his hatred for her) is correct. There is nothing between us—never has been," he said carefully. "I did not know—but she is neither my legal wife—neither is she my son's mother. Brian belonged to my sister—is my nephew *but* my child, adopted—and, yes, he knows. The—the woman has ruined his life—" he cut his sentence short. "I must say no more—"

"Oh, no, Daddy—I love you. I love you—and I know better than to cover my shame. Oh, Daddy, I love you! Star has made me see—"

Was there a dry eye in the house?

And suddenly it was all over. Aunt Em appeared, her arms laden with food. But Rachel, joined by Yolanda, hurried to the side door, followed by Buck and Howard, with Brian clinging and skipping between them. Some day they would put it all together. But for now Yolanda reacted differently to the nightmarish day. Hysterical laughter caught in her throat. How could things turn other-directional?

"Oh, we—we were not needed—everything was so clear—and yet so foggy! Suppose Aunt Em would have white thread? Just in case I *burst* out laughing? Oh, I am beside myself with joy—and—" she burst into unnatural laughter, "the end of the long, dark night—I need thread!"

"Maybe she has black thread," Rachel said senselessly. Then, finding her own insides turn over with laughter, "Will that do?"

"Not unless I want to—to be a black-eyed pea!"

Their laughter gave way to silence as the purple glow of twilight flooded the world then was washed away with darkness. It was quiet. Too quiet. Then again all was flooded by light as the small group turned the corner of the street leading to the Ames' house.

Every light in the great house was lit. And speechless figures were frantically hurrying to and fro. What on earth—?

One of the uniformed men ran forward to Howard, whispering...

Jules Dunigan had disappeared!

● ● ●

Again Lordsburg was abuzz. How could it have happened? And was it absolutely essential that those government agents button up their lips so tightly? Here the solid citizens were trying with all their might to give the past a decent burial, do some real spring housecleaning—sweeping out the cobwebs of suspicion and distrust. And just look at what happened. The news had heaped on more. Couldn't a body even trust those who preached justice? Well, maybe it was a good lesson for them all. The only real justice one could depend on was that of the Lord. He alone tempered His law with mercy. But the head-scratching went on: *Wasn't mankind expected to show brotherly love?*

Best just carry on the Lord's work. Just be ready to stay on the side of the law when called. The Good Book made it mighty clear that mankind was commanded to obey "those who have rule over you."

Aunt Em resumed the quilting bees, still secretive as to the receivers of the "Rose Garden," "Single Star," and "Double Wedding Ring" patterns. There were ladies who said Miss Annie and the reverend were getting sort of chummy-like... but, "you know how rumors spread," each prefaced before whispering it to another. That was as near as they came to gossip and membership flourished as it flourished in church. That young Brother

Patrick was a wonder! Modern as they came but had sense enough not to discard the baby with the bath water . . . knew how to laugh . . . but not afraid to pray for "those lost souls out there."

Amen! Amen!

33

Changes

Changing her calendar, Rachel wondered how it could be May. So busy had she been—as had the entire city—that the seasons blended to make a glorious spring.

The long autumnal rains had greened the dry stubble-fields, free of their burden of grain...reminded folk to haul in firewood, bleached from lying lazily in the sun...and the sun itself, a rayless disk, brightening as it sped across the shortening days burned away the thin, dry mist, flamed briefly bold and red; then, chastened and subdued, wove a purple-gold twilight. Had there been time to talk of small things, settlers would have made note of the falling of the first, sharp frost.

Rachel remembered the frost as she inhaled the violet-scented breeze of leafy May as it parted shadows in knee-high cornfields, ringed with dancing daisies. How wisely God had planned in providing for his children with bread, the staff of life. There had been a bumper crop of wheat. The best ever, Brother Davey declared, as he punched down rising rolls of whole-wheat bread. No wonder Nola's chickens packed their craws with the choice grain. Well, the dullards—like a heap of mortals—didn't possess enough brains to be grateful. But those red-combed hens could shell out the eggs in appreciation. And, come to think on it, whole choirs of hens and crowing roosters could harmonize better than some folks he knew who bellowed out on the hymns....

She would drop by The Eatery on the way to visit school, Rachel decided. Callie, helping full-time now, Rowie, Brian, and her own children—especially Star—had been insisting that Rachel visit. Suddenly it had occurred to her that school would be closing very soon. They were understanding of course—all of them. Nobody could do much in the way of extracurricular activities. They must "stick with the books," Miss Annie had declared. Brian giggled that teacher found time to crimp her hair and—now, don't tell, but I do believe she's hiked up the hems of her dresses! 'Course, that was before she and the reverend started boarding with Aunt Em and Brother Davey—their grand-parents—right?" Brian had mentioned the change to Mrs. Maxton and all but got his jaws slapped. Mrs. Maxton's bark was worse than her bite anyway, Brian had shrugged. She would have scared him before she moved in when she threatened to send him out behind the haystack to "meditate" for such remarks—"and that was on that first frosty morning..."

Frost! The word kept coming back to her mind. It caused goose-flesh to rise on Rachel's bare arms even though the sky was still warm with red-radiance of the trail left by the rising sun. The word hung in the air. Silver-white, frost covered the world last winter. All white? Yes, but—

That was it! White with the colors of the seasons blended into one. "The hues of all the colors in the spectrum are in white." Star's words. Could that account for the flash of white she had seen the night the canoes capsized? What difference would that make? Rachel stopped, allowing the now-brighter sun to warm her through and through. It made a difference because, yes, she was sure something caught and lingered in her mind just as Star had known there was something she needed of Patrick's "heal-ing" (admittedly through the power of prayer). Well, she could pray. Rachel dropped on her knees, inhaling the sun-warmed daisies, and let the words flow like an ancient psalm. Slowly, a vague memory—and yet not quite. There had been white motions, like a cloud descending to earth the night Julius Doogan was taken into custody. And then it disappeared! She would never recall more, for there had been no more. But memory of the white cloud hung in the air. It had meaning. What was it Star had said? "The heart remembers what the mind forgets"? Then someday she would know...

Rachel found Brother Davey sitting cross-legged on the floor husking and shelling corn for the mill. She waved him back when he tried to move his creaking joints and stand. He yanked danger-ously at his skimpy sideburns and eased himself back onto the cabbage-rose patterned carpet. "'Some like it hot, some like it cold,' some like it hot in th' pot ten days old!' 'Member th' ole English rhyme? Only me, I'm referrin' t'eatin'—"

"Nat'rally!" Aunt Em said good-naturedly from her chair drawn close to the oil lamp where she was darning her husband's socks. "Come on in, Dearie, 'n set uh spell. We need t'catch up like them." Her head bobbed to a shadowy corner of the porch of Cal Merriweather's barbershop (now boasting a peppermint-striped pole) where three elderly gentlemen sat, seemingly serene of heart, talking over old times. Rachel nodded, her heart filled with tenderness for this pair, who fitted such a seat-of-honor in her own past. But with those memories came a wave of sadness. Time was taking its toll. Brother Davey's cane by his side, Aunt Em's need of a light, even though her spectacles were the strongest the mail-order book afforded, and pride of hair once midnight-black now silver in the light of the lamp. Those underscored Rachel's thinking. But not for long!

"Back t'my likin', some folks praise th' wheat 'cause they want biscuit-dough bread. Me—I cotton t'cornbread dipped in cream gravy t'bacon 'n eggs. Glad th' Lord provides folks a'thinkin' otherwise so's them hens gobble up wheat. Lookit this ear uv corn, Rachel hon, its gold, like Star's rainbow—shinin' out th' glory uv ever' season—"

Talk of the rainbow changed the course of the conversation. As the elderly men chatted idly of the long-past, the three in the great living room talked over more recent happenings. The Galloways pounded Rachel with questions. Was there word of Willie Mead? No, Rachel had to admit, adding that his disappearance was the biggest puzzle of all—unless it was the escape of Julius Doogan. Brother Davey was convinced he had "inside help—else he couldn' uv streaked out like unto greased lightnin'" but who'd be telegraphin' fer Lordsburg? Rachel was sure Britches could handle it and that they could depend on the boy. Wasn't it a miracle about the change in so many . . . the women's change of living quarters and how it all worked out since that conniving Barb got herself caught along with Doogan . . . such a change in little Brian. Had Rachel ever studied on the fact that Star really *did* chase a heap of them rats out of here—and tolled the rest ("fer th' most part") out with that willow whistle Young Brother Pat whittled out of a branch hanging right over the bank where all the boats hid out? A regular little girl—well, not so little anymore—Pied Piper, she was.

"She's a wonder," Rachel agreed, misty-eyed. "Which reminds me, I'm on my way to the school—it's been ages—"

"Lemme tell yuh, they's lots uv changes—me, being on th' board 'n all," Davey said with pride, "I got th' insides uv ever'thang." Brother Davey made another attempt to stand, this time successfully—if one could call doubled into the four-legged position of a bucking horse standing. "Gim'me my cane, Emmy-Gal—"

Aunt Em shook her head at Rachel and her indulgent smile said a-man-has-his-pride. Rachel returned her smile, knowing that a woman needed hers, too. Once upright, the dwarfed but courageous man continued, "Yuh bound t'be noticin' some—well" his merry eyes twinkled, "s'prises—like th' Reverend Elmo's beholdin' t' Miss Annie and Mr. Bixby's behavin' like a man in love."

"Now, now, Davey-Love, iffen yuh keep on a-talkin' they won't be no s'prises—but I got two fer you, Dearie—"

Before Rachel could protest, the Galloways were all but pushing her upstairs—making only one stop to feed the always-hungry wood range and stir the stew for the lunch diners ("dinner" to them, of course, with supper being the evening meal).

The upstairs bedroom the Galloways had converted from a raftered-attic was light, airy, and scrupulously clean. Furniture, artfully placed to make the most of space, was of pre-mail-order period, solid walnut and of good design. A harpsichord leaned against the wall, its stance reminding Rachel that the ancient musical instrument was—it *had* to be—the old one used in the first log house of worship before Cole's shipment arrived from back East bringing the new one Aunt Em had played for weddings (a lump in Rachel's throat forced her mind back to her present surroundings). Braided rugs added to the brightness of sunlight beaming through the big room's multi-windows, immaculately clean and decorated with ruffled muslin curtains. One wall was lined with books, the opposite one accommodating a hand-painted matching china pitcher and bowl set. Amazed, Rachel commented on the faucet (a bit crooked admittedly). Running water? Had himself "uh thunder uv a time gettin' hit upstairs, water bein' contrary 'bout runnin' 'gainst gravity's pull," Brother Davey told her with pride.

"Big 'nuf fer two, huh, Davey-Love?" Aunt Em put a warning forefinger to her lips then covered the motion by pointing out the old-fashioned desk—complete with paper, inkwell, and pen staff—when Rachel looked her direction. "Yuh'd hafta know uh teacher lives here—'n Miss Annie brangs home wild flowers er leaves, even pun'kins, tellin' th' season. Oh, lookit this," she said in awe. Rachel looked and beside the sewing basket with its pin-filled cushion lay a wee pink-and-blue quilt with BABY spelled out in delicate French knots embroidered on top.

"Little Nola Em," Emmaline Galloway said with tears rimming her eyes. Then, straightening, "What did the specialist say 'bout the little doll's Paw? Maynard *is* a-gonna walk, ain't he now?"

Rachel's intake of air was jerky. "We'd better pray," she half-whispered. "Dr. Punkett held little hope—the other doctors are coming from Portland next month to help Howard—"

Aunt Em clapped her hands. "June! Thet's when th' 'vangelist is a-comin' with his foldin' tent show—travels like them medicine-show folks—'ceptin' his medicine's straight from th' Lord—"

"'N I better be tellin' yuh straight out, Rachel hon, thet Young Pat thanks purty much like 'im—then thar's our Star—"

"Davey-Love they ain't a-gonna be much t'sprise fer Rachel iffen we keep on tellin' all we know." But she was wrong!

●　●　●

The children welcomed Rachel with broad, bright smiles. "You were my mother's teacher, you and Mrs. Killjoy, 'way back," several said. Yes, "'way back" when there were no certificated persons and she and Yo alone could read, spell, and cipher. Such changes. Everything changed except God and His eternal love—and, hopefully, His children's faith.

Rachel chatted briefly with Miss Annie and found Brian's description accurate. She even blushed when Rachel complimented her on the decor of her living quarters. Miss Annie appeared about to say more when Mr. Bixby poked his head in the door and curled an inviting forefinger toward Rachel. It was recess and he wished to speak with her. The teacher had high praise for Star—her brilliance and her artistic ability. Mostly she painted remarkably beautiful rainbows. Some of the pupils thought a rainbow was a state flag; others, God's threat to send another flood! That, he said, explained his asking Brother Pat to teach a class. These misconceptions she must ponder on the way home.

She was buried in thought when the bushes parted and a woman in white blocked her way. *Miz Lily!*

"I know where my brother is," she panted.

34

"White Mystery" Resolved

Great puffer-belly clouds buttoned over the sun, the same tranquil breeze which toyed with the world of green below spawning little shadows from above. The late-afternoon earth lay silent except for an occasional plaint of a tree toad. Lover of nature that she was, Rachel neither saw nor heard. Her thoughts were too engrossed as they traveled back over the day. All of Lordsburg knew there was a strong possibility—or was it inevitable?—that there must be a reckoning with an untold number of Julius Doogan's gang. But had anyone suspected that Doogan himself would dare hide out right here among them?

The sooner, the better, she supposed as she all but ran toward home—and safety, a million regrets fretting her over-burdened mind. Some inner urge had all but pushed her from school without so much as seeing her own family. Now, she shuddered, they must come alone. But why punish herself needlessly? The situation was no more explosive than it had been for months. She had planned to stop by the Galloways, too. Sauerkraut and spare-ribs called for hot biscuits and she needed a new starter of sourdough. How ridiculous to think she would have time on her hands once she surrendered her mayor's gavel to Dr. Ames. Of course he was the logical one for mayor, knowing the populace as he did, as well as being a secret agent . . .

Secret agent? As such, why wasn't he informed of Julius Doogan's whereabouts? Could the sweet-faced woman be lying? She dismissed the idea. Howard had a brilliant mind. He would have a foolproof spy system in operation. And certainly he would never have allowed Brian to be exposed to the danger of Mrs. Maxton in his employ. He knew that she and Lily Dunigan were sisters and, as such, shared their secrets.

She stopped suddenly, her heart pounding like a bass drum. If the two women were that close, wouldn't Miz Lily have told her of Doogan's being here? The pounding increased tempo when it dawned on Rachel that Miz Lily was caring for Yolanda's husband . . . Rowie . . . and the baby . . . Should she race back? Oh, no, no! She could trust nobody except her own husband. With trembling fingers she unbottoned her high-top white kid shoes and ran for home in her stocking-feet with the speed of an Olympic racer.

Buck met her at the door with open arms. "What is it, Darling—what happened?" He scooped her up and laid her gently on the brocade settee at the entrance. There, jerkily, Rachel panted out her story.

For a moment, he was speechless. "Is that all Miz Lily told you, sweetheart—just that?"

Rachel nodded.

"And you didn't question her? She's our only hope—wait a minute," he said, uttering each word with deliberate spaces between as if thinking the senseless plot through. "Do you suppose—no, that is impossible—yes, it *is* possible—in fact, that has to be where—"

"Where what?" Rachel's mind was beyond reasoning out missing words.

"The house behind the Welcome Stranger may be where the evidence has always been!"

Rachel jerked herself erect. "But—but it's under lock and key, posted No Trespassing by the government—"

"Don't we know a traitor like Doogan could get a duplicate key? Now, here's what we'll do tonight—oh, here come our four trophies!" Hurriedly he laid out the plan, just as the children came bouncing in.

• • •

Midnight. The witching hour. Prayers and bedtime stories had taken longer tonight, as if the children suspected something. They were alert to change, adult in their thinking. Rachel doubted if she and Buck set their minds at ease, try as they would to behave normally.

Wishing they could have left earlier, Rachel, now squatting behind a clump of willows, decided there had never been a darkness so thick. With all her strength of will she smothered her apprehension, stilled her shaking. She *must* control herself. Even so, she felt a constrained silence lay between her and Buck like a smoke-screen. It was so *lonely.*

Rachel's sudden jump alerted Buck. "What?" His single word was barely audible as he reached for her hand. Before she could tell him that something cold and clammy had touched her, Scot was wriggling his nose into their clasped hands in affection. The dog! That meant the children! She caught at her fleeing courage and pinned it into place with a prayer. God would protect these wonderful children. He had a special plan for them. The Father they knew and worshiped was not a benign, remote figure. He descended in time of need to walk beside them, looking after them as they looked after anything that walked on four feet. Scot knew to walk stealthily and withhold his barking. No need to caution his young masters to remain as quiet as little mice in a pantry. They *knew. Oh, thank You, Lord.*

Wordlessly, the children knelt beside their parents and were drawn close. They needed comforting, not scolding. Anyway, Rachel found herself thinking, less reasonably than they, that numbers inspired her courage—even the warmth of the dog's lying down among them, head on his furry paws as if to say, "Situation normal."

A thin veil of mist shrouded the sky. Rachel felt sure that she had several birthdays in the dark-of-the-moon silence. Nothing happened.

And then—

There was a faint—ever so faint—rustle in the impenetrable dark behind them. Significant only because there was no breeze. Rachel's heart began working overtime. The fear was not for herself. No matter what happened to her and Buck, they *must* protect the children.

"Don't move," she whispered needlessly to huddled heads.

Star cupped her hand to Rachel's ear. "Have no fear, Mother Mine." Her murmur was like that of a brook. "It is only Mrs. Maxton—"

Rachel jerked her head back and peered over her shoulder, catching a glimpse of a figure in white. So that was the white—but what was this? *Two* women, followed by . . . and there she lost count.

"The lady in white is Miz Lily—"

Much later she was to learn that Mrs. Maxton had told her sister, who then told her employer—but Dr. Ames already knew.

Now as the group squatted beside them (waiting for the fugitives) Howard muttered such phrases as "foolhardy . . . I keep constant watch . . . and it's time—*Brian!* What on earth brought *you*?" "Not *what—who*," Miz Lily was whispering. "*I* did—we saw one of them men unmasked—*Mead!*" Yes, later Rachel would fill in the missing pieces. But for now she could only remain in a squatting position and bury her face against Buck's pocket prayerfully. They were together.

Suddenly hoofbeats blended with the flapping of great wings. *White* wings. And then the darkness evaporated in arcs of blinding lights from powerful lanterns and the wings became white bed-sheets draped over the riders' heads, turning them into highly visible ghosts. The ghosts were fumbling comically in an effort to draw weapons . . . shrieking . . . and disorganized. The authorities closed in from all directions. Sheriff Brimmerton's face was livid as he advanced toward the leader of what had to be Doogan's gang—Julius Doogan himself. With both hands gripping a gun tightly, the Sheriff's yell was that of an animal gone mad. "Fiend, *fiend!* Trying to drown that child—how yellow-bellied can you get?"

One of the searchlights turned on the leader, enlarging the owlish eyes blinking behind the cut-outs in the sheets which allowed the strange band to see but retain anonymity. The man made no reply.

Howard Ames might have been carved in stone. Less impetuous than Brimmerton, he assessed the situation. Undoubtedly, Rachel realized later, preparing himself for a king's-in-check situation, were life a game of chess. Now, however, she was aware only of the twins, Mary Cole, and Brian pressing against her skirt, as they lived out the nightmare. Star had inched closer to Buck and stood apart like a guardian angel.

In that brief standoff, Miz Lily grew inches taller in Rachel's eyes. There was no anger, no malice, just pity, as quietly, one-by-one she identified the sheeted men to the authorities. Then unexpectedly:

"Surrender, Julius!" Miz Lily commanded. "Swallow your pill—you're ill!"

Her nephew spluttered into virulent denial. She waved him silent. "Don't perjure yourself. No disguise can change you inside. We all *know*."

Somewhere a cock crowed—three times, ironically. A faint band of gold ringed the sky. A new day. Rachel forced herself to see visions of the children safe . . . perhaps dangling bacon-baited bent-pin hooks in the shallows of the fern-decked stream—*safely.* How could she know what lurked behind?

It happened so suddenly. Mask pulled back boldly, Willie Mead reached from the shadows, snatched Brian, and pulled him upon the horse with him. "I got 'im Boss! Now, you're home free!"

The commotion had aroused the Galloways. Brother Davey, in his long underwear and carrying a pitchfork, shuffled into their midst. "What happened? Ever'body flappin' like chickens with their heads chopped off—them outlaws—lemme at'em!"

"Out of the way, Preacher!" Brimmerton cocked his gun.

With the speed of light, Star was in front of Julius Doogan, arms spread out like Pocahontas' endeaver to save Captain John Smith. "Spare his life. Jesus would have. This man will do me no harm."

Julius Doogan groaned. "Throw down your weapons, men, and may the Lord have mercy on our souls."

Sheepishly, the men obeyed. A new day had dawned.

35

A Time of Healing

Rachel's heart was twisted to a pulp. But she was not alone. The entire city needed healing. It would take time for them to feel secure—even after they talked it all out, made it fit together. Bit by bit it was to pass. Admittedly, a few mysteries remained, but life was like that. The ministers and doctors were invaluable in helping them find the courage to carry on—and then step beyond. "Somethin' good allus comes uv th' bad. Jest take uh look at what th' Lord has'ta put up with, but He shines us up after we're burnt!" Aunt Em said with a good deal of validity. A shinin' example was the fact that all creeds, codes, and colors—and most of all, various denominations were drawn closer together through the horrible experience.

"Or be it them quiltin' parties?" Judson Lee grinned roguishly. Then, sobering, "Good fer th' saintly souls to be unburdenin' to each other. They be piecin' more'n quilts—just be lookin' at me family!"

Of course, there were those quick-acting folk who questioned the delay in "haulin' them dunghills in, seeing as how lawyers, lawmen, 'n th' like located th' hideout."

Howard Ames made no reply. If he was to continue his service, it must be in secret. Sheriff Brimmerton did his work well; but, after all, a man had to look after his reputation, didn't he? So best he "let his light so shine." He was no show-off, he said of himself. But with political ambitions, there was a lot to be gained in a show of merit.

"'All good things come to him who waits'—guess that's not

Bible, Brother Davey, but we men of the law assess these situations. You see, we had the case pretty well solved before letting our presence be known."

David Saul Galloway grunted. "No, ain't Bible y'er mouthin', call hit horse sense—still 'n all, 'Him what hes'tates is lost.' Come t'think on hit," Brother Davey scratched his head, "thet ain't Bible neither, but oughta be iffen we gonna talk on uh body's soul. Know whar yu'll be, come eternity, Sheriff? Wan'na brighter star in yer crown than th' tin one? How come *you* jest happened t'happen? No siree! Th' Lord planned th' timin'—'tweren't man's doin's!"

Sheriff Brimmerton looked thoroughly confused and somewhat uncomfortable. After all, how *did* it commence? Brother Davey, making the most of his advantage, closed in. "Well, now, Sheriff, hit's best yuh be knowin' they's a-gonna be uh revival 'bout th' time them doctors are hereabouts from Portland—let's see which 'uns heal Doc Maynard!"

● ● ●

Nature forgot about the winter past. The burst of summer-like sun turned the Oregon country rosy-pink as azaleas and rhododendrons tried to scale the walls of surrounding mountains. Shy violets, trillium, and lady-slipper orchids huddled together in the fern-green glades. And, like pastel umbrellas, the gnarled "Johnny Appleseed" fruit trees hung protectively over the valley, as if shielding tender blossoms and preserving more gentle memories of the past. Neither must the new closeness rediscovered be blown about "like a straw in the wind." Spring zephyrs looked northward, allowing the patient weathercocks to rest. Only the meadowlarks sang the glory of the season as children ran barefoot in search of wildflowers while their parents planned end-of-school picnics, looked ahead to the all-church revival, prayed for Dr. Killjoy's recovery—and, behind their fans, ladies whispered little happy suspicions. "Now, let's keep still . . . you know until we know . . . maybe even it's wiser to keep it secret—"

Men overheard and reacted with amusement and indulged their ladies. Some guffawed (those wearing dentures, holding them intact).

"Secret? Say that word was th' last word in th' dict'nary—served t'make wimmen more cur'us-like."

Buck repeated the words and together he and Rachel laughed. Could be a regular Grub-Street English novel. Yes, it was mediocre—still—and then her husband laughed at *her*. It was the first time she had poked him playfully since—well, how long ago? Rachel only knew that it felt good to laugh again....

• • •

The baking was finished. Ham was baked and sliced. Great loaves of risen-bread were pumping the yeasty odors over the valley once it was finished with them. All ladies were exchanging recipes over prize-winning pastries and cakes—all in readiness for tomorrow's end-of-school picnic boxes. No packing done—which was good—

The next day dawned sullen and in no mood for a picnic. But as Gram'ma Belcher said from beneath her black taffeta bonnet, worn day and night, "Oh, law-zee me, how's hit did rain—wuz lack Noar's Zark 'n th' belly uv uh whale!"

Visibility dropped to zero, but it was warm, almost sultry. Children, seeming to possess webbed feet, paddled over to the Joneses. It was a hard day to spend peaceably, tempers already whetted to just the right amount to cause friction.

Being more of a loner, David finally asked desperately, "What can I do, Mother? Every time I try to steer clear of them, they call me stale. Saul dogs my footsteps—and Brian crabs—Mary Cole and the others—"

"Enough!" Rachel, tired of jerking her head from side to side, said firmly. "Now, pretend this is a holiday and," she hesitated, out of her wits, "eat *all* your cookies!" They took her at her word.

Rain brings a ribbon to tie beneath the earth's chin, Star told the children and through her eyes they could see anything. She had heard the pull of the latchstring above the "raucous birds," Star explained to her father afterward, accepting two telegrams from Britches. The children sat quietly, *amazingly* so, as Buck read the yellow sheets.

He handed them to Rachel who read one brief message. With a significant look at the children, she read solemnly that Dr. Killjoy's surgery must be postponed. The Willamette Bridge had washed out and it would be between two and three days before it could be repaired: No way to cross.

"Does Uncle Maynard know?" David's eyes brimmed with tears, causing the entire group to cloud up and declare a good rain.

"Uncle Maynard and Auntie Yo sent the message by Britches."
Buck was already shoving his feet into his rainboots. "Mother will
share the other one," he grinned brightly, "and you'll feel better
for sure!"

Buck was right. The evangelist was safely across the river.
Some good sister from "over a piece" wired that the "saint"
would be here tomorrow!

"That and the picnic on the same day—there is God's rainbow.
And it wouldn't surprise me if the sun is overdue—*see*?" Star
smiled.

> "Our school will shine tonight;
> Our school will shine;
> Won't we look neat tonight,
> Dressed up so fine,
> When the sun goes down
>   and the moon comes up,
> Our school will shine!"

Back to the kitchen to make more cookies. And back to the roof
to reshingle it. Rachel was sure the children had blasted it off in
song.

• • •

Usually, the last day of school was the highlight of the entire
business of school. Perhaps it was today. If so, it was because
somewhere down deep the children, and beyond a doubt, the
adults as well, were so excited about the coming night. Undoubtedly the inspiration for the song, sung until Rachel's ear-
drums played a tune, and then—thankfully—carried away to
school. Not that her ears got much rest between.

Brother Cypress Humphrey came to Lordsburg preceded by a
fine reputation, although nobody seemed to know its source. He
brought a sparse flock with him to have boasted of thousands.
Some said millions had been healed and Brother Davey found the
ciphering peculiar. The night-of-the-picnic service was well
attended—some in "finery," while others in the unusual congregation wore apparel ranging from quietly conservative to dowdy.
And the number greater than both sums put together totaled
greater than "city folks." They came from far-distant fields,
parking with embarrassment out of sight. But hundreds of thousands? No.

There were those who quoted Brother Humphrey as claiming to own the world's biggest tent. Brian said solemnly he thought that Barnum with "The Greatest Show on Earth" owned the biggest tent. Rachel quickly extinguished the fires of comment from the other children.

Well, there was nothing like the numbers quoted. However, the bulging crowd was encouraging. Or maybe she should say "impressive"? Rachel, a little ashamed, simply wasn't sure how she felt about the crowd. While it was fine for the valley, it was less than memorable when compared to Cypress Humphrey's reputation for his crusades. The children were all eyes. Rachel looked Buck's direction and saw that he, too, was puzzled as they watched the evangelist, a wiry man with jet-black hair and a voice raspy from his marathon preaching. He was about 55, they agreed later. What puzzled the Joneses was that the quick-moving little man—about the size of Brother Davey—busied himself carefully scattering a portion of his team at random beneath the large but somewhat rickety tent. Ah, yes, the tent. Above the tall stage with a white iron rail, two red-painted crosses declared: *Prayer Changes Things* and quoted, "For the eyes of the Lord are over the righteous and his ears are open unto their prayers," 1 Peter 3:12. The only really handicapped person Rachel spotted was an elderly stranger bearing his weight on a sawed-off-broom handle that the preacher had seated near the front. His body was dwarfed—or was his problem visionary?

"Mother—Father—"

Rachel recognized Star's voice dropped to a muted whisper. But *father?* And she had dropped "Mine" from her usual Mother Mine form of address. But the greatest surprise was Star's moving around inside the tent. *Or was it?* To her surprise, the young minister stood beside her without embarrassment. It was Patrick who spoke.

"May I have your permission to take Star up front with me? We would like to observe what, if any, healing takes place."

Buck rose politely. "Permission granted," he said with a little crooked grin that had a hint of tears in it. Seated, he took Rachel's hand. Children must grow up, their eyes reassured each other. And where better that it all begin than in the house of the Lord? At that very moment they spotted Callie and Boneparte. Rachel was stunned. And then wondered why—

The organ, its back to the congregation, loosed long melancholy hymns and a few strangers (placed there? Rachel wondered) knelt on the hard dirt floor still wet with last night's rain. The evangelist centered the stage and boomed out raspily, "Are you seekin' Jesus tonight? Follow me. Me and *my* apostles preach like the Master. Pray with me!" His prayer was long and anguished, as his arms threshed back and forth overhead. The service lasted 90 minutes and Rachel, thinking back, said the prayer absorbed over half an hour of it. Sorrowful groans flowed from the kneeling supplicants, spreading throughout the tent until there was a chorus of charismatic responses in a "Glory...Hallelujah... *Thank You!*"

Rachel was strangely touched although she remembered little of the man's message except: "Too bad, too bad, *too bad* that people who claim to be believers become ill and go to doctors before trying the church!"

Rachel was startled. *Oh, thank You, Lord, that Maynard and Howard aren't here!* And then her eyes locked with Elsa Sanders and Elsa O'Grady, as they met hers in question. She was saved from trying to signal back something appropriate when she had no answer, for the healing had begun. The hard-preaching man was accepting a pitcher of oil from one of his assistants. "You are commanded to be baptized in oil—"

Her eyes felt glazed. Her palms were damp. Buck leaned forward and whispered, "Are you all right, honey? By the man's energy, urgency and ostentatious gesture, he might as well have had that congregation he's supposed to attract."

Was she all right? Rachel wasn't sure. Why should it matter so much? Of course, she knew the answer. Because it affected her family. One of the "angels," a lady in white, began distributing handkerchiefs to the knot of people gathered at the altar. What in the world?

Later the children, seated closer, explained that they were squares cut from worn-out sheets. "What was it all about?" Mary Cole asked later, "I thought they were just wiping sweat after all those warm-ups." "You're older," Saul said with disdain, "an' oughta be wiser, but, of course, being a girl—" Saul sighed a bit too deeply. Before he could exaggerate the exhalation David explained that the cloths were to wipe away the excess oil. "Then why go through that rigamarole?" Brian wondered. "That's easy—works just like a towel," Saul was quick to explain. "You know—wash then wipe the dirt off with a towel?"

Sheriff Brimmerton got up, went out, and came back, whispering something in Buck's ear. Buck's face blanched. Buck had to go. Rachel knew before he told her so rose with him. Nobody noticed when the three of them left. At the door, Rachel quietly asked the Galloways to remain, accompany the children home, and give her a report on the rest of the meeting.

"What's wrong? We'll go!" they said in unison, but Rachel shook her head.

"No! It may be nothing." But in her heart she knew better.

36

Sick of Body, Mind, Heart— or Soul?

The stretch of woods was flooded with moonlight. Rachel felt no great sense of peace and wondered why. Was it because she must strain her ears to hear the sheriff's voice as he explained that the doctors from Portland were here and wished to consult with Buck and Rachel in advance of Maynard's surgery the next day? She glanced longingly toward home but turned to the great house occupied by the Killjoys.

"It seemed important—something they wish to disclose to you before telling the doctor and his missus. I am sure I know because I am in possession of—" Mr. Brimmerton fumbled in his pocket, found nothing, grew agitated, and left his sentence unfinished.

The heavy white door swung open and a figure stepped into the ghostly silence. So somebody was watching for them? Suddenly the light from inside picked up the shine of something directly beneath her feet, which the moon had missed. A chain, expensive-looking even in the dark, and studded with jewels. It looked familiar, but nobody she knew intimately wore diamonds. And diamonds the gems had to be. With a pounding heart, she scooped the necklace up in her palm. It gleamed like an evil omen. Glancing up, she recognized Howard in the light. Had he seen?

"Rowie—you should be in bed," Howard Ames said. Then, dropping behind those filing in the door, he lowered his voice to address Rachel. "See if you can influence your friend to let this child out. He cried all evening because the other children went to the tent show—"

201

"Revival," she corrected tonelessly. "You know his mother's fears—"

Howard Ames turned palms up. "Overlook that—I know Yolanda's still paranoid about Doogan, although the Portland surgeons knew about the case and reassured her that there will be no more of the man's crawling through the holes. He's docile as a lamb—and in tight federal security. That's nothing we must keep secret—talk to her before Ambrose does—"

"I think Yo's more afraid of Barbette—"

He was about to say more when the two doctors appeared at the door. The older of the two looked like a horned owl, Rachel thought foolishly. Wisps of hair were brushed carefully over the top of his bald head, ending in upcurled tufts like the pointed ears of the nocturnal bird. She was sure his eyes, behind thick-lensed glasses, shone yellow in the lamplight. It was his companion who stepped forward and motioned to the fern-decked sunroom off the foyer. There was little time to observe his appearance, but one glance told Rachel that he was very young and instinct told her that he wished time alone with her. To advise her on how to prepare Yolanda—perhaps for the worst? *Oh, please, no, Lord . . .*

It was. "Mrs. Jones?" The earnest-eyed young man extended his hand. Rachel accepted it wondering if any sound came from her lips.

"Tonight and tomorrow will be difficult for Mrs. Killjoy, particularly with her temperament. Life has left scars—so many of them that I question her ability to handle another loss. Not that I expect one, but we *are* only clay. Doctors can only aid God. I would like to share an experience I had last week. It is very upsetting, but at the same time, perhaps, it will be comforting in a strange sort of way. May we be seated?" Rachel nodded and eased her trembling body into the chair he pulled from behind a tall pot of pink begonias. "I am Dr. Ambrose," he began.

Time was short. They could be interrupted any moment, so Rachel did not ask any questions. Yet she remembered his words because they were written on her heart. . . . He had been called to the women's prison in Salem where one of the inmates had attempted suicide. He did not know if he would be able to save her from the poison somebody had slipped to her. Eyes fixed, permanent. Even the lids refused to blink. Rachel shuddered, seeing the ashen face plainly in the lemon-light the moon spread among the shadows, but refusing to allow herself to recognize the features as those of Barbette Ames. When Dr. Ambrose said that she made it by a "hair's breadth," relief poured over Rachel's body, but her mind was in confusion. What did this have to do with Yolanda? His next words told her. The first episode was only the introduction.

"The second time she was successful—having hanged herself."

Rachel's mouth was suddenly filled with down, wadded so tightly she was unable to move her tongue in speech. Barbette dead, at her own hands. How could he be sure it was suicide? Julius Doogan was capable of all evil....

The young man's voice was shaken with emotion. "It was my first experience with suicide and I had to struggle to keep from being sick—but it was as if God took me by the shoulders, shook me and said, 'My son, do you not realize that I have chosen you for My service? That doctors must be ministers?' Can you believe that I accepted Him then and there ... in that dismal room ... with the grotesque body of a dead woman lying before me? Life took on a whole new meaning. The experience drove home my first clear definition of what it means to minister to those sick of body, mind, heart—and soul."

How much time passed Rachel did not know. Neither did she care why he was telling her this. She was fascinated now with his testimony. The young doctor talked on as if he were all alone.

"As a doctor, the Lord calls on me to hold, or bear, the ambiguities of pain, confusion and suffering—even try and share the burden of the bereaved without understanding it myself. Christian doctors bear a burden that is impossible without the hand of God. Only He can lead His servants to handle this tension, the gap that lies between awful reality and an unknown future that may not bring solace. Will you and Mrs. Killjoy pray for me, Mrs. Jones?"

Rachel managed to find her voice. "Yes, oh yes! Will he live?" Her voice broke with a little gasping sob.

Dr. Ambrose laid his hand over hers kindly. "Yes," he said confidently, "I feel he will! Thank you for listening to me—but, my goodness, I left the talk unfinished. I must hurry as I want Miz Lily to join us men with the patient—if you will prepare his wife. She is confident, and I want to keep her that way. Wives are often the prime factor when it comes to pulling their husbands through. I want the lady's mind as worry-free as we can keep it."

"I understand. So?"

"Tell her what I have told you in gentle language. The purpose is to comfort Mrs. Killjoy, not upset her further. There is another matter which I feel belongs in your hands. The deceased left a suicide note—that's why there was no question—and a comparison of handwriting verified it. Your sheriff has it—along with a necklace—"

So that was what Mr. Brimmerton was searching for? Rachel held her free hand out. In her palm the jewels were shining-eyes-in-the-night.

"Barbette Doogan made money her idol," he said quickly. "I was unaware that you were in possession—which makes no difference. Just see that it gets to the proper owner, Dr. Ames. Tell him that the woman whom he thought was his wife—in name only, as I understand—had a chest of furs and jewels which the government confiscated. This piece she held back because it belonged to Brian's mother. She felt that he should have it. You see, my dear," he said, letting go of her hand, "God placed a bit of good in us all—"

Rachel was dumbfounded. But he was right. Always she would remember the points at which Julius Doogan was a real hero.

"I understand," she said again.

"Yes—yes—I know you do. And now you and I have work to do."

He smiled for the first time. Rachel smiled back. They would both succeed!

• • •

Miz Lily was wearing a starched white uniform. It was the first time Rachel had seen her as a nurse. With her usual sweet-face smile, she informed Rowie that Mrs. Maxwell was making cookies in her kitchen.

"He has been restless—and I thought you might wish to talk with his mother. I hope your children will stop by, else my sister must go."

"Aunt Em's in charge, so go ahead with your conference," Rachel smiled back. The three went their separate ways. How good that Brian was happy.

Yolanda was happy, too. She met Rachel with arms wide open, eyebrows raised in question. "Hi, Sweetie!" Rachel greeted her jauntily, thinking that she would prefer doing the operation to preparing Yolanda.

"You look as confident as the doctors. Oh, Yo, how wonderful for God to send us such doctors! But they deserve our prayers and the Lord certainly is entitled to a prayer of praise! Let's pray with just the two of us here—like old times." Yolanda dropped to her knees and they prayed.

"Now everything is in the hands of the Great Physician," Yolanda said, her face placid and her eyes shining with triumph. "He'll make it!"

"Of course. That's called faith! Now—some 'girl-talk' before the rest of our rooting section comes trooping in. You'll want to hear my report, then theirs. Take a gander!" Rachel extended the necklace.

"My stars and garters!" Yolanda burst out. Rachel forced a laugh and prayed that she would find the right words.

37

Believe the Impossible

Rachel and Yolanda talked in their old animated way, uplifting one another and building strength together. Yolanda admitted in her prayer that she could feel no remorse in the demise of the woman who had broken her heart in so many pieces but begged forgiveness.

"I feel relief to have been open with God—He knows anyway—and now I will work on conquering my fear. For Roland, I mean. I am glad Star has spent so much time with him—he's not afraid. And the baby's too little to be aware. Now," drawing her legs up, crossing her knees, and folding the skirt—gray satin with pink tube roses embroidered at random—around them, "tell me about the revival opening night. Was it grand?"

Rachel described it factually, without an opinion. She still had no conviction whether the man was for real. But "opinions" were filing through the door. "We might as well have held the revival here," Yolanda laughed almost gaily when what looked like the entire congregation trooped in, excitement glowing in their faces.

"You should've seen how many were cured!" Saul burst out. "You mean how many *claimed* to be!" Brian contradicted. "Huh, David?" "I'm supposed to be wiser—you said so, Saul, so I'll tell you what *I* think—" Mary Cole began.

"No, remember your manners, Darling," Rachel reminded her. "Let's hear what the others have to report. Aunt Em, Brother Davey, Reverend—oh, come on in, Patrick, Star—all of you. Yolanda's in the kitchen—"

"So's Mr. Brimmerton, he likes Mrs. Maxwell's cooking," Brian announced wisely. The others weren't the only ones who were the custodians of privileged information, his expression plainly said.

The adults were surprised when the sheriff, licking his lips and bearing an enormous bowl of assorted cookies, followed a pink-cheeked Mrs. Maxwell, who kept her eyes downcast, as she brought in the tea service. "So *they* are to receive the quilt?" Rachel whispered when Yolanda brought her cup. Yolanda's lips moved like those of a ventriloquist, "No—not now anyway—but I think I *know* who..." as she moved on.

"How was the rest of the service?" Rachel picked up the conversation.

There was a flurry of responses. Brother Davey pointed out that he didn't know nary one what claimed to be healed right on the spot. Aunt Em knew one, she admitted, going on doubtfully to say that he did not make use of the ramp but left his wheelchair below the altar—and besides she'd never known Old Gus to use such a vehicle. They all puzzled over the meaning of what Brother Cy meant by calling himself a "Jesus-man." The reverend reminded them all that theirs was not to judge—that it was only the visiting minister's manner of expression. After all, weren't they all Jesus people? Well, yes, they said guiltily.

Rachel searched Star's face. Neither she nor Patrick had spoken. They sat pensively without accepting refreshments, until someone spoke of the large number who responded to Brother Cypress Humphrey's call for those to come forward who felt the "Lord's call" to join him in "going about to heal the sick." Rachel bit her lip when Callie said softly that she had expected Star and Patrick to go forward. They possessed God's gift and everyone knew of their special power. It was Patrick who spoke.

"Do you truly believe," he said slowly, "that God demands us to make a special declaration, 'Yes, I have the power to heal?' or isn't a testimonial of faith in God enough? Whatever gift I possess He gave me—my gift to Him is what I do with it. Star must form her theology—"

"Amen, good brother!" Brother Davey said, tapping his cane. "Right, Reverend?"

Luke Elmo obviously preferred to keep his opinion to himself, but a glance around the room told him an answer was expected. "I believe in intercessory prayer for healing, of course. I do not feel that I am blessed with the gift of healing. But I believe there are those who are. I *know* there are." The reverend paused to clear his throat. "This seems the right time to tell you—and I'm not finding it easy—you see, I shared my witnessing the miracle of healing at my previous church when young Brother Patrick here was little more than a child and was told to leave the church—that I was preaching witchcraft. But I know what my eyes saw. I hinted at Brother Patrick's possessing the power of healing—performing it—"

"Only to some degree," Patrick said quietly. "But it *is* hard to explain—something God Himself does through me—and then only to those who pray with complete faith that He can and He will. The person who is healed in body or in spirit is gifted too—all of you are if you have faith. I will proclaim that I have felt God's power passing through my hands—even if I'm thrown, to the lions!"

Brother Davey could keep still no longer. "Amen, good brothers! But yuh gotta have th' faith uv uh mustard seed. Maynard in there's a-gonna rise up 'n walk I betcha!"

"Now, Davey-Love, it's doubtful-like if th' Good Lord wants us gamblin' on His power—believin' is a-plenty. He 'preciates that tho'."

Sheriff Brimmerton looked, Rachel decided, as lost as Ned-in-the-First-Reader. They might have been speaking Latin in the Vulgate. "I'm remembering back on Star's terrible experience. Maizie, these cookies are something to write home about." He stuffed another in his mouth while his companions looked around the room puzzled. *Mrs. Maxwell's name was Maizie?* "And I guess I would've expected her to go forward. Why not, my child?" Obviously, he had switched from Mrs. Maxwell to Star.

"I do not know," she said sweetly. "My hands hold a certain inexplicable power. But God has not told me when and how to use it. I will serve just as all of you are serving in your own way. Mrs. Maxwell's gift is cooking—*verdad*? Miz Lily serves the sick—yes? And those who teach—and, oh, prithee, remember the power of parents and—"

The door opened and the three doctors stepped into the room. Buck and Miz Lily remained with Maynard. There was total silence.

The three medical men were too sober. Something was wrong. Yolanda, whose spirits had been so optimistic, rushed to the senior doctor. "He's worse, isn't he? Something has happened, hasn't it? I want to see my husband!"

Frederick Greer removed his thick glasses and blinked against the light. "He jerked his neck and dislodged the bullet. Complicates matters. Time will tell. He's in shock now." He returned his glasses. "Have you space where we can wash up, Mrs. Jones?"

"You mean—? You're going to operate tonight, aren't you?" Her voice was rising. Howard, his face dark with worry, led the visiting surgeon to the washroom and took clean towels from the hall closet.

"I want to see my husband!" Yolanda bolted forward only to have Dr. Ambrose's arm shoot out and bar her way. She respected his wishes, but, white-faced, she ground out the words, "He's paralyzed, isn't he, maybe permanently blind? Oh, he's going to make it, he has to make it!" She sank to her knees, arms hugging his legs.

The young doctor helped her to her feet, led her to a chair.

"Nobody said that, My Dear," he said gently. "Doctors make no claim to miracle-making; but we must dismiss the idea that miracles stopped with the Apostolic Age. Miracles need faith. Believe in the impossible—and the incredible *can* happen."

38

We Move
to Hold It Fast

"Let's join hands in silent prayer," the Reverend Elmo said softly. All bowed except Star and Patrick. Wearing an otherworldly look, Star laid a sheaf of sketches on her chair and walked toward the patient's door. Patrick followed. Rachel bowed her head, but prayer was impossible. From the corner of a trembling eyelid she sensed that someone else had entered. An involuntary glance revealed Miss Annie. Dimly she was aware that the teacher seated herself beside the reverend. Foolishly, recollection of the mystery quilt returned. Rachel dismissed it as a fragment of curiosity... memory drifting in to open the safety valve to her sanity. In the face of all this, what difference did it make?

Strange about time, wasn't it? It seemed to Rachel that the two young people were with Dr. Killjoy for eons and that it took only a short time to perform the surgery. Actually it was just the opposite. But it was that fleeting moment beforehand which determined the outcome.

It was Buck who filled her in...

The conversation between Star and Dr. Greer was short. "Who told you to come here?" he growled. "The Lord," was her reply.

The doctor jerked a medical book from the lamp table and opened it to read the passage describing the case as if to prove himself right. "At that point," Buck said in the telling, "our Estrallita didn't *half*-listen—she didn't listen at all—and wouldn't you have supposed she'd have looked at the diagrams, proper as she is and with her love for illustrations?"

Yes, she would have supposed, Rachel thought, remembering the sketches Star had made: A man lying in a patch of tall grasses, motionless, lifeless. A single stroke of the pen and the man was unexplainably *alive* in the second picture.

Inside the sickroom, Star dropped to her knees.

"Uncle Maynard, it is Star. May I lay my hands on your back?"

Maynard stirred, moaning slightly. Dr. Greer was annoyed. "He's unable to hear you! I've injected tincture of opium—and, if you'll leave—no way can he respond!"

Star laid her palms gently on the flat of Maynard's back. Patrick covered her hands with his own from the opposite side of the bed. Eyes closed, their lips moved in silent prayer and then they were still. "My back feels warm," Maynard said clearly and, with a smile, fell asleep.

Frustrated, the doctor pushed Buck, Star, and Patrick from the room and then followed. Yolanda sprang forward, "Doctor, tell me—"

"I make no predictions. Ask this young lady—she claims to have a pact with the Almighty!"

He jerked his head back and closed the door, but not in time to close out Star's words. "He will live," she said humbly.

• • •

The calendar turned from May into warm, balmy June with a smile. The visiting doctors remained in Lordsburg "just to be sure." Aunt Em observed to Rachel that Frederick Greer likely as not kept hoping complications would develop with Maynard's operation just to prove that he was right. Downright stubborn-like he was, not a whit like young Doc Ambrose. Norman and Patrick had become "really good pals" and, she hinted, he just might be coming back. Could be reasons other'n *that* friendship. Unless she missed *her* guess, he had eyes for Miss Callie.

Norman would be a welcome resident, Rachel mused. Nevertheless, the bright bee-loud day that saw them off, she breathed a sigh of relief. That meant that no doctor's orders would matter. Yolanda would have to hire someone to hog-tie her husband to keep him from returning to his practice. Memory hurled her back to the miracle of it all...

• • •

Goodbyes followed Star's declaration. Yolanda, comforted, thanked each of the guests in turn. No sympathies were expressed, because nobody doubted Star's words. Yes, yes, if there was anything they could do, she promised, her smile at Rachel saying that they would do it all anyway. Rachel, of course, would keep vigil with her. Buck split all the children between the Galloways, the Reverend, and Miss Annie.

When the team came from Maynard's room, the older doctor was rubbing his liver-spotted forehead in perplexity nearing anger. "By all the rules of common sense, he should be totally paralyzed if not deader than a doornail!"

Yolanda gave what Aunt Em would have called "the scream of a panther." Dr. Greer looked non-plussed when she threw her arms about him in wild abandon. These people were stark raving mad, all of them.

"This is the critical time, of course." It was a statement delivered in the sourest tone imaginable, and nobody in the room, in which dawn was laying rosy fingers on everything it could touch, saw fit to answer. The shine on the face of Dr. Ambrose and Miz Lily made it unnecessary. Their expressions said clearly that Star was right.

Later Buck was to complete his account of the bedroom scene before he was ordered out by saying that the senior doctor did all he could to stomp out Star's prophecy. Maynard might not survive the surgery...one slip of the knife would paralyze him... render him blind...anything bad was possible If he should happen to pull through, he could still be in a coma. Certainly he would drowse for days. And when the shock wore off, he would hate the world, curse the whole human race, and drown in self-pity. Hope and optimism would be shut out like wolves from the sheepfold.

None of these things happened. Maynard regained consciousness before the suturing was completed. Critical condition or not, he demanded to see his family. And wild horses couldn't have kept him in bed by the third day....

Aunt Em broke into Rachel's reverie by bringing an enormous basket of saucer-sized ginger cookies with sugar and spices sprinkled on top the way the children liked them. There was no reason why the ladies couldn't resume quilting Wednesday, she said with a gleam in her eye. And now here they were. There was an undertow of excitement.

The mid-summer day held its breath, cooled only by a wood-bladed, motor-operated ceiling fan Brother Davey had rigged up. It was a bit off-center necessitating a constant change of chairs around the quilting frames. But the grape juice was refreshing—

and there was enough to talk about to keep the ladies' minds off the heat. It was the custom to do conversational warm-ups—comparing the number of jars of "garden stuff put up," how much fruit jelled and jammed, kraut "put down," and who had company coming—before getting down to the business of news.

Brother Davey, seeding raisins, was seated conveniently near the door, his better ear turned toward it, just in case a comment was needed.

"Did the ladies know that the traveling evangelist had joined forces with a clown act?" Miss Annie asked, then blushed when asked where she got her information. "Luke—uh, that was Reverend Elmo heard it," she said, blushing all the more. Brother Davey saved her further embarrassment by commenting that laughter was the best healer—made sense—yep, shore did.

Elsa O'Grady announced that Mandy Burnside was "in a family way" and downright scared . . . needin' prayers . . . you know, her age 'n all. . . . Yolanda laughed at her "foolishness." Nothing to it, a pushover, she said.

Maizie Maxwell snipped off a thread and said she was glad the sheriff decided to remain. When curious heads popped up, she—like the teacher—turned pink and tried to explain that it was nothing personal, mind you. "As Lily knows, that senior doctor's sort of under suspicion—Mr. Brimmerton saw him digging around—so if he comes back. . . . On the other hand, Sis trusts him. Might not be digging bringing him back—oh dear!"

"Dr. Greer wasn't the one," Callie said a bit too quickly. "It was Dr. Ambrose—ouch! I pricked my finger!"

There was a round of laughter. "I guess," Rachel smiled, we'll have to postpone a shower for Mandy until we see who will be receiving a quilt—rather *several* quilts in their hope chests!"

Speculation began. It could be this couple, that couple, or some others, Aunt Em reminded them, a bit of mystery in her voice.

"Women, bless 'em," Brother Davey said indulgently, "oughta be trussed up—full uv curiosity as uh turkey stuffed with dressin'."

"I would'n be sayin' more, Davey-Love, seein' as how one pair's ast ahead fer yuh t'be performin' th' cer'mony."

"*Who*?" David Saul asked as he leaped from his listening post.

"Aha! *Now* is curiosity stamped '*Ladies Only*'?"

There was another burst of laughter as Brother Davey made a hasty exit—forgetting his crutch.

The conversation turned to life in general—its richness, its sweetness, and then questions. Which was more beautiful: "apple-blossom" marriages or vows taken when fruit had been kissed by God's gifts of sunrises and sunsets? The maturity of years could not be begged, bought, or borrowed. Couldn't be book-learned either, excepting through the Bible. The rest came from other folks. The good of them. And, yes, it would be "hollerin' down th' rain barrel" to claim that the bad of them didn't leave *something*. And how blest were those to whom the Creator sent a star...whose light was the soft-noted flute that piped away the evil...and healed the heart...*Estrallita*.

Rachel took leave misty-eyed but singing inside....

The day's warmth lingered as evening came. The world was flooded with moonlight and the tender sounds of strolling lovers—among them, Rachel and Buck. There was the magic of children's laughter, and, if one listened closely, the ethereal sound of a flute, rendering the tongues of mortals silent. "Be still and know that I am God."

Rachel gripped her husband's hand harder and his eyes outshone the moon. They were witnessing the fruits of Dr. Ambrose's miracle: "Believe in the impossible—and the incredible *will* happen."

Once in a while such an image emerges, however briefly, as clear as that cloudless moon—its lines delineated by truth and sharpened by experience. We move to hold it fast before it slips irretrievably from sight....

And the heart remembers.

MEMORABLE BOOKS
by June Masters Bacher

The Love Is a Gentle Stranger Series

An adventurous saga of the American frontier and a young woman's quest to find a new beginning.

Book 1 *Love Is a Gentle Stranger*
Book 2 *Love's Silent Song*
Book 3 *Diary of a Loving Heart*
Book 4 *Love Leads Home*
Book 5 *Love Follows the Heart*
Book 6 *Love's Enduring Hope*

The Journey To Love Series

The continuing story of Rachel Buchanan and Colby Lord along the Frontier Trail to Oregon.

Book 1 *Journey To Love*
Book 2 *Dreams Beyond Tomorrow*
Book 3 *Seasons of Love*
Book 4 *My Heart's Desire*
Book 5 *The Heart Remembers*

The Love's Soft Whisper Series

Courtney Glamora is sent to the rugged Columbia Territory where she becomes a pawn in a family feud.

Book 1 *Love's Soft Whisper*
Book 2 *Love's Beautiful Dream*
Book 3 *When Hearts Awaken*
Book 4 *Another Spring*
Book 5 *When Morning Comes Again*
Book 6 *Gently Love Beckons*

Quiet Moments—A Daily Devotional for Women
The Quiet Heart—A Daily Devotional for Women

Contact your local bookstore or Harvest House Publishers for more information about books by June Masters Bacher:

Customer Service
Harvest House Publishers
1075 Arrowsmith
Eugene, Oregon 97402

Dear Reader:

We would appreciate hearing from you regarding this Harvest House fiction book. It will enable us to continue to give you the best in Christian publishing.

1. What most influenced you to purchase *The Heart Remembers*?
   ☐ Author
   ☐ Subject matter
   ☐ Backcover copy
   ☐ Recommendations
   ☐ Cover/Title
   ☐ _____

2. Where did you purchase this book?
   ☐ Christian bookstore
   ☐ General bookstore
   ☐ Department store
   ☐ Grocery store
   ☐ Other

3. Your overall rating of this book:
   ☐ Excellent   ☐ Very good   ☐ Good   ☐ Fair   ☐ Poor

4. How likely would you be to purchase other books by this author?
   ☐ Very likely
   ☐ Somewhat likely
   ☐ Not very likely
   ☐ Not at all

5. What types of books most interest you?
   (check all that apply)
   ☐ Women's Books
   ☐ Marriage Books
   ☐ Current Issues
   ☐ Self Help/Psychology
   ☐ Bible Studies
   ☐ Fiction
   ☐ Biographies
   ☐ Children's Books
   ☐ Youth Books
   ☐ Other _____

6. Please check the box next to your age group.
   ☐ Under 18   ☐ 25-34   ☐ 45-54
   ☐ 18-24   ☐ 35-44   ☐ 55 and over

Mail to: Editorial Director
Harvest House Publishers
1075 Arrowsmith
Eugene, OR 97402

Name _____

Address _____

City _____ State _____ Zip _____

Thank you for helping us to help you in future publications!